RECOVERING RAMONA

A Novel

KRISTIN RUSSELL

Nashville

RECOVERING RAMONA

Published in Nashville, Tennessee by 12th South Press

PO Box 121836

Nashville, TN 37212-1836

For information on book club guides, signings, or visits,
please email: info@hairinmycoffee.com

Cover Art by Benji Peck

Library of Congress Control Number

2010916891

ISBN 0-615-41932-1

ISBN 978-0-615-41932-9

Printed in the United States of America

ACKNOWLEDGMENTS

IT TRULY TAKES A VILLAGE FOR AN INDIE AUTHOR...

Rann Russell's patience, organization, and Mr. Mom talents made this book possible. I am beyond grateful for gifts of advice and encouragement from these people: Scotty and Darlene Smith, Scott and Bayley Smith, JoAnna Kremer, Ben Pearson, Kathy Helmers, Paul Griffith, Stephen Parolini (my novel doctor), Jenny Stika for crossing t's and dotting i's, Meredith Smith, Dan Raines, Rosanne Cash, Jenny Lawson, Heather Demetra, Kristin Barlowe, William Otto, Kim Thomas, dear Maggie Anthony, Andi Ashworth, Ruby Amanfu, Miranda Whitcombe of Frothy Monkey, Matt and Carrie Eddmenson of Imogene & Willie, Smokin' Josh and Mike of Grimey's, and my Green Pea Salon peeps who support and put up with me (I love you guys): Kelly Mason, Jen Deaderick, Erika Wright, Anna Thiele, Kathleen Marr, Jean Owens, Jessica Nienebar. I love the independent and artistic community of 12th Avenue South in Nashville, and am so proud to be a part of it.

Many thanks to my PATRONS:

Deborah Barnett
Julie Couch
CJ Hicks
LaDonna Bowers
Gail Vinett
John Deaderick
Amanda Shoffner
Katy Parker
Sarah Braud
Betsy Wright
Alexandria Wegner
Darlene Smith
Maggie Anthony
Mary Katherine Simmons
Laura Reynolds
Juli Mosley
Sue Smith
Jeanie Dayani
Amy Brown
Susannah Smith White
Paige Seals
Ruby Amanfu
Jane Haynes
Bayley Smith
Jan Maier
Laura Hirt
Kellie Conn
Deena Blackstone
Angela Cay Hall
Robyn Jones Clark
Sherry Lowe
Stephanie Garrett
Stephanie Hastings
Kristine Marshall
Tess McCloy
Keri Pisapia
Kristin Barlowe
Julie Adkison
Mindy Grimes
Keely Scott
Emily Urban

For my mom,

and anyone who is a mother, has a mother, or is motherless

RECOVERING RAMONA

Chapter 1

Claudia's universe spun like a well-loved record on repeat until Alex bumped the needle, sending it screeching across the grooves they had co-written as a map of their lives together. The past few years, she had worked hard to achieve balance between her career and her relationship, using one to create distance from the other, thus placating her instinct to bolt. So far, it had worked. Now looking down at the ring on her hand, her body limp and clammy from the adrenaline and alcohol leaking through her pores, she replayed the events that led up to this new apprehension—the needle stuck on the bridge of the song, sounding improvised and strange.

She had skipped lunch that day so she could get all of the actors' hair done on time. By the time filming finally wrapped, it was five o'clock and she was starving. She didn't want to ruin her appetite for the dinner Alex had planned—

it had taken weeks for them to find a date night that worked for both of them—but she had to eat something or she would morph into an ugly monster, swiping ravenously at anyone who crossed her path. She grabbed a granola bar off the craft service table and tried not to inhale the whole thing in one bite. She coughed a little on the dry grains and reached for a water bottle. One of the lighting techs surprised her when he asked if she was okay. She choked even worse, inhaling the water but waved to him assuredly while her eyes teared up as she tried to keep from spewing water into the glass bowl of tortilla chips.

Alex showed up only a few minutes after six, though Claudia had grown used to his twenty to thirty-minute margin of tardiness usually caused by an overrun phone call with a client. As promised, he brought one of her black dresses (his favorite with the low back) and a pair of hardly worn heels. Claudia usually opted for comfort over allure, especially when she stood on her feet all day, which were most days.

"Are we in a hurry?" Claudia asked, taking the hanger and box from Alex's hands. "Can you at least tell me that, Mr. Secretive?"

"Um, we're on a little bit of a schedule," he said, and twisted the toe of his shoe into the carpet and smiled.

"Got it." Claudia peeked around the edge of the door while closing it, leaving Alex to wait outside. She glanced at her shiny nose and smudged eyeliner in the mirror and rolled her eyes. Even though she was in front of a mirror all day, she rarely looked at herself. It was all about making the talent's hair look as perfect as possible, and she always seemed to disappear behind the mythic reflections.

She took off her jeans and black t-shirt and slid the dress over her head. The paint on her toenails was chipped, but it didn't matter once she stepped into the heels. It only took a couple of minutes to whip her hair into a loose bun, powder her face, and brush on some lipgloss.

"Can you help me?" she asked Alex, opening the door. "This feels so official, 'Date Night'."

"Wow, look at you, Audrey Hepburn." Alex took the straps from Claudia's hands and tied them in a bow just below her nape.

"Really? I don't look tired?" Claudia turned around, opened her eyes wide and blinked.

"You look perfect," he said.

"How was your day? Let's talk about something else," she said, and waved away the attention.

"You're funny how you can't take a compliment."

"Your day?" He could still make her blush.

"Right. It was good. I got Javier Bardem."

"What?" she grabbed his arm, "You say it so casually, like it's no big deal. Babe, that's amazing news! So that's what this is all about tonight?"

"Nope, this has nothing to do with work tonight, I promise," Alex said, corralling her as he opened the car door.

After she sat down, Claudia smoothed the front of her dress and leaned over to give him a kiss on the cheek before she buckled her seatbelt. Then she pushed her hand through his shaggy hair and rubbed the back of his neck.

"I need a cut," he said.

"I know. You're always the last. Sorry. It looks good kind of long though."

"You're the boss, but I'm starting to feel a bit like Billy Ray Cyrus or something."

"We'll trim it tomorrow. I know it's driving you crazy. Oh yay, turn it up," she said glancing at the satellite radio tuner.

He shook his head a little, smiled, and turned up her favorite Rolling Stones song, "Ruby Tuesday."

Claudia sang along loudly and off-key. The song always made her want to spin in circles and run around barefoot in a field in Brighton or Something-Shire.

"Unbelievable," Alex said, still smiling and shaking his head.

"What?"

"Nothing—it's—nothing. I'm just happy we're finally doing this, that's all." He sighed and tapped the beat on her knee.

Claudia went back to singing as Alex pulled through the studio gates, waving at the guard. He took the 405 to Sunset, and Claudia was praying that he wouldn't stop there. She was in no mood to wade through that craziness of tourists, freaks, and hipsters. By then, they could have stopped at In-N-Out Burger and she would have been happy. All she wanted was food and fast. Alex kept driving. It appeared that they were going home to their North Montana neighborhood, but when he drove past their street, she finally understood that he was deliberately trying to throw her off course. She tried to remain pleasant and not show her mounting low-blood-sugar irritation as he headed for Santa Monica. Claudia happily thought they were going to Roku, her favorite sushi restaurant, but Alex drove right past Ocean Avenue onto Highway One. While the sun pierced the interior of the car on its way down into the ocean, she searched her bag for her sunglasses, hoping her fingers would find the M&Ms she bought at the movies the other day, but then remembered she had given them to Louisa during the disappointing second half of the film. She was just as disappointed now.

"You okay?" Alex asked her when she sighed.

"Hungry, that's all," she said smiling at him, rubbing her growling stomach. The granola bar had only momentarily satiated the monster.

"Not too much longer. It'll be worth it, I promise."

Perhaps he was springing for Nobu?

Alex put on his blinker. Claudia looked to the left and saw a parking lot in front of the ocean where all the surfers left their beat-up Jeeps and trucks.

"Trust me," Alex said as he turned into the lot. He put

the car in park. "I know you're starving, but look at that," he pointed to the glowing orange sand and the pink sky above it. "We gotta stop."

Claudia couldn't argue. This was why she loved him, his boyish spontaneity. He jumped out of the car and ran around to the trunk before she could unbuckle her seat-belt. When she got out of the car, he produced two slender glasses and a bottle of Moet & Chandon.

"Oh, and you just happened to have a cold bottle of champagne in your trunk?" she asked.

"I always keep some back there—I thought you knew that about me," he said, doing a bad James Bond imitation and smirked.

Claudia laughed. "Oh right, how could I forget?"

When they got to the sand, Claudia slid off her heels. Several pelicans were pecking in the shell-rubble the tide brought in, and there were a few remaining junkie surfers milking the last bit of high out of the mediocre waves of the day. She smiled at Alex's wrinkled brow and crooked mouth as he wrestled with the cork. They both squinted, waiting for the pop and then sighed when it released, like a post-coital exhale. She wrapped her arm around his waist while they sipped bubbles and stared at the froth the ocean chased toward their feet. For a brief moment, she forgot her hunger and end-of-the-day exhaustion and remembered how four years ago, they had stood on this same beach together for the first time. She remembered how raw and burned her lips had been from kissing him so much the night before, and yet she reached for him again and again.

"More?" he asked, when she drained her glass.

"I'll be drunk before dinner."

"Fine with me," he shrugged. "Cheap date," he smiled. "Okay, okay, I get it," he said when he saw the look on her face, "this woman needs food." He rubbed her shoulders and lightly kissed her on the mouth. He turned to walk back to the car and she followed beside him. "Oh, I almost forgot," he said, and stopped, standing still.

"No, no, no, I'm on the verge of fainting," Claudia said, realizing she sounded whiny and childish, but didn't care.

"Hold these." He handed her his glass and the bottle of champagne.

She brushed some loose strands of hair away from her eyes, and when she looked at Alex again, she saw a small black velvet box resting on his palm. Claudia stared at it for a second. She bent her head to the side and looked up at Alex's brown eyes, squinting into hers. "Oh my God," she said, swallowing hard. He opened the box. His fingers removed something red and shining and lifted it up into the soft light.

She gulped the sea breeze into her lungs. A ruby, an old one—rose-cut, two carats at least, set in gorgeous filigreed platinum. He held it in front of her, his fingers quivering, and that was when she noticed that he had chewed his normally manicured fingernails to the nub.

"I . . ." He couldn't find the words, which usually came so easily to him. The man could sell a rotten apple to an orchard keeper.

"Yes," she said, and took his head in her shaking hands. She kissed his mouth, and it tasted like salty champagne. "Yes," she said again, more for her sake than his, just to ascertain that the word was actually coming from her own lips and not another, more graceful and competent woman standing somewhere behind her.

"Oh, thank God," he said, and dropped into the sand running his hand over his damp face, still holding the ring in his fingers.

"Um, can I have it?" Claudia asked and laughed, looking down at him.

He leaned his head against her stomach and slid the ring onto her finger. She dropped to her knees to join him.

"Your dress . . ."

"It's just sand," she said.

"I swear when that damn 'Ruby Tuesday' song came on the radio, I nearly lost it and just handed you the box right then. You like it?"

"I love it. It's perfect." Claudia held her hand at a distance and smiled as the ruby glinted. "Babe?"

"Yeah?"

"I know this is the perfect moment that we will be telling everyone about over and over, and I really don't want to ruin it because we both know I tend to do that sometimes, but can we please go get some pizza or something?"

"Just ten more minutes and you can eat. I promise."

In the car, Claudia put her left hand on Alex's knee and smiled at the ring, and then at him. The whole thing had caught her off guard, and a thought pricked the edges of her conscience that maybe she had said yes to something that she didn't quite understand. Her parents hadn't exactly bequeathed her with trusty marital footprints she could follow; but when Alex turned onto Topanga Canyon Drive, she knew exactly where they were headed and exactly what she would order, and that certainty squashed the small nagging doubt like a mosquito slapped in mid-bite.

When they stepped through the door of Froggy's, she was surprised to find a small group of their friends waiting expectantly, shouting their congratulations when the couple walked out onto the patio. A buffet table was set with platters of king-crab legs, fish tacos, flatbread, and grilled veggies. Buckets of beer and pitchers of Mojitos were already being enjoyed by the guests.

Louisa sidled up to Claudia and grabbed her hand to look at the ring.

"You helped him with this, didn't you?" Claudia asked her.

"Nope, not me," her tiny, pixie-like friend said. But there was a mischievous sparkle in the large brown, Vietnamese-American eyes.

"Okay everyone," Alex called. "She said yes and she's beyond starving. Let's eat!"

Claudia was unabashedly first in line and found a seat next to Charles, Louisa's husband, and their eight-month-old son, Ben. Their friends stepped forward to look at the ring and gush their happiness, but she couldn't wait any longer and stuffed her mouth with a taco. With her right hand, she held her food, and whenever someone approached her searching for the coveted jewel, she would smile and show them her left hand. "Mmmmm, I know! Yesh, totally surprised! (gulp, gulp)." Everyone was on the way to being drunk anyway and manners were on the way out the door.

The sun went down behind the mountain, and the fairy lights roped around the trees growing throughout the patio sparkled. Claudia held sleepy little Ben and danced with his head on her shoulder to keep him from crying so that Louisa could finish her food. Charles showed Alex the completion of his second tattoo sleeve. "Took five hours yesterday for Snake to finish it," he said. Jason and Frank had to go to a birthday party in the Hills and blew kisses to both Claudia and Alex. Deirdre was without Greg, and there were whispers that they might be breaking up—again. Tom and Derek were around the corner smoking cigarettes, keeping an eye out for their wives who both disapproved.

Claudia sat on Alex's knee, buzzed from the Mojitos and said, "This is our family, isn't it? We're like an adoptive agency for lost souls."

Alex kindly chuckled at Claudia's quasi-drunk rambling.

"Yes, baby."

Claudia crunched on some ice and leaned her head on his shoulder, wondering why her real family couldn't have been more like this.

Chapter 2

In the morning, Claudia's eyes were still blurry from the long night of celebration, and she curled up on the sectional with a steaming mug of coffee and the remote control. She scrolled through the channel guide station, and not wanting to search too hard for anything, selected the documentary channel where there was usually something interesting on. She yawned and squinted and stretched, patting Foster's golden head that rested on his paws. She wasn't paying any attention to the screen, but when she heard a voice say, "People need to know that we have our own lives. We work, fall in love, and want to be involved in community. That's what this program is about. I just want to help others with disabilities know about all of the choices we have now." Was it really her? Little Gracie? Claudia's heart flooded with pride and awe and shame. She should have stayed in touch with her friend. "Alex!" she yelled, even though she heard the shower running. He didn't answer. The program had moved on to another young adult with mental disabilities talking about the same organization, but Claudia was still thinking of Gracie, and a particular day.

"Stop it!" Claudia had yelled. The boys were pointing and laughing at the puddle that seeped into the middle of the bus aisle. "If you'd leave her alone, she wouldn't have accidents!" It wasn't like Gracie didn't face enough ridicule on a daily basis. Claudia had voluntarily taken the job of looking out for her next-door neighbor. Every day, she made sure that Gracie got to their classroom and didn't leave her Coke-bottle glasses on the playground. It was a tall order for a six-year old like Claudia, but it was nothing like Gracie's job of surviving the bullies every day, she thought. And anyway, whenever Claudia felt sad, Gracie had the ability to make her laugh and forget whatever had caused the upset. Like the time Claudia's mom never came to pick them up from Susan's birthday party. After calling Claudia's house repeatedly, Susan's mom finally took them home when it started to get dark outside. Gracie sang her favorite song, "Do You Believe In Magic" the whole way, and though most of the words were made up gibberish that didn't have anything to do with the real lyrics, Claudia couldn't help but smile and hum along. When they got to her house, Claudia's dad apologized to Susan's mom, saying Claudia's mom had a migraine and had shut the phone off and that he had just gotten back from the office.

"Come on," Claudia said, and herded the urine-soaked Gracie in front of her so she could follow closely behind. She heard the boys and some of the girls laughing, and turned around and glared. Gracie skipped off the bus and into her front yard like nothing had ever happened. "Bye! See you tomorrow!" she said, running to her red front door.

Claudia dropped her backpack on her small bed and took off her shoes and changed her pants, which were wet from sitting next to Gracie at the time of the accident. "Mom!" she yelled. There was no answer. She walked out of her room and found her dad sitting at the kitchen table. "Hi, dad!"

"Hey, pumpkin," her dad said in a tired voice.

"Why are you home early?" Claudia grabbed a cookie from the box on the counter.

"Sweetie—"

"Where's Mom?" Claudia dropped her cookie when she noticed that there was something wrong with her dad's face. Crumbs stuck to her bottom lip.

"She went to the doctor, baby, so she can get rid of her headaches. She might be gone for a while. It's just going to be you and me for a little bit, okay? Like when we went camping in the summer."

"Uh-huh." Claudia's small face wrinkled between the brows, an expression of concern too old for such a young girl. It was the same expression she saw on her father's face.

"She wanted me to give you this," he handed her a thin paperback.

Ramona the Brave, Claudia slowly read out loud. She had wanted to tell her mom how she had been brave on the bus, protecting Gracie from those jerks. She looked up at her dad, a question glistening in her damp eyes. Is it my fault she had to leave? But she found no answer in his weary eyes. Claudia set the book down on the kitchen table and ran to the back yard, the screen door slamming behind her. She picked up an old tennis racket, the strings broken, and swung at the towering oak tree in her backyard. Pieces of bark fell around her feet along with the rest of her world.

"Ring around the rosy, pocket full of posies," Claudia sang the words to the nursery rhyme over and over. If you're brave she'll come back sooner, she told herself. Just be brave. She pushed the tears away with the back of her hand and ran off to find Chloe, her cat.

Now that Claudia had seen Gracie all grown up, she envied the courage her nearly forgotten childhood friend had found. She couldn't imagine tackling those kinds of life obstacles and exposing the world's ignorance. "I'll be outside," Claudia called to Alex, who was still in the shower and probably didn't hear anything she said. She was wearing her old jean cutoffs and an oversized vintage Led Zeppelin t-shirt.

Foster followed her out the door, panting and wagging his golden tail. She turned on the hose and filled the bucket with bubbles. Her car hadn't been washed in months, and a thin film of the mysterious Los Angeles smog clung to its body. She was considering selling the Accord and buying something new, but needed to take it in for a checkup before she listed it and just hadn't made the time. As she sloshed the bubbled water onto the car with a rag, she remembered her first car and how she had lovingly washed it every Saturday. Ramona was a blue 1986 240GT Volvo that her father bought for her sixteenth birthday. When he handed her the keys, it was as if he was handing Claudia a passport to happiness. She imagined not only an escape from the turmoil of her broken family, but also tremendous possibility for adventure. She knew they could conquer anything together. A heavy guilt still weighed on Claudia that she had abandoned Ramona when she sold her—maybe she had even abandoned part of herself. But there was no other way to get out of the downward spiral that was the microcosm of Landry, Texas. The few thousand dollars from Ramona afforded her several months rent and countless boxes of Ramen noodles for her rough initiation into Los Angeles. Even though she wasn't physically with her during the transition, Ramona had still played an essential role in Claudia's escape.

"Louisa's on the phone," Alex said, standing with a towel wrapped around his waist and damp hair.

"Ask her what's up? I'm kinda a mess here," Claudia held up her dripping hands.

Alex spoke into the phone and then said, "She wants us to all go for brunch."

"Tell her one hour. Babalu?"

Alex relayed the message, and then said, "She says Kreation."

"Okay. We have all that champagne left over from the party. Tell her we'll bring a bottle," Claudia yelled.

"She heard you." Alex hung up the phone.

"Catch," Claudia said, faking like she was throwing the wet rag at him, trying to get him to drop his towel.

He barely flinched. "Nice try," he said.

Claudia hosed down the car and ran inside to change.

The Sunday crowd at Kreation wasn't as bad as she had expected, and they were seated within minutes. Little Ben sucked on his bottle while they looked at the menu. "Banana pancakes," Claudia said, and Louisa slapped her menu down on the table and nodded at the waitress in agreement. It was a well-practiced routine. Charles and Alex both had the organic egg and farm sausage scramble, although Charles put so much hot sauce all over his plate, Claudia wondered how he could taste anything underneath the liquid red umbrella. "Helps me breathe better," he said, motioning like he was meditating. In reality, Charles was the type who would never make it through a yoga class because he would either crack up at the person bending down in front of him with their butt up in the air, or he would try to make everyone else laugh by farting during the relaxation at the end of class.

"So—what did your parents say about the engagement?" Louisa asked, while Ben pounded his tiny fists on the table and reached for the small opened pitcher of cream, which Louisa quickly rescued. Everyone pushed the forks and knives out of his range, and Ben made do with the napkin Charles handed him.

"Dad and Betsy are thrilled, of course. Dad's been pushing for this since they came to visit two years ago for the golf tournament and Alex rented the Ferrari for the day. Alex won him over as soon as he handed him the keys and then took him to Pink's hot dogs. Betsy said she wants to come help organize everything—look for the dress, the place, all that. She's sweet, but it gives me a headache to think about it."

"And your mom," Louisa said, looking up carefully from her Bellini, (their server had graciously provided fresh peach puree for the champagne).

Claudia looked at Alex, who gave her a comforting glance, and then looked back at Louisa. "I haven't told her yet."

"When was the last time you talked to her?" Louisa inspected Claudia's face closely.

"Oh, I don't know—Christmas, I guess."

"Is she still married to that same guy?" Louisa asked.

"If you mean Tim, the dealership-cheese ball, then yes. She never married the other one—the guy with the barbeque place. Broke off the engagement."

"Is Tim the one she met at the wacko religious conference in Colorado Springs? The one with the black toupee and red hair sticking out underneath?" Charles chimed in, hunched over his oozing plate.

"Yep, that's the one. I'll never get it." Claudia took a deep swig of her Bellini, which stung her nose. She rubbed her sweating palms down the legs of her jeans.

"Have you set a date yet?" Louisa chirped. "No, Ben. Don't eat the napkin. Here, have some pancake."

Claudia put her head down on her folded arms resting on the table. "Geez, guys, we've been engaged for all of two days now. I haven't thought about any of the details. Maybe this is why I always said I never wanted a wedding. Maybe we'll just elope."

"No way. My mom would disown me," Alex said. "I don't think she'll know what to do with her time now that she doesn't have to worry about her baby getting married anymore. Oh yeah, next she will be bugging us for grandkids."

"Yay!" Claudia raised her fists in mock jubilation. "Why do weddings have to involve so many people? I thought this was just about you and me," Claudia said. Alex reached across the table for her hand and squeezed it.

Charles and Louisa looked at each other and laughed, but then Louisa saw the concern on Claudia's face and straightened up.

"Sweetheart, it will actually never be just about the two of you again. You're taking on each other's crazy family members, even the ones who are dead, because they have all shaped your lives in one disturbing way or the other. And then if you ever have a kid—well, we won't talk about that yet. We'll just stick with what is on your proverbial plate."

Claudia looked down at her pancakes and realized she wasn't as hungry as she had been a couple of minutes ago.

"Come on guys, you're not really helping my cause here," Alex said looking at Charles and Louisa. "You need to tell her all the blissful things about being married. Like how much fun you two have together and how you've never regretted it."

Ben squawked.

"Look Claude," Louisa said, "We're just giving you a hard time. At the most, it's only a few times a year that you guys will have to deal with the chaos of mashing your families together. Just do what I do and keep a steady flow of Xanax in your bloodstream. Then it's not so depressing, but kind of amusing."

Claudia leaned her head on Louisa's small shoulder and let out a loud sigh. "You'll have to give me some of your stash for when I call my mom. Or you could just call her for me." Claudia looked up and blinked her eyes at her friend.

"Here," Louisa handed her a few little blue pills. "Take one now with that Bellini, and you can just get it over with today. Done. Next!"

Claudia tossed back the pill.

"I've never even met the woman, and now you're all making me nervous. Give me one of those," Alex said, reaching for Claudia's hand.

"I think you should get doc Rogers to call in a 'script," Claudia said, "Because you ain't gettin' any of mine." She took another bite of pancake. "Look, we're already becoming pill-poppers. Imagine what we'll be like on our tenth anniversary."

Charles laughed.

"Looks like someone is past their naptime," Louisa said.

They all looked at Ben, who was swaying in his highchair, half-laughing and half-crying—drool running down his chin.

"That's what Alex does when he's tired," Claudia said.

"She's right," Alex said.

Soon after they got home, Claudia tapped her fingers on the counter and bit her bottom lip while she listened to the phone ring—once, twice—she hoped that voicemail would pick up and she could just leave a quick message.

"What's wrong, is everything okay?" Maryanne asked breathlessly when she picked up after the third ring. She didn't even say hello.

"Yes, Mom. Why?"

"Well, I just never hear from you. I figured something awful must have happened for you to actually call your mother out of the blue."

"You know it goes both ways, Mom. You could call me."

"Well, we've just been so busy now that we're on the board, and Tim's bought another dealership. There just hardly seems to be enough time in the day, does there?"

"You're on the board of what?"

"Crestview Baptist, of course."

"Mom! The church where the Bill-something preacher was arrested for tax evasion and sexual misconduct?"

"Oh Claudia, you're so dramatic—that was years ago. We have a new pastor now. A young guy from California, actually. The blessings are just pouring in under his teaching. You'd like him; his worship team plays the drums and everything."

"I doubt I'd like him. Anyway, there's something I want to tell you," Claudia took a deep breath and then said quickly, "I'm getting married." Claudia squinted her eyes shut and waited for the response.

"Tim, can you get the door, sweetheart? No, I'm not dressed," Maryanne said in response to Claudia's news.

"Mom—did you hear what I said?"

"Hmmm? Oh, yes. Married. I heard you."

There was silence on the line.

"Okay, well, I just thought you might like to know . .. bye." Claudia hung up the phone and rubbed her eyes. If she felt this stressed talking to her mom while on Xanax and two Bellinis, she couldn't imagine what it would be like sober. Yes she could—she remembered. A shiver ran up her spine.

She walked into the living room where Alex was watching football with Foster on the coach. He was swallowed by the cushions, slumped, with his knees spread wide, a beer in one hand.

"I'm glad that's over with," Claudia said, looking for solace.

"What did she say, babe? Oh, Oh, Oh, get it! Yes!" Alex stood up and pumped his fist into the air.

Claudia knew it was pointless trying to have a conversation with him while the game was on. It seemed that no one was going to listen to her today. She walked into the kitchen, stared at the sink full of dirty dishes, pushed up her sleeves and turned on the faucet. With every dish she rinsed and shoved into the dishwasher, she pushed out a little bit of her frustration. By the time she had the silverware in, she could breathe evenly again. She dried her hands and looked at the ring. Maybe they could just let Alex's mom throw an engagement party for them in Rhode Island and that would satisfy her need to show off Alex. Then they could go to the courthouse without telling anyone—except maybe Charles and Louisa —but if Charles and Louisa were there, then their other friends would have to be too, and oh—it was hopeless. Wasn't she supposed to feel giddy and elated right now instead of wanting to compulsively tweeze each downy hair from her arms and then after that, perhaps move on to the grays that were sprouting up seemingly overnight?

She took a load of her laundry to the washing machine and was greeted with a musty, moldy smell when she opened it. Alex had left his wet clothes in overnight. So this was how it was going to be now? Was she supposed to look after everything now that they were getting married—like his mom did for his dad? Except Pam had a maid come regularly and an interior decorator to update the décor annually; she'd be happy to remind him of that. She worked full time, and they said the next step in her career would be editorial styling and then possibly her own product line. She didn't have time to run around picking up after him. She filled the removable compartment tray on the washing machine with detergent, slammed it shut and pushed start. She didn't bother shouting goodbye over Alex's exuberant whooping when she grabbed her purse and walked out the door.

Claudia was the only person she knew who still made mixed-tapes, only now they were CDs. Alex had bought her an iPod for Christmas, but she couldn't get used to programming things onto her computer and then transferring them over. It actually seemed like more work and was less tactile and therapeutic than opening the plastic jewel boxes she knew by a quick glance at the cover art. In the glove compartment of the Accord, Claudia had a library of over twenty discs, labeled emotively on the spine, so there was a soundtrack for every mood she might experience on her wavering wide spectrum. She slid "Peace Train" into the player, in hopes of quelling her nerves.

Going south on the PCH, she tried to erase the disappointment of the awkward exchange she had had with her mother. She should have known better than to expect anything after all of these years. The thick walls of cynicism she constructed around her life served her to some extent, but still, she couldn't keep the stubborn sprout of hope that one day things could possibly change with her mom from popping up through the deep soil of her imagination every once in a while.

She thought about how far she had come since she left Landry. It had already been ten years—she couldn't believe it when she stopped to count. She and her friend Deena had piled everything they could fit into their hand-me-down suitcases, including their plans to be the best hair and makeup team in all of Hollywood. Claudia wondered how Deena was now. It didn't take long for the poor girl to get sucked into the back-alley Hollywood scene. After Deena left their apartment with the popcorn ceiling and moved in with her cokehead boyfriend, she and Claudia lost touch. Claudia occasionally saw Deena's name in a gossip magazine's credits, but the two no longer crossed paths.

As she drove, Claudia continued her nostalgia along to John Lennon's "Imagine", by recounting all of the L.A. apartments she had inhabited. There was the rat hole in the valley that she shared with Deena, the tiny place off La Cienega with Chris and Becca, the reggae room in Venice where she never slept, the four-month house sitting job in the Hills that she never wanted to leave, the studio in Marina Del Rey where she finally settled down on her own—until she moved in with Alex six months later. And now, her name would go on a mortgage. She felt a wave of nausea.

This sleepy music would no longer do. Once the road straightened out and she could look away for a moment, she reached into the glove compartment, and pulled out "Rebel Rebel".

Documents scared her—the intended permanence of them and how much it cost to undo them. She remembered the year that her parents split up—she was nine. It seemed like all they did was hand papers back and forth via lawyers to be signed. She knew she wanted to be with Alex and no one else, but it was the details, the legality of it all that seemed to detract from that sentiment. What name would she use after the marriage? Was she going to take Alex's last name? Why hadn't they talked about any of this yet? Claudia Franklin, Claudia Franklin. Claudia Nichols-Franklin? It wasn't that she was dying to keep Nichols; it just seemed so strange to one day have a completely different last name. Maybe she could ease into it—hyphenate and then later shorten. *"No you won't fool the children of the revolution,"* she tapped out the T. Rex glam-rock beat on the steering wheel and chewed on her bottom lip. She had already passed Newport Beach—might as well go on to Laguna while she was at it. "Sheena Is a Punk Rocker" charged her onward.

It was dark when she finally got home from her road trip, all of the angst drained from her mind and body. Alex was in his office on the phone. Claudia laid her head on a sleeping Foster, who was in the same position on the couch as he was when she left several hours ago.

"Want to order in?" Alex asked when he walked in the room.

He didn't ask where she had been. "Sure," she answered.

The food arrived within fifteen minutes—one of the best things about L.A., Claudia thought, was the endless variety of quickly delivered ethnic cuisine. They sat on the couch with boxes of noodles, chopsticks, and glasses of wine—hers white, his red.

"There's a great new script that I'm trying to sell Javier on." Alex sucked a noodle into his mouth.

"Oh yeah? What's it about?"

"The writer is an unknown newbie, so I'm really having to fight for it. Javier's character is a professor. The female lead is a brilliant poet with severe dyslexia; so she can't write the poetry down, only recite it from memory. He takes her under his wing and . . ."

"They fall in love."

"No. He realizes that she is much more talented than he will ever be, and he submits her poetry as his own."

"That's terrible."

"I know, right. But his wife finds out and weighted down by her conscience, tells the truth about her husband's lie. The dyslexic girl goes on to win awards, and then opens a school for children with learning disabilities."

"That sounds pretty cool. Think he'll do it?"

"I think so. We just have to make sure the part is dark

enough for him. He's a little worried it might be too much like a Lifetime movie."

"Hmmm." Claudia chased a mouthful of MSG with some more wine.

"I'm going to the gym early, so I'm gonna hit the sack. You staying up?" Alex closed the small box.

"Yeah, for a little while. I'll be in soon." Claudia said.

When Alex leaned down to give her a kiss goodnight, Claudia noticed a thinning area on the top of his head she hadn't seen before. Was he already starting to bald? She also thought his breath smelled unusually malodorous, but she smiled at him, kissed him lightly, and inwardly slapped herself on the hand for being such a critical bitch.

Chapter 3

Where're Charles and Ben?" Claudia asked, leaning over Louisa's countertop, munching on some cheese that Louisa had just finished shredding for the casserole.

"Look out the window," Louisa nodded at the glass while she chopped onions and used the edge of her sleeve to wipe at her watering eyes.

Claudia walked over to the window and covered her mouth while she laughed. Charles had Ben sitting on the large seat of his Harley and was snapping photos with his camera-phone, jumping in just as Ben looked like he was going to topple over and hit the ground, only to prop him up again for another shot. "What'll he be doing to your son next?"

"Teaching him to play drums and mix drinks at the bar, I'm afraid. It's hopeless, really. I might as well accept it. Can you hand me the cheese, please? But I have to say I've never seen him more proud of anything in his life. You'll see when you guys have a kid; you'll discover a side of Alex you never knew was there. There's nothing sexier than a man who's in love with his kid. "

"Want me to stir the onions?" Claudia asked, after handing her the bowl.

"Yeah, that would be great." Louisa added the cheese to the egg mixture in the bowl.

Claudia stood at the stove and watched the boys outside. Louisa was right; Charles obviously loved spending time with his son. It didn't seem like a chore with him as she had witnessed with other dads, begrudgingly pushing their kids in the swing at the park while they checked email on their phones. Ben was bouncing up and down on the Harley seat in sheer bliss. Claudia tensed when he lost his balance again, and then she sighed when Charles's big hands caught him just in time.

"Anymore thoughts about eloping or planning a wedding?" Louisa seasoned the yellowish mixture with salt and pepper.

"I don't know, Lou." Claudia looked down wistfully at the onions in the skillet. "Betsy sent this package in the mail the other day—it was really sweet and everything—she had torn out pictures from magazines of wedding cakes and bouquets. She bought me one of those little notebooks that has a file for every category of the wedding, you know, the church, caterer, photographer, etc. I know that she's trying to help make up for how clueless Mom is, but it just all seems so damn condescending, like 'poor little Claudia, she just needs a woman's guidance', you know? It makes me feel icky."

"Alright." Louisa looked at Claudia with her hand on her small hip. "I guess I'm going to have to drag it out of you. What's going on with you? You haven't seemed right since you and Alex got engaged. This isn't you. All of a sudden you're Miss Irritability."

Claudia stirred the onions and frowned into the pan like the answer was there, browning. "I know. Everything was great before. We were perfectly happy, and I was fine with our plans, or rather, lack thereof."

"And now?" Louisa asked.

"It's like the smallest thing Alex does drives me crazy. I'm noticing all this stuff I didn't notice before. God, that feels good to admit."

"Like what?"

"Well—it's so terrible, promise you won't think I'm a jerk—but the way he eats, the way he brushes his teeth and doesn't clean the spit-out toothpaste out of the sink. How he lets Foster get on every single piece of furniture and doesn't care about the shedding. There is yellow fur on every piece of black clothing I own, and you know how much black I wear."

"You've always loved Foster."

"I know! That's what I'm saying. It's like someone flipped

a switch, and the light is revealing all these annoying little quirks that were hidden before. Are they bad things? Not really—but can I live with them forever?"

"Uh-huh," Louisa said, flashing her round brown eyes and biting the side of her mouth.

"What does that look mean? You are judging me, aren't you? Claudia raised her voice in incredulity.

"No, I'm not judging. I'm just thinking—it's not Alex. He hasn't changed. It's you. You're freaking out about getting married."

"I'm not freaking out! I'm just fighting the stereotypical wedding frenzy. There is a whole industry built on the delusion that every woman should look and feel a certain way, and that way carries an exorbitant price tag that could feed an entire small country for a year. I'm trying to be thoughtful about it all and make sure we are doing the right thing here, that's all."

"And all I'm saying is, you've moved to a million different places since you've lived here. You won't settle down in a salon—you like to freelance because it's not permanent, and you can always find a different show if the one you're working on starts to feel familiar. Alex is the longest relationship you've ever had and to tell you the truth, I've been waiting for you to freak out ever since you moved in with him three years ago"

"Well thanks for the vote of confidence." Now Claudia's eyes were the ones stinging, even though the onions had long since caramelized, and no longer gave off a pungent odor.

Louisa wiped her hands on a dishtowel and walked over to her friend. She leaned her head on Claudia's sagging shoulder.

"Hey—it's okay. We've all got our shit, you know?"

"You don't," Claudia moped.

"Are you forgetting what happened three years ago? My freak out?"

"That was just a seven-year itch, and you guys worked through it. It was just a flirtation."

"It was more than that to me."

"Yeah okay, that was a really rough time. But you both survived, and now there's Ben and everything's great. You're a better couple for it."

"After a lot of heartache. But you will be better too on the other side of this. Whatever happens; whatever you decide to do."

"Lou? Why are you such a good friend to me?" Claudia asked.

"Because I'm stubborn, and I won't let you chase me away." Even though Louisa was tiny, her spirit filled the room like an exuberant gospel choir.

"Thanks for that," Claudia said.

"Burning!" Louisa looked at the pan Claudia had turned her back on.

"Damn it!" Claudia pulled the skillet off the stove and

pushed it into the sink.

"It's fine," Louisa said. "Onions give Charles the farts anyway."

"Mmmm, sexy," Claudia laughed, and ran the water over the burnt mess.

Charles came flying through the door, swinging a crying Ben through the room and then into the nursery. "It's a nasty one," he yelled from the back of the house. "Oh God," he made a gagging sound while he changed Ben's diaper. "Seriously, you should come see this epicness."

Chapter 4

Hey sweetie, I just wanted to let you know I'm on my way home and see if you wanted me to pick anything up from the store or anywhere. I love you." Claudia hoped that Alex wouldn't be working late that night. Louisa's words had whittled their way into her conscience, and she was feeling guilty for the snappy replies and all of the eye rolling she had been inflicting on Alex during the past couple of weeks.

Before she left Charles and Louisa's home, she put the CD titled "Vivify" into the stereo. While singing along to the Flaming Lips, she reminded herself what a constant and calming force Alex had been for her throughout the past four years. She had been waiting for the other shoe to drop, for him to meet a younger, more attractive girl who wasn't as complicated; but he hadn't. He wanted her, apparently for better or for worse. She couldn't quite get her head around it and this, she realized, was why she was indeed, as Louisa had so kindly put it earlier, freaking out. *"Do you realize—we're floating in space,"* she listened to the rest of the song before putting the car in park in their driveway. Alex's car was there.

She walked inside and found him filling Foster's bowl with water. Something about the way his hair obscured his left eye as he leaned down unexpectedly stirred her longing. She set her purse on the counter and walked over to him. "Hey—" he said, but she stopped him from saying anything else by kissing him. He pulled away slowly and smiled at her, his hands resting on her hips.

"Wow, hi," he said, and kissed her again. "There you are. I was wondering where you went."

"Did you forget—I told you I was . . ."

"That's not what I meant."

"Have I really been that bad?" Claudia looked down and saw that Foster was dripping water all over her sandaled feet. She patted him on the head and shuffled her feet away from his panting mouth.

"Yeah, pretty bad."

"I know. I'm sorry. I thought maybe you hadn't notice."

"I just figured you needed a little space. Sorry I didn't get your call earlier, I was stuck in a long phone meeting with Bob."

"Oh, that's fine. And—I don't want any space from you right now, at this moment," Claudia kissed him again and pulled him toward the bedroom.

"I guess I'll take what I can get," Alex said, following her.

Claudia realized that it had been a long time since she had pursued him like this. She closed the door behind them so Foster wouldn't follow them onto the bed. That could be one of the reasons things were less lively in the bedroom lately, it got pretty crowded with a golden retriever and two adults on a Queen sized bed. It was cozy, but not exactly a stimulating ménage a trois.

It was only a few minutes later when Claudia heard something outside. She ignored it at first, but then it persisted. It wasn't a car alarm, because the rhythm of the beeping was irregular. She then realized someone was honking a horn over and over again.

"Ignore it, they'll stop." Alex said, and pulled her face back to his.

"But it sounds like they're right in our driveway."

"It's probably just Lucy's boyfriend, drunk again."

"He drives a scooter with a wimpy horn," Claudia said, pulling her shirt back over her head.

Alex sighed and followed her to the front door saying, "You're not going out there, are you? I'll deal with it."

"I just want to see what's going on," Claudia peeked between the shutters of the front windows. She gasped and covered her mouth with her hand. "No, no, no, no, no. Absolutely not."

"What?" Alex said, walking to the door. His jeans were on, but his shirt was lying in a heap on the bedroom floor.

"No! I'll get it," Claudia said. "Put your shirt on, quick."

"What? Who is it? The Pope?"

"It's my mom. And Ramona." Claudia whispered, the whites of her eyes glowing in the dark.

"Your mom and who?" Alex whispered back, and then asked, "Why are we whispering?"

"Dear God, what is she doing here? Go get dressed." Claudia motioned to Alex frantically while she walked to the door.

Maryanne was still honking Ramona's horn when Claudia opened the front door. "Can you believe it?" Maryanne screamed and jumped up and down.

"No! I can't! I uh, okay—I don't know where to start. How uh . . . Wow! Where did you find Ramona? What are you doing here?"

"Well you remember you sold her to that Billy Perkins, and then he got one of those new low-rider trucks, and he sold Ramona to Nancy's youngest daughter, Jane, you know the one covered in freckles? I'm sure I paid them more than Ramona's worth, 'cause they jumped at the offer, didn't try to negotiate or nothin'. Tim said it was a mistake to buy her back, and we could get you something better at the dealership for the same price; but I just couldn't think of a better wedding present, can you?"

Claudia touched Ramona's driver side door and then glimpsed around her insides. She was still in good shape. Ten years and two different owners hadn't done her too much harm. And somehow her mother hadn't destroyed her in transit.

Maryanne saw Alex at the front door and said, "Well, hello there, you good looking thing. You finally did the right thing, didn't you? Come here and give me a hug."

"Wow," Alex said, moving toward Maryanne, looking like he didn't quite know what angle to go at her from. "It's so nice to finally meet you."

"Mom, how many cups of coffee have you had?" Claudia asked. She hadn't seen her mother this excited in years. But then of course, she hadn't seen her at all in years. Maryanne wrapped her arms around Alex's shoulders.

Claudia was impressed with Maryanne's performance—no one would ever know that she had disapproved of Alex ever since they moved in together.

"Enough to get me through twelve hours of driving today!" Maryanne said.

"You did the drive in two days? That's crazy, Mom. I don't know if I could even do that."

"Well, I was just dying to get out here and see you two, and show you Ramona, of course."

As the three walked inside the house, Claudia turned around and looked at her old friend. She was covered with dust and dead bugs clung to her windshield, but it was nothing a good wash couldn't take care of. She was anxious to see how she ran.

"So that is your beloved first car out there, huh?" Alex

said glancing out the door.

"Yep. That's her."

"You'd never known a girl could care so much about a car, Alex. Claudia had pictures of Ramona on her walls—she wouldn't let any of her friends drive her."

"Why didn't you ever give the Accord a name?" He asked.

"I don't know. I don't have that kind of relationship with the Accord. I guess it was just that time in my life. I knew that no matter what was going on, I always had her to take me away if I needed it." Claudia said, and watched her mother look down to the floor and clear her throat. "Come on Mom, sit down on the couch. You must be exhausted. I'll get you some water."

"Or we have beer and wine?" Alex offered.

"She doesn't drink," Claudia said quickly.

"It's one of the many things the Lord convicted me of years ago," Maryanne said.

"Oh, sorry—" Alex said. "Well, we have a guestroom, I just need to clean some things off the bed."

"Oh, that's okay. I booked a hotel over on Wilshire."

"What? Why?" Claudia asked, although she was secretly relieved.

"Oh Claudia. You know I love you, and I'm glad you two are finally going to do the right thing and get married, but I can't stay here and support your decision to live in sin until then. It wouldn't be honest. I'd be betraying everything I claim about my faith. Avoid the appearance of evil, the

Bible says."

Claudia looked at Alex and rubbed her forehead. Then she laughed a little in disbelief because there was nothing else that could be said. There was an awkward silence while Maryanne looked back and forth between them, smiling condescendingly, like she felt sorry for their lost souls.

"Well, after the wedding, you're welcome to stay here," Alex jumped in.

Maryanne nodded politely. The three of them stood for another moment without saying anything.

Well, I guess I might as well tell you now, Claudia," Maryanne broke the silence. "Ramona isn't your only wedding gift," she fluffed her overly teased and sprayed hair and grinned. "I booked us a package at a real nice spa. We are long overdue for some good ole mother-daughter time, wouldn't you say?"

"Wow Mom, I don't know what to say. That's—that's a really nice gesture. Which spa did you book? I know a lot of people who work at the ones around here, maybe I could get a deal for us."

"Oh, well, it's not one here. It's a little ways away."

"Where is it?" Claudia asked.

"Just over in Scottsdale." Maryanne glanced at her bright coral fingernails, away from Claudia's eyes.

"Mom! That's six hours away!"

"I know, but that's not too bad. It'll be fun to take a road trip like we used to when we went to see your Granny

Maeve and Pawpaw Cruise."

"I hated going to their house. It smelled like mothballs and Pinesol," Claudia said.

"Listen, just do this one thing for me, please. It's all I ask. I just want us to have some time together, time to—" her voice trailed off and so did her gaze, and Claudia followed her mother's misty eyes to see if there was something she was actually looking at, or if this was just another one of her dramatic devices to manipulate concern. It was the latter.

"I don't know, I have work," Claudia said.

"On the weekend?"

Claudia was silent while she tried to think of a viable excuse. Doctor appointment? Jury duty?

"I'm going to be in New York anyway," Alex said and shrugged.

"What? You didn't tell me about that!" Claudia said. Whose side are you on here—Claudia asked him in a glare.

"Yes I did, last week. You said, 'Okay' and rolled your eyes," Alex said.

Claudia knew that this was a real possibility, even though she didn't remember it. She turned to Maryanne, who was looking at the couple with a smug expression, as if this little exchange revealed all the inevitable cracks in their relationship.

"Okay, fine. We'll go to Scottsdale. But can you at least try to lighten up on the whole preachy thing? I can't take it."

"Alright—I can do that, sweetie. Ooooh! This is going to be so much fun! I brought my camera so we can take lots of pictures! Well—I am just about beat like the thinnest piece of country-fried steak. A girl must get her beauty rest. I don't want those spa technicians thinking I don't at least try to take care of these old bags under my eyes."

Claudia thought that Maryanne should be more concerned about a different kind of baggage than what was under her overly made-up eyes. "Okay, Mom. Well—I work all day tomorrow until late tomorrow night, so you might be on your own."

"Oh don't worry about me, sweetie. I have some shopping to do. Ramona and me, we'll be just fine. I'll pick you up bright and early Saturday morning, okay?"

"Okay," Claudia said, wondering what exactly she was getting herself into.

"Bye Alex," Maryanne flickered her fingertips. "You two be good now. You know it's never too late to start doing the right thing, and I know you know what I mean." She looked down her nose at both of them.

"Okay Maryanne. Goodnight." Alex said, and waved.

When Claudia closed the front door, she immediately poured herself a large glass of wine and turned on Alex. "Why didn't you help me out there? You lead me right into her little scheme."

Alex laughed.

"What?"

"I've just never seen you this wound up over anything before."

"I'm not that—" Claudia realized her voice was shrill and stopped to take a breath and lower it. "Look, the point is you're supposed to help me when it comes to my mom, not work against me. That's the rule. We are a team. I don't want to spend the weekend with her. Louisa is taking Ben to the zoo, and I said I would go with them."

"Babe, I'm sure Louisa will understand. And anyway, I don't think you really have a choice here. Your mom is practically abducting you. If you say no, she'll find a way to get you in that car. Speaking of which, how weird is it that she tracked down your old Volvo and re-bought it?"

"Well, you haven't seen Landry. It's tiny. I'm sure she saw Ramona all over the place. And it was Dad who bought the car for me, after the divorce."

"It sounds to me like she's trying to make up for some things in the past. You should give her a chance."

"Yeah, maybe," Claudia said.

"She's the only mom you've got."

"Okay Dr. Phil. But I would gladly trade her in for a newer model."

"Come on, let's go back to bed." Alex tugged her hand, and gave her the get-down-to-business look.

"What? Are you kidding me? I'm not in the mood anymore, not after all of that."

"See, she's already getting to you. You've got to let it all roll off."

Claudia rubbed the back of her neck to get rid of the tension that had suddenly set up house between her shoulder blades. "Oh my God, what if I end up being just like her?"

"I believe those are every daughter's famous last words." Alex laughed, but then saw the sincere concern on Claudia's face and added, "Babe. You won't. You won't leave our kids the way she left you."

Chapter 5

Piper didn't want to hold her head still while she fought over speakerphone with her boyfriend, and Claudia's frustration grew each time she went to pin a piece of hair and lost her grip. It was like playing pin the tail on the donkey—in more ways than one.

"I don't need to ask Greg where you were last night, he'll say whatever you tell him to. The point is, you said you were meeting me and you didn't show. Not. Acceptable."

"But—"Claudia heard the boyfriend say, but then Piper hung up and flung her phone onto the counter beneath the mirror.

"Ugh!" she yelled, and leaned her head back.

"Sweetie, I know you're really upset right now, and fighting with the boyfriend will ruin even the strongest girl's day, but—I really need you to sit still so I can finish your hair or Tom is going to be pissed at both of us. You know how crabby directors get."

Piper held her hands up to her face and started crying.

"Oh no, sweetie—" Claudia said, but was interrupted by the intern at the door.

"Sorry," he said, only slightly cracking the door open, "but security just called, and there's a woman at the gate who said she's your mom?"

Claudia held a section of Piper's hair in her hand while Piper continued to weep into her palms. Her makeup was going to have to be completely redone, and Claudia was already running late with her hair. "Um," she said, "Yeah, she's in town. Tell them to let her in." Claudia closed her eyes for a brief second. She had just been thinking the day couldn't get any worse.

She took a deep breath, refocused all of her attention on Piper's hair, and changed her game plan. Instead of completing the complicated updo she had scheduled for the scene, he decided a nice, low ponytail would have to do. She hurriedly teased the hair at the crown and covered it with a cloud of hairspray. Then she smoothed the top, gathered it all into her hand, secured it with an elastic, and sprayed again. "There, you're done. Go ask Candace to touch you up."

"But I thought—" the girl said.

"This looks much better, trust me," Claudia said.

Just then, there was a light rapping on the door.

"Come in," Claudia said, as Piper stood to leave.

Maryanne stood beaming like a tourist in front of the Grand Canyon, a huge smile spread out across her face. "Now, I know you're working, but I won't be a bother one bit. I just couldn't pass up the opportunity to come see where you work," she said. "I remembered you said it was the NBC studios, and then I Googled directions on this fancy phone Tim got me for my birthday, and it was a cinch."

"Yeah. Uh—okay, well, I'm still kind of in the middle of things here, but I guess if you wanted to take a seat over there, that would be fine."

"You won't even know I'm here," Maryanne said, and fondled the laminate pass hanging on a cord around her neck.

Chris came in next, and it seemed that Piper's bad mood was contagious and spreading throughout the studio because he walked through the door huffing. He immediately scowled at Maryanne in the chair on the other side of the room, and then looked at Claudia as if to say, who the hell let the crazy lady out of the zoo?

Maryanne stood up and walked over to them, offering her hand and saying, "Hi there, I'm Claudia's mom. I'm just watching."

Chris shook her hand and smirked. "Hi," was all he said.

Claudia flinched, and was glad that after Chris, she could break for lunch. She shot a look at Maryanne that said, "please behave," and then took out a bottle of Surf Spray and the hairdryer.

"They said it was too flat yesterday," Chris said. "They want it to be like Robert Pattinson, or something—stupid poser," he mumbled, and looked down at whatever he was texting.

"Got it," Claudia said. She tried to avoid looking at Maryanne's goofy smile while she worked to make Chris's hair perfectly messy. It didn't take long. She gave him a good coating of spray; he looked up in the mirror with a nod of semi-approval, muttered a "see ya," and was out the door.

"This is just so exciting," Maryanne said to Claudia. "It's so—official around here. What's the show for?"

"It's called *Fire and Ice.* You probably haven't seen it. It's one of those new teenage-dramas with lots of premarital sex and drug overdoses."

"Oh. Well, anyway, it's just great that you've worked so hard to get here. Where do you want to go for lunch?" Maryanne asked.

"Do you feel like sushi?" Claudia asked.

"Raw fish? Oh no, I can't do that. I heard you get tapeworms from that stuff."

"I've never gotten a tapeworm—not that I know of anyway. Um, okay, I know a place I think you'll like. I don't have a lot of time though, so we need to hurry."

Claudia and Maryanne walked to Claudia's car parked in a reserved spot, right outside the back entrance. Maryanne had parked Ramona in the visitor lot, which was quite a hike.

They were fortunate to be seated quickly at Bistro Garden. It was a place that Claudia never would have normally chosen, but she knew the perfect white tablecloths and the lush greenery throughout the restaurant would thrill Maryanne. Also it was a big place, and loud; so she would be safe from any long, in-depth, too-serious conversations with her mother.

"This looks fancy," Maryanne said.

"It's my treat," Claudia said, as they followed the hostess to their table.

Maryanne carefully spread her napkin over her lap and gasped when she looked at the menu. "Eighteen dollars for a hamburger?" she whispered in shock.

"Mom, I said it's my treat. Get whatever you want. Things are a little more expensive out here, that's all," Claudia said.

In a few minutes, their waiter brought water and asked for their orders.

"I'll have the grilled salmon with the corn salsa," Claudia said. "And if I could get asparagus instead of the sautéed spinach that would be great."

"Certainly," the waiter said. "And for you, Ma'am?

Maryanne looked up from the menu and said, "I'll have the half-sandwich with a cup of soup. What's that? Oh. The turkey-breast and the French Onion. No, I'm fine with water, thank you very much."

"Mom," Claudia said, after the waiter walked away, "Is that really all you wanted?"

"Yes. I'm really not that hungry after all," Maryanne said.

"Well, you'll have to try some of mine."

They looked around the room and commented trivially on the décor and the piano player.

"Claudia," Maryanne said, a new intensity in her voice. "Is that Mr. De Niro over there?"

Claudia was taking a sip of water and almost spit it out, laughing. She had mastered the Los Angeles casual glance over the shoulder so as not to look like a naïve tourist—exactly the way Maryanne looked, mouth agape, eyes wide, and even worse, pointing. Claudia slowly turned back after glancing, like she was assessing the architecture and said, "Yes, Mom. That's Robert De Niro."

Maryanne was so excited that she forgot about her not-so-hungry act, and not only finished all of her soup and sandwich, but also half of Claudia's meal.

After Claudia signed the receipt, she had a hard time tearing Maryanne away from the table, but when she saw the camera coming out of her mother's purse, insisted that they had to leave that very second.

Chapter 6

Louisa pushed Ben in the stroller and from slightly behind, Claudia could see his little feet happily kicking and bouncing up and down. A stream of half-naked roller-bladers swerved dangerously close to them as they flew past in a blur of glistening tan skin. A grizzled caricaturist sitting behind an easel studied a teenage girl with braces and bad skin. Set up next to him was a couple selling sterling silver jewelry and knock-off sunglasses.

"I mean, what would you do? Would you drop everything and go on a trip with your mom if she showed up out of the blue?" Claudia asked Louisa, narrowly avoiding the steroid bodybuilder walking toward her.

"Well, considering she is in Vietnam and has been buried there for ten years now, I'm guessing I would be a little surprised, and I would probably go if she came all that way."

"Okay, I know. But I mean, what would you do if you

were me?"

"Well, I can tell you being a mom myself—I can't imagine how it would feel if Ben ever turned me away. That has to be the worst thing that can happen to a mother."

"But you're a good mom, Lou, that's the difference," Claudia said.

"Ice cream?" Louisa asked.

"Yes, please."

They walked into the small gelato shop, and approached the icy case. The buckets of muted pastel cream and vivid sorbets offered momentary sugar rushes and anesthesia for tired tongues.

"A scoop of pistachio in a cup, please," Louisa said.

Claudia's eyes roved over the options. "Hmmm. This is always so hard. They all look so good. Okay, I'll have the dark chocolate with sea-salt caramel."

They positioned the stroller between them at a small table, and Louisa gave Ben a tiny taste of the light green stuff. He smiled and shimmy-shaked with pleasure, his eyes growing wide—another sugar addict was hooked for life.

"Look," Louisa said. "You're a big girl. You've built a great business for yourself and you've got a strong relationship. You don't have to do anything you don't want to do. It's all a choice, there's no right or wrong."

Claudia swallowed another spoonful of chocolate and nodded, trying to imprint Louisa's words onto her consciousness. "But all of a sudden I feel like I'm five again when I'm around her. Like all this pressure to do the right thing, you know? It just weighs me down."

"I can tell," Louisa said. "Hey, will you go with me over to the Promenade? There's a dress in Anthropologie that I like, but it might be a little too Betty-Rubblish— it's so hard for short girls to find good dresses. I need your help or otherwise I'm going to end up wearing mom jeans and orthopedic shoes for the rest of my life."

"Oh God, don't go orthopedic, Louisa, whatever you do." Claudia took Louisa's empty cup and stacked it in hers, tossing them in the trash. "Let's go."

As they walked to the car, Ben pointed at a mime trying to lift an immovable invisible box off the ground. The mime strained and strained until finally he fell backward in defeat, unable to move the obstacle. Ben squealed and laughed, but Claudia felt sad watching the show.

That night, Claudia drove Alex to LAX and tapped the steering wheel with her fingernails while he tried to wrap up another lengthy phone conversation.

"I don't think I'm going to go with her tomorrow," she said as soon as he hung up.

"You're going. It's only two days, and years down the road, you will be glad that you spent the time with her." Alex sounded like a recorded self-help mantra by this point.

"I've already spent some time with her. I don't think I can handle more than two-hour segments. What if it only makes things worse between us? Pandora's box and all that."

"Just try to keep it light. Maybe you two just need to laugh together."

"Yeah. If only she drank . . . that would loosen her up." Claudia knew he was so sick of hearing about it, but she wanted a clear, black and white answer to her dilemma.

"Well, I'm sure when you guys get naked in a mud bath together, that will help loosen things up." Alex laughed.

"Oh God. This is going to be terrible. I'm not going," Claudia said.

"This is me, Babe," Alex pointed to the terminal.

"Okay." Claudia's stomach was gurgling on her afternoon latte, no dinner, and a tall order of anxiety without whipped cream.

"Promise me one thing. You'll take the Prius this weekend. I don't want you driving that old Volvo until it's reliable. And I think we should finally sell the Accord, so there's no use putting any more miles on it."

"You know the seatbelt hits me weird in that car—it always leaves a mark on my collarbone."

"Promise."

Claudia leaned over and kissed him goodbye. When he pulled away to open the door, she pulled him back in the seat. "Don't leave me with her."

"You'll do great. And then we can move on and talk about the wedding."

"Okay." Claudia nodded with resolution, but felt slightly dizzy at the word 'wedding'.

"I'll text you when I land. You'll be asleep, I hope," Alex said standing next to the open door.

"I doubt it." She forced a smile like a middle-aged airline hostess and waved goodbye, watching him walk through the automatic doors to the check-in line.

When she got back to the house, Claudia went straight to the "stuff drawer" in the kitchen and pulled out the pack of cigarettes that she reserved only for nervous breakdowns. She thought it was a good sign that she only smoked one pack every year or so. If the number went up from that, she told herself she would speak to a doctor about anti-anxiety medication, because that would mean she was having more than her allotted amount of nervous breakdowns. There was no doubt in her mind that tonight definitely deserved a smoke—stale though it was.

She paced around the back patio with the cigarette between her fingers. Foster watched her walk back and forth like she was a tennis ball on the court. She took a deep drag off the cigarette and dialed her father's number.

"Did you know anything about this?" she asked him.

"Your mother drove out there? In Ramona?"

"Okay, obviously you didn't know. What should I do?"

"Darling, you know I am the wrong person to ask how you should deal with your mother. I never figured it out. I hope you can though."

"Do you think she's finally lost if for good?"

"I don't think she's dangerous, if that's what you mean.

As bad as it got with all of us, she never did anything to physically harm you or me."

"The key word there is physically," Claudia said.

"Claude, you're going to have to forgive her at some point, you know. Otherwise, you will turn into a bitter, miserable old lady. You're too smart for that."

"Alone. You left out that part. I'll end up alone."

"I'm sorry baby, but it's true. My doctor finally convinced me to cut down on my stress level—leave the office at the office instead of bringing it home, try to communicate more clearly with Betsy, go for walks. It's made a difference. My blood pressure has dropped ten points. You just can't ignore things forever."

"But everything was fine until she showed up," Claudia said.

"Was it? And is it that she showed up out of the blue that's made everything bad, or is it that she didn't show up until now?"

"Have you been talking to Alex?" Claudia asked.

"No, but if he's saying the same thing to you, then he's bright, like your old man."

"Okay," Claudia said with resignation.

"You're a good kid. You'll know what to say to her when the time comes."

"Can you promise me that?"

"Yeah. Pretty much," he said, "But I don't envy you one bit." Claudia heard the smile in his voice.

"Oh, come on, you're not even a little jealous?"

"Goodnight, sweetheart. Get some rest. Tell Ramona I said hi—and your mother if you think of it."

"Okay, Dad. Love you. Thanks."

Claudia lit another cigarette and looked over at Foster who had given up on watching her charades and was sleeping with his head cradled on his paws.

"I guess that is that," she said to the sleeping dog. "I hope Lucy will be around this weekend to feed you."

Chapter 7

Louisa yawned when she shuffled through the door, took a mug from the kitchen cabinet and poured a cup of coffee. "Morning," she said.

"I left the note on the counter for Lucy next door, and I wrote down your number for an emergency contact," Claudia said to her while she crammed a couple of more shirts into her already bulging duffle bag.

"Um, you guys are only going for two nights, right?" Louisa said, staring at the bag. "You look like you're packing for a month."

Claudia looked at Louisa, and then at the bag, sighed, and put her hands on her hips. "Yeah," she laughed. "Oh, this is ridiculous! Why am I so nervous?" She rubbed her face.

"Because you're a little bit of a nutcase like me, and that's why I love you," Louisa said.

Claudia looked up when she heard the honking horn. "Shit."

"Go! Foster will be fine with Lucy. I'll check in on him too."

Claudia hugged like she was a child begging her mom not to drop her off at preschool.

When she got out the door, Claudia stopped to take in Maryanne's ensemble of a brightly printed shirt draped over pleated capri pants, orange nails and lips, large sunglasses, big hair, and bedazzled flip-flops.

"Isn't this fun?" Maryanne squealed.

"Yeah, it's great," Claudia said, trying to feign enthusiasm. "Mom, I think we should take Alex's car. It's quite a drive to Scottsdale."

"Oh no. Absolutely not! Ramona has to go with us. I brought her all the way to you and now you don't want her? If I had known you didn't care about her anymore—maybe I wouldn't have—" Maryanne looked off forlornly at that elusive spot in the distance she was always searching for.

"Mom! Of course I care! I just thought the Prius might be more reliable."

"I see," Maryanne said, looking down, with all the mother-guilt-manipulation she could muster on her crestfallen face.

"Okay, fine. You win. We'll take Ramona. Whatever keeps the peace."

"Good. I'll put your bag in the trunk then. I assume you

want to drive?"

"Yeah, I do," Claudia said, and felt a flurry of excitement rush in her chest.

Maybe she wasn't being totally selfless in breaking her promise to Alex. When she put her hands on the steering wheel, her adolescence came tumbling back like the way she and Gracie used to haphazardly roll down the hill in their backyards, and she remembered listening to The Verve's "Bittersweet Symphony" over and over during those first days that she had Ramona. She waved to Louisa who was getting in her car to leave, and before she turned the keys, she leaned over her mom in the passenger seat and checked the glove compartment just to make sure that by some crazy chance, one of her old mixed tapes from high school wasn't left in there after all these years. But there was nothing in the cracked box except tissues and three packs of Doublemint, her mother's favorite brand of chewing gum. The scent infiltrated the car, and Claudia felt nauseous as she remembered the times she was forced to sit quietly next to Maryanne in church, listening to the sound of her jaw pop as it worked the gum, and the sickly sweet smell formed a bubble around them that she longed to pop.

"Okay, then. Here we go," The heft of the tank reacted slowly when she pushed her foot on the gas pedal.

"I printed out directions at the hotel," Maryanne said, as Claudia pulled out of the driveway.

"I'll be fine for a while. I've been to Scottsdale before."

"Oh, okay. Goodness, there's just so much I don't know about you, Claudia. I want you to tell me everything." Maryanne clapped her hands together in her lap for emphasis.

Claudia cleared her throat and squinted at the road ahead. "Oh. Um, well—I mean, you know the big things. You know where I live and that I'm getting married."

Maryanne looked at her hands in her lap and disappointment shadowed her face like a dark funeral veil. "Yes, but I want to know about your work and what you dream of for your future," she looked up at Claudia, who gave no response. "It can wait. I'm glad you're here with me. That's enough for now."

"Are you still working in the office at the school?" Claudia asked when the silence became unbearable.

"Mmm hmmm," Maryanne nodded. "At least for a little while longer."

"I guess you're pretty tired of it. You've been there for what, over twenty years now?"

"Yeah, it might be time to move on to something new," Maryanne said.

"Is there something else that interests you?" This felt like a really bad first date.

"Oh. I don't know—I guess I haven't thought much about it, yet. Have you started looking for a wedding dress?" Maryanne pulled hard in the other direction in the subject-tug-of-war.

"No." Claudia fixed her sight on the road ahead. Tug, tug.

"Well, maybe we can do that when we come back?" Maryanne asked.

"Maybe. I don't even know what style I want, Mom. I think I need a little more time before I jump into all of that stuff. Who knows? Maybe I'll walk down the aisle in a pair of jeans just to piss everyone off."

Maryanne laughed uncomfortably. "Oh, don't be silly, Claudia. I'm sure Betsy has plenty of her own ideas for you. That woman can be so conniving," she said this last part still wearing a smile.

Claudia sighed. She wasn't going to discuss Betsy with Maryanne. "We have plenty of time. We haven't even set a date yet."

"Really?" Maryanne said in surprise. "Well. I don't know why not, there is so much to do—you have to be organized about these things." Maryanne looked at Claudia, who continued to look straight ahead at the road.

"It's my wedding, Mom. Leave it. Okay?" Claudia said, in as calm of a voice as she could muster.

"Well, I guess I should just learn to keep my mouth shut. If you want my advice, you can ask for it. I know you don't value my opinion very much."

"Sounds like a plan." Claudia tried not to let her mother's passive-aggressive comment get under her skin and searched her brain for a song that would fit the moment. She came up with the obvious Frankie Goes To Hollywood's "Relax", cringed, pushed the imaginary stop button and then played Janis Joplin's "Summertime". While Maryanne babbled about Tina Hampton marrying some loser from their old high school who worked at Tim's car dealership, Claudia concentrated on the lyrics and Joplin's gravelly voice that were silently playing at full volume in her head: *"You're gonna rise, rise up singing, you're gonna spread your wings child. . ."*

"Claudia, did you hear what I said?"

"Yes, Tina went on a cruise to Jamaica for her honeymoon."

"No. I asked if you remembered Gracie, our old next door neighbor? You know, the little girl with Downs?"

"Mom—of course I remember Gracie. We were together all the time, until you and Dad split up and sold the house. And I saw her on TV the other day talking about her organization."

"The Lord has just blessed that poor child with so many opportunities. Not all of them can function as well as she can, you know. Usually they can only bag groceries or small things like that. It's such a heavy burden."

"Mom, you can't talk about people like that, disabled or otherwise. You can't throw them all into a homogenous lump. Especially not out here, okay? Not only is it cruel, but you'll end up on the news for being politically incorrect. It's almost just as bad as pulling a gun out on the freeway in road rage."

Maryanne looked shocked, her bottom lip protruded as she looked down and frowned. "Well, I wasn't aware that you and Gracie kept in touch. I was just trying to make conversation, but that seems impossible."

"We don't stay in touch."

"Why not? It sounds like you really loved her."

"I did. But after I left, it was just easier to leave everything behind. Start over, so I wouldn't be reminded of—things."

"I understand that. You know, before I came back, I thought about continuing on to a new place, starting fresh."

Everything inside of Claudia grew hot. She tried to hear "Summertime" again and breathe deeply, let it slide off her shoulders; but she couldn't. She paused, and then slowly said, "Please don't ever compare your decision to leave Dad and me with mine to move away from Landry. I didn't have a family depending on me. It was the right time for me. You left at the wrong time."

Maryanne opened her mouth to say something, but then closed it and looked out the window. Claudia pulled her hair into a ponytail, using her knees to steady the steering wheel, which she knew terrified Maryanne, but she continued to squeeze her legs around it until her hair was satisfactorily secured. She heard her phone beep and saw a text from Alex, "How's it going? Missing you, x." She wanted to text him back and say she was trapped in parental hell, and that she was about to turn around. She fought the urge, chose safety instead and chewed on the inside of her lip while she steadied the wheel. It was silent inside Ramona for close to an hour until they got to Palm Springs.

"Can you turn the AC up, darlin'? I'm starting to sweat." Maryanne pulled her shirt away from her chest and fanned her face and neck.

Claudia checked the dashboard and looked at the faded temperature dial. "It's on the coldest setting. I can try to make it blow a little stronger, I guess." Claudia pushed the air dial to the highest capacity. The breeze was steady, but still weak compared to the AC in the Accord and Prius. "It's an old car, Mom. This is as much as she's going to give."

"That's fine," Maryanne said, mopping her forehead with a tissue from the glove compartment and breathing slowly.

"This is why we should've brought the Prius," Claudia sighed. Anyway, tell me about this place in Scottsdale," Claudia said, trying to distract Maryanne from complaining about the heat. "Where'd you hear about it?"

"Oh. Well, it came highly recommended from my friend Susan. She said it changed her life."

"A spa changed her life?"

"Mmmm hmmm. Said she learned a lot about herself there."

"Like what? That she loves getting massages and facials?"

"So sarcastic, Claudia. You know, that really is not an attractive trait."

Inwardly, Claudia was wailing like Janis Joplin during her most orgasmic, high-pitched riff. She searched her mental playlist for another song and focused on the Pixies' version of "Head On". She could hear the guitars charging in for the intro, and she tuned out Maryanne's panting and fanning. She softly hummed and accidentally laughed out loud when she thought of what Maryanne would say about the song. *"I'm taking myself to a dirty part of town, where all my troubles can't be found,"* she felt her lip curl up like Billy Idol. *"I said, yeah yeah yeah yeah yeah."*

"What's that?" Maryanne sat upright and pointed out the windshield. Claudia shook herself out of her rock daydream. A thin trail of white smoke was coming out of Ramona's hood. It quickly turned into a thick cloud and billowed so fast, Claudia could barely see out the windshield.

"Pull over!" Maryanne screamed.

"I'm trying to!" Claudia looked in the rearview mirror, and got over to the right lane. There wasn't an exit in sight, so as soon as she could, she pulled over to the dusty side of the road.

"Get out! Get out of the car!" Maryanne shouted.

Both women opened their doors and ran ten yards away from the car, into the dry red earth that only ten miles ago was green and fertile.

Ramona sat with her doors open, the smoke trailing away from her hood. After a couple of minutes of waning smoke, it was clear that Ramona was not going to explode, and

Claudia and Maryanne returned to her side.

Claudia looked at her phone, wondering what she should do. If she called Alex right now, he would be angry that she broke her word about taking the Prius. She was angry with herself for falling for Maryanne's guilt trip, the oldest trick in the antiquated mother-daughter handbook. She Googled AAA's number on her phone, even though she wasn't a member.

"Would you like me to connect you for no additional charge?" the operator asked.

"Yes, please." Please connect me to something, anything right now would do.

She was waiting on the line when an old truck pulling a trailer pulled up behind them.

"Hello, how can I help you?" the man from AAA said. "Hello?"

"Yeah, I need um, I'm sorry, can I call you back?" Claudia hung up the phone before getting the number.

Maryanne was walking toward the person getting out of the truck. Claudia ran to catch up with her. She never knew what might pop out of Maryanne's mouth, and she felt the need to constantly censor, particularly with strangers.

When Claudia caught up, she saw a woman with long silver hair pulled back into a bun approaching them. Stray hairs escaped the bun and created a fuzzy halo around her head. Even from a distance, Claudia could hear something jingling. The woman's skin was dark and deeply wrinkled like the shell of a walnut. It made her hair appear even whiter although it was flecked with the red dust. She wore a long skirt that flowed around her ankles when she walked and a sleeveless shirt that bared her lean, leathery arms. As she came closer to them, Claudia saw that the ropes of necklaces the woman wore around her neck were responsible for the jingling sound.

"Well, at least it's a beautiful day to breakdown," the woman said and laughed.

Chapter 8

Claudia had a hard time finding humor in being stranded on the side of the road during the hottest part of the day. "Beautiful day, my ass," she muttered.

"It was the weirdest thing," Maryanne said to the woman, "All of a sudden, smoke started pouring out of the engine. I thought my time for glory had come for sure. It happened so fast. Oooh, praise the Lord you were behind us!"

Claudia squinted skeptically at the wild haired woman smiling at Maryanne.

"I can offer a suggestion, if you'd like," the woman said. "My name is Kate, and my brother Ron owns a service station just up at the next exit. He's fair, and I'm sure he could tow your car quickly."

"Oh, how about that?" Maryanne smiled at Claudia. "You see Claudia, angels really do exist! Praise you, Jesus!" She clasped her hands together and looked toward the sky.

Claudia didn't think the burnout hippie she was looking at was an angel, but the longer she stood under the incinerating sun, the less she worried about what kind of person this woman was. "He won't do anything to the car until he talks to me first, right?"

"Of course," Kate said. "I'll call him. Can I use your phone?" she pointed to the one in Claudia's hand.

Claudia thought they had made a great discovery in finding the one person who didn't have a cell phone these days, but instead of asking questions, she handed hers over to the woman, who reached for the phone expectantly. Her fingernails were edged in brown, a rough callus rubbed Claudia's palm in the exchange. "Yep. Next exit down," Kate said into the phone after a couple of seconds into the conversation. "Alright. Okay, thanks, Ron." She hung up the phone and handed it back to Claudia. "He has to make another stop first, but it won't be long."

"Oh, hallelujah," Maryanne said, fanning her face. Her red chest was covered in beads of sweat.

"I live just a mile or so from Ron's shop. Why don't we go back to my house and you two can get out of this heat? People who aren't used to it shrivel up like little raisins in minutes."

"That sounds wonderful—getting out of the heat," Maryanne said.

Claudia looked at Ramona. "But we'll just leave her here? That seems kind of sketchy."

"She's not driveable, and the chances of someone else coming through here and taking the trouble to hook her up to a tow truck are pretty slim, I'd say," Kate said. "But suit yourself. If you want to wait, go ahead."

Claudia looked again at Maryanne who was pleading with her eyes like the saddest hound dog. She looked like she was going to melt into a gooey puddle of Mary Kay.

"Okay, let's go," Claudia said, reluctantly.

"That-a girl," Kate said, and walked around to the driver's side of the truck.

Claudia retrieved their bags out of Ramona's trunk and carried them to the back of the truck. She noticed for the first time that there were two horses in the trailer attached to the truck. They were both nodding in a warm slumber, completely unconcerned with their whereabouts. Who were these people? A brother mechanic and a sister farmer? Had they landed in Green Acres? Obviously not, because there was hardly anything green about the place. A blue plastic tarp covered with dust lay in the truck bed, and Claudia grimaced when she pulled it over their bags, knowing that it wouldn't do much to keep them clean. She didn't care about her old black duffle bag, but Maryanne's carry-on suitcase was new, with a light rose color background, and printed with a Laura Ashley-esque floral pattern.

Maryanne was already sitting next to Kate in the truck, the air conditioner blowing her wilting hair straight up and away from her face. After she climbed in and sat down next to her mom, Claudia closed the truck door behind her. She peered into the side mirror as they pulled onto the freeway and watched Ramona become smaller and smaller, until there was nothing left of her but a blue dot. She felt the same ache as when she handed over Ramona's papers to the new owner in exchange for hard cash. She felt like a terrible, mutinous friend—like a Judas.

When Claudia saw the brown twisted trees and the cacti, (for God's sake, there were even tumbleweeds), she thought she had been dropped into a Dr. Seuss book. Kate turned onto a red dirt road, and dust billowed around them, nearly obscuring everything from sight. After the dust settled, and ten minutes of bumping along the primitive road with no buildings in view had past, Claudia said to Kate, "I thought you said you live just a mile away."

"Yeah, that's right, a mile from Ron's shop. That's twenty miles from here. We're both right by the park entrance."

Claudia opened her mouth to ask what park Kate was referring to, but then she took another long look at the landscape and thought about how far they were from the Palm Springs exit. "Oh wow. We're in Joshua Tree, aren't we?"

"Not yet. Fifteen minutes and we will be." Kate's silver necklaces chimed with each bump in the road.

Maryanne was uncharacteristically silent, and turning a light shade of green.

"I always wanted to come here, but never made it," Claudia said. She had heard that lots of musicians visited Joshua Tree back in the sixties and seventies to explore the psychedelic spiritual movement, which she understood meant they basically took loads of acid and peyote and could go as mad as they liked in the desert, away from civilization.

"This place has a way of pulling people in. Looks like that's exactly what it's set out to do with you," Kate said.

There was something Claudia liked about Kate's hippie-speak, but then it also sounded like a script for a bad movie—like she could be an extra in *Shaft*.

"Are you okay, Mom?" Claudia turned to Maryanne, who was steadying herself with her hand on the dashboard and staring straight ahead. It seemed to take every ounce of her concentration. She nodded and swallowed hard.

"Look in my glove compartment," Kate said. "There are some ginger chews in there that will take care of any car sickness." The truck continued to bump and bounce along small potholes and rocks.

Claudia reached around a large flashlight in the glove compartment, found the bag of chews, unwrapped one, and handed it to Maryanne. She also took one for herself; her throat was shriveling up like a slug covered in salt. The ginger's spice hit the back of her tongue first, and then her nasal passages. Saliva rushed between her jaws as she worked the chewy candy between her teeth. Maryanne sat back in the seat and sighed. She closed her eyes.

"How long have you had that Volvo?" Kate asked. "Been a while since I've seen one that boxy."

"Since I was sixteen. Well, that's not entirely true—she's been lost and recently found—now it seems she's sick and needs to be healed," Claudia muttered, and Maryanne, with her eyes still closed, smiled in approval of the metaphor.

Kate laughed, deep and throaty. "Well, Volvos last forever, and I'm sure once Ron lays his hands on her, you'll witness a miracle. There it is," she pointed ahead to a small service station with two pumps and a crackerjack box of a convenience store, as they drove slowly past.

"This reminds me of the little town where I grew up. We only had one gas station, one market, and one post office—there wasn't much else," Maryanne said.

"Unfortunately, we have been attacked by the god-awful strip malls on the other side of the park entrance, but the locals avoid them. They're really for the tourists, and we do our best to let visitors know about the local places around here."

They passed a few trailer homes and a cabin or two. Claudia noticed a collection of old cars in one of the grassless yards—a truck with missing tires, a Mustang without a windshield—the hood of an old Cadillac opened to reveal an empty tomb where an engine had once been.

Kate turned by a lopsided mailbox fashioned out of scrap metal and an old breadbox. Claudia's eyes scanned the curious artifact and then immediately jumped to the more bizarre monument of Kate's home at the end of the rutted drive. The structure topped the list of the most eccentric homes she had ever seen, even after living in Los Angeles for ten years. It was a round building and was the same shade of red as the ground, as if the desert itself had given birth to it. There were no corners or edges; the surface was a continuous smooth, organic line. The windows looked like they had been scooped out of the moldable clay, and sealed with liquid glass. Even the door was an asymmetrical curve, like a child had drawn it. The roof was woven thatch, something Claudia had only seen on the Travel Channel and *Gilligan's Island*.

"Oh my gracious," Maryanne said. "Well, I've never. My girlfriend Susan would just go to town taking pictures of this. She's the photographer for the *Landry Local,*" she said, as if Kate was familiar with the little paper.

Claudia felt weak. Three hours ago she was talking to Louisa in her cool, clean kitchen. Now she was in an absurd desert mirage with her crazy mother and a mysterious woman who was quite possibly even crazier than Maryanne. She wanted to call Alex, but she had to wait until she was alone. She needed to hear his calming voice and no longer cared if he said, "I told you so".

Kate pushed the unlocked front door open and said, "Make yourselves at home. I need to let Franny and Zooey out of the trailer."

Claudia took tentative steps ahead of Maryanne, as if she were scoping out dangerous territory. Inside, the home was relatively modern and clean. The furniture was artisan crafted and simple—a wooden framed sofa with colorful silk cushions, an armchair, and a custom bookcase that curved around the clay walls. The living room was open to the kitchen, which was outfitted with modern appliances suitable for any wannabe gourmet. Maryanne sat down on the couch and put her head in her hands. "Oh, I'm so glad it's cool in here. Whew!"

Claudia glanced through the glass sliding doors to the large, open backyard and saw Kate tying the two horses to a wooden rail under a lean-to stable of tree branch posts and a corrugated metal roof. Two sheep were walking around the stable. In the back corner, Claudia spotted a chicken walking out of an old doghouse. She jumped when she felt something wet touch her ankle and found a medium-sized mutt with his tongue hanging out of his mouth. He smiled at her and wagged his tail; his chocolate colored fur was speckled with grey hairs.

Kate stepped through the sliding glass side door and into the kitchen where Claudia was standing. She washed her calloused hands in the sink, and then poured three glasses of cold water, handing one first to Maryanne and then Claudia. "Naptime," she said. "Guestroom is to the right off the hallway." She took her glass of water and disappeared down the opposite end of the hall.

Maryanne stood up, and without saying a word, walked in the direction of the guestroom.

Chapter 9

Yeah, I'm here," Claudia said to Alex over a bad connection. "Can you hear me now?"

"Sorry, just got out of the cab. I swear the driver was drunk. How's the spa? Have you and your mom pulled each other's hair out yet?"

Claudia sat down on the brightly colored sofa next to the dog that was already snoring. Apparently naptime ran like clockwork at this house for all of the creatures. "Babe—we haven't made it to the spa yet."

"Why? Did you leave late or something?"

Claudia sighed, and then sped through the account of the day's disaster. She didn't want to stop because she knew what was coming and wanted to get it over with as quickly as possible, without any speed bumps.

"I'm sorry, you're where? With who?" Alex laughed. "Babe—are you kidding me?"

"I know, I know. Go ahead and say it."

"Apparently I don't need to, you already know. But—I don't have a ton of sympathy for you right now, Miss Liar Pants. He started singing, "Please allow me to introduce myself," and laughed again.

"Oh, shut up," Claudia said playfully, appreciating his reference to the song "Sympathy for the Devil".

"Well, it's a shame you guys are missing out on a whole day of pampering because of this."

"Ugh. I am going to need a five-hour massage after today," the knots that appeared in her shoulders as soon as Maryanne showed up in Los Angeles were now calcifying into rocks. "How's everything in New York?" she asked, trying to forget her predicament.

"Oh you know—fast and pissy. I think there aren't enough trees to get oxygen to people's heads, so that's why they always sound like they're about to implode. I'm going to see Helen on Broadway tonight, and I'm sure that will be great. I don't know how long I can hang at the after-party, though. I need to at least show my smiling face for a while. God, I sound ancient, don't I?"

"No. You're just a grown man who knows that all of that bullshit doesn't really mean anything."

"It's a part of the job—but it does wear me out. You know what I want us to do when I get back Monday night? Put on our sweats; stuff our faces at El Cholo, and see some weird indie movie at the Wilshire Theater."

"You never want to go see movies at the theater," Claudia said, curious.

"And you hate cutting my hair because you do it all day. But I miss doing the things we used to when we first started dating."

"Yeah, we did do a lot more then, didn't we? Okay, deal—sweats, Mexican, movie. Oh, Babe—that might be the car guy on the other line. I'll call you later."

Claudia switched lines and stood up from the couch. The brown dog shifted, yawned, and hung his head over the edge of the cushion; a pink tongue stuck out of one side of his mouth.

"Uh, Miss Nichols?" a man's voice said, "This is Ron Saubel."

"Hi, yes, you got my car to the shop okay?"

"Yes. I did a quick once over."

"Okay."

"Well, there is coolant in your oil," Ron mumbled and then cleared his throat.

"What does that mean?"

"It means there's a leak."

"Can you plug it or something?"

"Nope."

"Wrap some duct tape around it just to get us home?"

"Afraid not, I'm going to have to order a new valve."

Claudia scratched her scalp. The word "order" did not bode well.

"Should be here tomorrow by lunchtime. Won't take long to change out. An hour. Maybe two."

"So we're stuck here for the night?" Claudia looked outside the window at the red and brown landscape.

"You could look at it as a vacation instead of a sentence. Lots of people visit here, you know. It's not all that bad. I mean, our family has lived here for hundreds years and we still like it."

"Sorry, I didn't mean to offend you," Claudia said. "I guess we'll just talk tomorrow then."

She wanted to scream after she hung up the phone. She should have said no the moment her mother showed up. No, you can't stay here. No, I don't want to go anywhere with you. No, you can't buy me off with my stupid old car. NO, you can't make up for everything that happened in the past, damn it!

She paced around the room. She walked over to the bookcase and scanned the titles on the spines of the books: Jack Kerouac, Ernest Hemingway, a bunch of self-help nonsense, Jung, Plath, Vonnegut. She pulled out an old copy of *Franny and Zooey*, one of those books she had always meant to read, but never got around to, and had been reminded of again by Kate's horses. She opened the cover and flipped through the pages. She felt something stiff preventing the book from flipping smoothly, like a bad deck of cards flowing clumsily out of a dealer's hand.

The faded photograph she pulled out of the book was

wrinkled from where it had been folded in two. Claudia looked closely at the photo and gasped when she made out a very young, dark-haired Kate standing next to whom she would recognize in any era of his long reigning rock stardom, Keith Richards. On the other side of Kate stood a tall, longhaired man who looked vaguely familiar to Claudia, though she couldn't quite place him. The picture had obviously been snapped at a show, as a crowd stood behind and below the figures. Actually, it looked like it was taken from onstage. What was Kate doing hobnobbing with the Stones? Claudia ran her fingers along the edges of the yellowed image, and then hid it back inside the pages of the Zooey chapters where it secretly lived. She knew the photograph wasn't supposed to be seen or remembered; otherwise it would be in a frame on the mantle, like the ones of Kate and Ron when they were children.

She slid the Salinger book back onto the bookcase and chose another one: Stephen King's *Salem's Lot.* She didn't get very far into the story—only to the point where Ben Mears rediscovers the Marsten House, when the book fell from her hand and her head dropped next to the drooling dog.

Chapter 10

Claudia lifted her right arm lying over her head with her left hand and tried to shake it awake. It was completely numb from lying above her head. She heard clanging in the kitchen several feet away, and then recognized Kate's raspy voice calling, "Come here, Jackson Browne! I dropped some apple!" The drowsy dog next to Claudia jumped to attention and ran into the kitchen. Claudia followed him, stumbling to the counter where Kate wielded a swiftly moving knife.

"Where's my mother?" Claudia asked Kate, and then covered a yawn.

"I believe she's still sleeping. She must really need the rest." After her eyes focused, Claudia could see Kate was now shredding zucchini into a bowl. "I just talked to Ron. Looks like you guys will be staying here for the night, huh? I had a feeling you might be."

"We don't want to impose on you—there has to be a hotel

around here somewhere, right?"

"Mmm hmm. An old motel, but you don't want to stay there," Kate grimaced and continued scraping. "There's plenty of room here."

"You seem pretty comfortable with strangers staying in your house." Claudia watched Kate chop some cilantro. "I mean, for all you know, we could be some kind of mother-daughter thievery operation."

"And for all you know, I could be a murderer," Kate said, wiping the cilantro off the edge of the knife. "But yet, if we walked around wondering what was lurking behind every new person we met, it'd be a pretty lonely life, don't you think? Ron and I grew up having a lot of people around; it's all we've ever known. Our grandparents were native Cahuilla. Our mother was white, but she didn't stand a chance against our father's family. People everywhere, all the time—grand-parents, babies, distant cousins, friends, and yes, occasional strangers. Even though we weren't a secluded tribe anymore, we still lived like one, know what I mean?"

"That sounds nice, actually. Your own little village."

"We all need one," Kate said, and looked up at Maryanne as she entered the room, her hair smashed flat against her head and jutting off to one side like a flying saucer.

"Why didn't you wake me, Claudia?" she mumbled. "How's Ramona?"

"Still sick. We have to stay the night, and Kate has offered to let us stay here. I hate to say it Mom, but we probably won't make it to Scottsdale until early tomorrow night. That will leave only Sunday for treatments. I've got to be back at work on Monday. Have you called the spa to let them know what happened?"

"Uh, no. I haven't called yet. I'll go do that now—excuse me." Maryanne shuffled out of the kitchen back toward the guestroom. Claudia looked after her, wondering why she needed privacy.

Kate put a pot on the stove and filled it with some kind of grain and water. Her thin brown arms were weightless in motion, her wrists circular in their movement. She was the kind of person who might float away if it wasn't for her fiery spirit, binding her to the ground. There was a force within her that came from fighting life's tide. Claudia recognized it because she held the same force within herself. As she watched the silver-haired woman move around the kitchen and prepare food for the three women, Claudia softened toward Kate.

"It's okay," Maryanne said, returning to the kitchen, her hair re-fluffed and her lips painted the awful orange color. "They were very understanding. Oooh, it smells delicious in here. What are you making, Kate?"

"Curried Quinoa and Zucchini fritters with goat cheese. My client gave me the recipe for the fritters last week and I can't stop eating them. I'm addicted!"

"Well, I can't say that I've ever had either of those things, so I look forward to trying them both," Maryanne said.

"What can I do to help?" Claudia asked. "I'm a great chopper. That's what my friend Louisa always has me do."

"Great! Why don't you chop the rest of the herbs on the cutting board over there? And then you can mix it all in with the goat cheese. I add a little milk to make it creamier. I've just started adding dairy back to my diet after three years of being a strict vegan." Kate brushed a long strand of silver away from her face with the back of her brown hand.

"How did you not eat dairy? I don't think I could live without ice cream," Maryanne said. "Do you eat meat now, too?"

Claudia laughed to herself. She couldn't think of one vegetarian restaurant in Landry. It was all steak, all the time.

"Oh, no." Kate shook her head. All of the animals here are for living, not killing. She nodded out the sliding glass door. I'll take the eggs now, but that's it. Ingesting something that's been slaughtered is bad energy for me, personally. But I don't judge. Ron practically lives on hamburgers."

"I see," Maryanne said. She nodded her head slowly, as if she were deeply pondering Kate's unheard of philosophy.

Claudia held her breath, wondering if Maryanne was going to launch into a Biblical explanation of why animals were given to humans for nourishment. She interjected, seeing the wheels behind her mother's eyes turning. "Kate, what do you do? You mentioned a client gave you the recipe for the zucchini? What kind of client?"

"I'm a massage therapist—and a healer, though that's not

for everyone. Some people just aren't open enough for it, yet."

Claudia swallowed. Things could get bad fast between New-Age Kate and Baptist Maryanne. It was a recipe for disaster. "Oh wow, look at that! We are going to a spa for massage and we landed in the home of a practitioner; that's wild," she said, and realized she laughed too loud for it to sound authentic.

"That is very funny, indeed," Maryanne nodded, still armed with her Texan manners. "You don't happen to do pedicures and facials also?" A shallow, polite chuckle followed.

"No," Kate said, wrestling with a wine cork.

Claudia watched her mother's face fall into a grimace when she saw the bottle. She was an adult, making her own choices, Claudia reminded herself. She was no longer the little girl kept from a world full of secrets. There was a lot about the world that she now knew better than her mom.

Kate handed a half-full glass of red wine to Claudia, and then sat down with one herself. Claudia and Maryanne both looked puzzled that she hadn't offered one to Maryanne. "I'm sorry, I assumed you're not drinking. Was I wrong?" Kate asked seeing the surprise.

"No," said Maryanne. "Did I mention that I don't drink? I don't remember having that conversation."

"No, I don't think you said anything." Kate took another sip of her wine and walked over to check the pot of oil.

"Claudia? Will you put some paper towels on the platter over there? It's time to fry these puppies."

Was this woman clairvoyant or just stark raving mad? Either way, Claudia was officially on Kate's team now—between the photo of Keith Richards, the common bond of being in the service industry, and now the wine, she was a true Kate believer. She had to know more about her. She relaxed and decided to let Kate make Maryanne squirm as much as possible.

Kate dropped the zucchini cakes into the oil where they sizzled and disappeared into clouds of tiny bubbles. "Maryanne, would you mind salting these after I take them out?" Kate asked.

"Not at all. I'd be happy to." Maryanne stood up from her stool and smoothed the front of her shirt. Her toenails radiated color like the old miniature Christmas tree bulbs, shining against the black rubber and rhinestones of her flip-flops.

Claudia leaned against the sink and watched Kate flip the browning cakes over in the oil. The room filled with a tangy golden scent and Claudia's stomach growled. She swallowed some more wine.

When Kate removed the fritters from the pan and dropped them onto the platter bedded with paper towels, Maryanne pinched a small amount of salt from a ceramic bowl and carefully sprinkled the granules over the small warm treasures. "Like this?" she asked Kate, who nodded in approval.

"Claudia, will you fluff the quinoa? And over there, in that bowl I have the dressing. The apples, walnuts, and raisins need to go in too. Got it?"

"Yep." Claudia loved how with casual direction, Kate had transformed her and Maryanne (neither known for their culinary skills) into an efficient kitchen staff. It helped take the tension away from the glaring differences between the three women. As they worked together on what would nourish each of them, they became an unlikely team of caretakers. She looked at her mother who was still attentively salting the fritters, and for an instant, the first time in she couldn't remember how long, she felt a granule of tenderness toward Maryanne.

Chapter 11

They set the table outside, within view of the animals dipping their heads into the feed buckets. Again, Claudia noted that an unwritten schedule seemed to be in play for Kate and everything that lived on her property. She set glasses of water sweating with condensation at each of the places. Before she released her glass, she took a long swallow. Ever since they stopped in this place, her throat felt dry and hoarse. She was used to the humidity coming off the ocean, a lush green environment that offered shady vegetation and ample places to hide. The desert was flat and open. There were mountains, but they towered in the distance like stern authority figures. The trees bore no shade, the rocks held no bush. Everything here was exposed to the light.

When they finally sat, the sky was the color of orange marmalade, the air quickly cooling as the sun said its welcome farewell. Kate refilled the two wine glasses, and

Maryanne gazed into the napkin on her lap, so as not to witness the travesty. After she set the bottle down, Kate put her hands in a prayer position in front of her heart, and Maryanne did the same, closing her eyes. Claudia watched the two women in anticipation as they bowed in silence. After a long pause, Kate finally spoke, "Namaste," she said. Claudia barely stifled a laugh before it escaped her throat and had to cough a little to cover it up. "Namaste," she echoed, and couldn't look at Maryanne's confusion at the short prayer because it would send her into howls of laughter.

Kate passed the bowl of quinoa around the small table and then the fritters. Claudia scooped a generous helping of the herbed goat cheese onto her plate and passed the bowl to Maryanne. All of the food's intense flavors jumped through the clean air into Claudia's nostrils, and she reminded herself that it wasn't polite to inhale an entire plate of food in fifteen seconds flat. She couldn't remember the last meal that tasted as good—maybe it was because she participated in its creation, or maybe because they hadn't eaten anything since breakfast. Whatever the reason, she was mindful of each bite and how good it felt going into her stomach, taking away the hungry ache.

"Kate, is most of your family still around this part of the country?" Maryanne asked, after she swallowed a small bite of fritter.

"Our father died twenty years ago and our mother moved back to Boston, where the rest of her family lives. I don't think she ever liked it here. She tried to stay after he passed on to his next life, but it was obvious that she wanted to be with her sisters. Ron finally told her she had to leave, she was so miserable, and it was only then that she gave herself permission. Besides Ron and me, there are still some cousins around, but everyone else either died or left."

"Oh, I'm so sorry. That must be hard to have once been such a tight-knit family, and then have only your brother around," Maryanne said.

What would her mom know about having a tight-knit family, Claudia wondered and helped herself to some more quinoa.

"Oh, I wouldn't say we were tight-knit. There were just a lot of us. Dad had a drinking problem, which was what killed him in the end, and Mom was so codependent that she didn't know how to live if she wasn't cleaning up his puke. And everyone—grandparents, aunts, and uncles—they all carried massive chips on their shoulders from being pushed on and off reservations forever. And of course, no one liked the fact that my dad married a white woman."

"Oh, I see," Maryanne said.

"Sounds like Christmas was a blast," Claudia said.

Kate laughed. "There were good times. But like most families, there was also plenty of the other kind. What about you two? Do you have a big family?"

Claudia and Maryanne looked at each other. Claudia chewed her lip, and left Maryanne to answer. "Claudia's father and I divorced when Claudia was eight.

We didn't have any other children. I . . ." Maryanne's voice strained. Her face contorted and her chin quivered.

Are you kidding me? You're going to do this right now? Claudia couldn't look at her mother when the tears spilled down her heavily made-up face. She wanted to push the pause button and hitchhike her way out of the insanity.

"I'm sorry," Maryanne said. "It's just . . . Oh, it wasn't supposed to happen this way. I was going to wait until we got there."

"Wait for what? Until we got to where—the spa?" Claudia clenched her fork and her knuckles went pale.

Maryanne sighed and stopped her running nose with a napkin and dabbed the mascara beneath her eyes. She breathed slowly, apparently trying to calm herself. "Just listen, okay? I didn't mean to lie to you. But when I got to your house with Ramona and saw your face, I couldn't tell you. I had to lie, God forgive me. I knew it was the only way we would eventually be able to talk about things."

"What do you mean? Tell me." Claudia said, pushing her chair away from the table, but still sitting. She crossed her arms in front of her; a flimsy shield for what she feared was coming.

"We're not going to a spa tomorrow. We are going to see a counselor, because I'm so tired of not having my daughter in my life. I want us to be friends, and I know that there is a lot we need to work through," Maryanne looked from

Claudia to Kate and said, "I'm sorry. I know this must be really awkward for you, but Claudia and I haven't—we're not very close, you might say."

"I'm fine. You two are in a safe place," Kate sat securely in her chair.

Claudia rubbed the tightness in her neck. She chewed her lip some more, trying to process what Maryanne had just said. She reached for her glass of wine and swallowed a large mouthful. Then she let out an abrupt laugh. "You tried to trick me into therapy? Do you even see how screwed up that is?" Claudia's laughter ended in a tense glare.

"I didn't think there was any other way you would go with me," Maryanne said.

"Did you think of maybe sending me an email—or mailing a letter about how you were feeling? Maybe start with an apology? I mean, it's just so classic, isn't it? You've never talked to me about anything—and now you want to, but it's all starting out with a lie!" Claudia's face was red, her voice high; etiquette no longer mattered.

"At least I am trying. I know that it was wrong to lie to you, but I had to do something. It seems that you don't even care if we ever have a relationship!" Maryanne's tone rose to meet Claudia's and became a yell.

"Why now, Mom? Why do you want to have a relationship with me all of a sudden?" Claudia leaned back in her chair, now several feet away from the table. She inched further and further away the more upset Maryanne got.

Kate drank from her wine glass, silently taking in every word of the argument between the two women. Neither Claudia nor Maryanne looked at her. It was like she had instantly disappeared—a ghost.

"Because—because I've always wanted to have a relationship with you, but I never knew how, because you're getting married and starting your own family, because I hope to be a part of my grandchildren's lives one day, because I never meant to hurt you—I could go on and on, Claudia. Does it really make that much of a difference why now and not sooner?"

"Yes, it does," Claudia said. "Because there were plenty of other times I needed you and you weren't there. Like when you left and everyone made fun of me in first grade for wearing mismatched outfits. Dad had no idea how to dress me, but he did his best. Or the day that Chloe, my cat died. You were gone for that too. And then you came back, but you didn't come back to stay, and you and Dad got divorced and when I visited you on the weekends, you were never around. You were always at work or a meeting. I ate more peanut butter and jelly sandwiches than any kid I knew; breakfast, lunch, and dinner at your house—that's all there was to eat. I told Dad when I started my period, not you. And then you had the audacity to make me go to that stupid church you joined with all of those freaks. Do you have any idea how many times I read *Ramona The Brave*? Even when I was in high school, I kept reading it over and over, like a freak, trying to find the answer in those pages. I was sure there was something I had missed—some reason why you chose that book to give me when you disappeared—a secret message scribbled somewhere or something. And then you show up in Ramona, like it's some kind of bond between us or something. I named her Ramona because that's the book you gave me when you left, and in Ramona the car, I could finally get my revenge and leave you instead of always being the one left behind. And you don't even see the irony, do you? How dare you sit there and pout like I am the one who did all of this to you. I won't take responsibility for your mistakes." Claudia stopped and took a breath. She was on the edge of her chair.

Maryanne opened her mouth, and then closed it. Her eyes filled again, and she covered her shaking lips with her hand. Claudia was also shaking. She couldn't believe she had spewed all of that onto not only her mother, but also this strange woman she didn't know. When she was younger, Claudia rehearsed what she would say to Maryanne if she ever had the freedom or found the courage. But that was a long time ago, and now she never would have expected to say the things she had guarded for so long—things she didn't even know she remembered or still felt.

Maryanne stood up and turned toward the sliding glass door. She looked at it for a few seconds, as if contemplating where she would go if she walked through it. Then she turned in the other direction and walked to the back of the yard. Claudia and Kate watched Maryanne grasp the top of the fence and look into the distance over the rocks and Joshua trees. The mountains were dark silhouettes against the sky that had ripened from orange to raspberry.

Claudia felt her phone vibrate in her pocket and saw the text from Louisa: "How's the spa? R u relaxed and rejuvenated yet?" She couldn't help but roll her eyes and smile at the absurdity of the question and timing. "I need to return this," she said to Kate, and left the table. She walked through the glass door and went into the bathroom.

"I thought you would be under the sprawling hands of a giant Norwegian man right now," Louisa said when she picked up the phone.

"You have no idea how much I wish that were true," Claudia said. She was sitting on the closed toilet lid. She told Louisa in all of four sentences what had happened that day.

"Do you want me to come get you?"

Claudia thought about it in silence, and then sighed. "No. I mean, yes, I want you to—but I know I shouldn't leave."

"Whatever you say," Louisa said. "But you can always change your mind. Are you going with her to the counselor tomorrow?"

"Hell no!" Claudia said. "As soon as Ramona is fixed, I'm going home. Chaos seems to follow Mom and me. It's hopeless at this point in our lives to try to change that. And anyway, you know it's some religious weirdo she hired for us to talk to."

"I can't say that it's the best way to enter therapy with someone, being tricked into it," Louisa agreed. "It's too bad it had to go this way. If she had just been honest . . ."

"That's the story of my life, Lou."

"I'm so sorry, honey."

"Thanks. Can I come over tomorrow night? Alex won't be back until Monday."

"Of course. We can have a margarita slumber party after Ben goes to bed and watch *Mad Men* reruns. In that case, maybe we should make it martinis instead."

"As long as whatever we drink makes me forget about all of this for a minute, I don't care what it is."

Claudia put the phone back in her pocket and looked at her tired face in the mirror. Her eyes were red and dry from the dust. The eyeliner she put on that morning had spread into two smudged rings of gray around her eyes; she looked like an aging, depressed raccoon. Alex was probably getting dressed right now to go to the Broadway show. She didn't want to ruin his night by telling him about the drama that had already ensued between her and Maryanne. Let him enjoy the imagined drama of the stage instead. She wet a washcloth and mopped around her eyes. The cool water soothed her tight face and brightened her complexion. "That'll have to do," she muttered, switching off the light.

She found Kate and Maryanne standing next to each

other in front of the kitchen sink. Maryanne was washing the dishes in soapy water and handing them to Kate. Kate dried the dishes with a large kitchen towel and stacked them carefully. Neither one of the women spoke, but they had a peaceful rhythm between them; the tension of the table outside had not entered the room.

Claudia found her wine glass on the counter and drained the last drops before she walked outside to watch the plum sunlight disappear behind the dark mountains.

Chapter 12

Claudia heard Kate's necklaces coming through the door, but didn't turn around. She watched Jackson Browne bite one of the sheep on its ankles and chase it around the yard to the chorus of bleats. A horse, Claudia couldn't tell if it was Franny or Zooey, rolled in a cloud of dust lit dimly by the light spilling out of Kate's domed house, like the gooey insides of a scorched marshmallow.

"This is their favorite time of day," Kate said, standing next to Claudia.

"I can see why. It's so much cooler now."

"Things come to life at night in the desert. Maryanne wanted me to tell you that she went ahead to bed," Kate said.

"Yeah, that whole conversation was pretty exhausting for me too. Everything about today has been. You don't happen to have any cigarettes, do you?"

"I don't think so. If I do, it's only because someone left them here. It's been a while since I've had a party, though."

Claudia remembered the photo she found in the book earlier. She imagined that Kate had had more than her share of parties in her day.

"Hang tight. I'll be right back," Kate said.

The skin on Claudia's arms contracted into small goose pimples. The temperature must have dropped at least thirty degrees from what it had been earlier, during the hottest part of the day.

When Kate returned, she handed a small hand-rolled cigarette to Claudia. Or at least that was what Claudia thought it was until she caught the unmistakable pungent scent of the dried leaves.

"It's better for you than tobacco," Kate shrugged, and handed her a lighter.

"I'm pretty sure that's arguable, but what the hell, I'll take it all the same," Claudia said, and lit the joint. She held the smoke inside her lungs until it burned in her throat and then she exhaled slowly. She handed the joint back to Kate.

"Okay if I grab that blanket off the couch inside?" Claudia asked. She was finally beginning to relax. She thought about sending Louisa a text to tell her.

"Of course," Kate said. "Grab the other one in the basket for me." Kate pulled two chairs away from the table and turned them toward the animals and the now invisible mountains.

Claudia returned, sat down, and after she covered herself with the blanket, took the joint again between her fingertips.

"She's doing the best she can," Kate said.

"You don't know the whole story," Claudia held the smoke in her lungs.

"I don't have to. It's obvious that you are both deeply wounded and that she is trying hard to break through it all. That is a tough job for anyone. Impossible, in fact, unless the other person is willing to also do the work."

Claudia nodded and looked into the black distance. She didn't want to think about Maryanne anymore. "I was checking out your books today. I promise I wasn't trying to be a snoop, but an old picture fell out. I think I recognized you with Keith Richards?"

Kate balanced and twisted the joint lightly, a cloud of smoke blended into her silver hair. She laughed and coughed a little. "Yes, I knew Keith. What were we doing in the photo you saw?"

"It looked like it was a concert—I think you were standing on stage with him and another guy."

"Oh my God, I can't believe you found that one. I was wondering where it went. That was Altamont. Talk about a crazy day."

"Wait, wait, wait," Claudia waved her hand in disbelief and marveled at how it appeared to be in slow motion. "You were at Altamont? The show where the Hells Angels killed that guy during the Stones' set?"

"Yeah. We just barely made it out of there. I shouldn't have been on the helicopter with everyone—it was a mad rush and somehow I got swept up with everyone. We barely made it off the ground, the 'copter was so overweight. Gram and I were standing behind the stage while the guys played. Everyone was nervous, because the energy in the crowd was so bad. When the kid pulled that gun the guys were playing 'Under My Thumb.'" Kate stopped to take another puff. "Next thing I knew, Gram grabbed my hand and we were running with the band off stage. We didn't know the Angels killed the poor kid until we were well in the air."

"Wow," Claudia said. "You were, like—a part of music history that day. I've seen *Gimme Shelter* several times. Wait! You were probably in the movie and I didn't even know! That is craaaaazy! The other guy you were talking about, Gram? Is he the other one in the picture with you and Keith?"

"Yes. That was him," Kate pulled her knees into her chest under the blanket.

"He looked kind of familiar. But I don't know, sometimes I feel that way about photographs of people I've never seen. Was he in a band or something?"

"Oh yeah, many bands. Back then it was The Flying Burrito Brothers. Before that, it was the Byrds."

"Oh, riiiiiiight!" Claudia smacked herself on the forehead. "Gram Parsons! He did a record with Emmylou

Harris, right? He was like a country-rock dude."

"I think you are the only twenty-something I've met who's even heard of Gram Parsons." Kate undid her bun and let her hair fall around her shoulders. She massaged her scalp and closed her eyes.

"Really? Well, I guess I've never fit in with my generation. I always wanted to be a part of the sixties, you know, the whole peace movement. But wait, I still don't understand how you knew those guys. I did ask you that, right? Did you answer me? I'm sorry, I can't remember. I haven't smoked pot in a long time and that stuff is really really good." Claudia rubbed her face to make sure it was still there.

Kate laughed and cleared her throat. "When did I first meet Gram? I almost can't remember when I didn't know Gram. I guess I was fifteen when he started coming to Joshua Tree. I poured beer at my uncle's tavern and Gram would flirt with me and always left a big tip. Then when I was a little older, everyone who came to town wanted weed. My family always used peyote in our ceremonies, but we needed money, and it wasn't difficult to grow marijuana. It wasn't a big deal—not any different than all of the other herbs we used for medicine. So we'd sell it to the musicians and hippies who came to the tavern during their stay in the park. I took care of Gram whenever he was in town and set him up with the best stuff for cheap—he gave me free tickets to shows. I'd go see him whenever and wherever I could. He knew, of course, that I was in love with him, but he treated me like a little sister. He was protective of me and called me his Indian Angel." Kate smiled and her voice trailed off when she looked up at the stars.

"That's so beautiful," Claudia said in a whisper. She squeezed the back of her neck and looked up as well.

"That's it," Kate said, and stood up, the blanket wrapped around her shoulders. "I can't watch you fuss with it any-more. You've been pinching and straining your neck ever since you got here. Let's go inside."

Claudia followed Kate and tripped on the edge of her blanket dragging on the ground. She pushed a hand out in front of her to catch herself and laughed when she realized she wasn't falling. Kate led her through the kitchen, down the hallway, past her bedroom and another closed door that Claudia noticed had a coded lock box on the outside, into a very small room with only a massage table in it.

"Go ahead. Get your kit off," Kate said, and left the room.

It seemed to take hours, but Claudia managed to get each article of clothing off her body. She lay face down on the table and covered herself with the top sheet. The cool cotton tickled the nerve endings all over her body and she shivered. After a few minutes, Kate came back in and lit a candle. Claudia was already easing into the tranquility of the room and the mellowing of her high. She heard Kate rub her hands together, and then felt their warmth on her back. At that point, she stopped thinking. The questions she wanted to ask Kate about Gram and Keith and the sixties disappeared from her mind. The worry lines between her brows softened. She sank deep within herself and let the rest go.

She was floating in a pool, nothing beneath her but water. It was effortless—as if she was being carried by invisible hands; like the time she played light as a feather, stiff as a board at Gina's slumber party when she was thirteen, but there was nothing scary about this. She felt safe, cared for, and covered. Her fingers and toes moved back and forth in the liquid, feeling the silkiness move between and around them. Something low and rhythmic drummed in her ears—a kind of swishing sound. She felt the sound move through every part of her body and reverberate within her heart. She couldn't see anything in the liquid, but she didn't need to. She felt all that was around her and inside of her. It was all the same. She wanted to stay in this place forever.

"Claudia? Claudia?" Kate whispered above her.

Claudia felt something wet on her face. She lifted her hand to wipe whatever it was away.

"Take your time. It's okay. Breathe. Wiggle your fingers and toes, your wrists and ankles. That's right. Gently wake up your system. Slowly."

"What is this?" Claudia asked, rubbing the moisture from her face between her fingers and opening her eyes.

"Tears, dear. It's perfectly normal. Happens all the time.

We must have unlocked something."

"Oh. Okay."

"Be sure to take your time getting up. Don't be surprised if you feel strange for a while. Of course, that could be the pot too, but sometimes Intuitive Massage has lasting effects. I'm sleeping on the couch tonight. You're taking my bed."

Just before she disappeared into a deep sleep, Claudia remembered a startling fact from her rock history trivia. Gram Parsons was the musician who died tragically in his twenties of an overdose in Joshua Tree. She thought about asking Kate if her memory was correct, but something told her it wasn't a good idea, and her body felt so heavy, she wasn't sure she could move it again.

Chapter 13

This should help you wake up," a voice said, and Claudia smelled strong coffee as a blurry hand placed a mug on the low table next to the bed. She squinted to adjust her eyes and registered Kate's face standing above her. "There's something I want you and Maryanne to see before you leave today. We will have plenty of time before Ron has your car ready, but we need to get moving."

Claudia pulled herself to a sitting position and took a sip of the black coffee. "What time is it?" she asked Kate, who had turned to leave.

"Almost nine."

"I slept so hard."

"Wonderful. Your back was such a nightmare, I was afraid you might suffer from some bad dreams while you slept."

"No. I don't remember dreaming at all."

"Good. That is truly deep rest when you're not conscious of your subconscious; that is when healing really occurs. We are leaving in twenty minutes. I'll let you get ready." Kate walked out of the room.

Claudia took another sip of coffee and then scooted to the edge of Kate's bed and stretched her back. Her body ached like it had been steamrolled—but in a good way. Though her muscles were bruised, her joints moved freely. She shuffled to the bathroom and looked at her face in the mirror. Her eyes were still pink and dry from the pot. She recalled bits of the conversation with Kate about Altamont and shook her head in disbelief, reaching for the toothbrush.

After she brushed her teeth and washed her face, Claudia walked into the kitchen. Maryanne sat at the kitchen table and smiled at her with a look of trepidation. Through the disjointed fog of the night before, Claudia remembered Kate saying, "You are both deeply wounded," and smiled back at Maryanne.

"You two fair-skins definitely need to put on sunscreen," Kate said, and placed a bottle on the table.

"I already have some on my face, I wear it everyday," Maryanne said proudly. "My friend Jackie sells Arbonne, and it really is the best. But I'll certainly put some of this on my arms and legs, thank you, Kate."

Claudia thought that even if Maryanne didn't have sun-screen on underneath all of the makeup, there was no way that the sun could break through the plaster coating. After

Maryanne finished with the sunscreen, Claudia took the bottle and smoothed the thick white glop on her face and neck, her arms and legs. When she was bent over, rubbing the lotion around her ankles underneath her socks and running shoes, she saw her mother's legs, pale and lined with spider veins. They looked so old. The last time she remembered seeing her mother's legs were when they occasionally peeped out of her long Sunday dresses.

"Okay," Kate interrupted Claudia's thought detour. "I've packed lunch for us and plenty of water. If it's okay with you ladies, I'm going to divide all of this up among three backpacks and we can each share some of the load."

Both Claudia and Maryanne nodded in agreement.

"Kate—is this a difficult walk, where we are going? Because I have to admit, I haven't made it to my aerobics classes lately and I'm a little out of shape." Maryanne grimaced.

"You'll be fine, I promise."

When Kate went to the refrigerator for a forgotten item, Claudia whispered to Maryanne, "do you have any idea what this is all about?"

"No," Maryanne said and shrugged her shoulders.

The three women climbed into the truck, and Jackson Browne hopped into the back of the bed, wagging his tail. He licked the window where Claudia sat on the other side, turned around smiling at him. Kate drove in the direction of the mountains. Several miles down the dusty road, Claudia realized Kate's house was deceivingly close to the park. The larger the mountains loomed, the thicker the Joshua Trees grew, their spiny leaves jutting in different directions into the air.

"So this is what people come to see, huh?" Claudia asked, looking out at the park.

"This is what most people see when they're here. There are many things hiding in this place, that very few people ever have the chance to experience. One of these things, I will show you today." Kate nodded and smiled, crow's feet framing her dark eyes.

She drove the truck up through the inclining grounds, bumping along the rocks. Claudia slid into Maryanne's shoulder as Kate steered around a sharp curve, and then found a flat area to park. There were signs for hiking trails, and two other cars parked nearby in the dirt. Kate parked, got out of the truck, and let down the back latch for Jackson Browne. Claudia followed Maryanne out of the old Ford, and the three women strapped on and adjusted their backpacks. Kate looked suspiciously around the grounds and up onto the trail.

"We need to go before anyone else shows up," she said, and started walking in the direction of the trail. But when they reached the spot marked with a sign: a graphic of a miniature person walking uphill with a stick, Kate continued on past it. "Maryanne, you follow behind me, and Claudia, you close behind her. That way, if you slip, or get tired, we'll be sure to catch you, Maryanne. Does that suit you?"

"Yes, thank you, that sounds great," Maryanne said.

Claudia filed behind her mother and they followed Kate's quick pace. "Once we get past this area, we can slow down. Not many people know about this trail, and we try to keep it that way," she said.

Claudia was glad to stretch her legs and get the blood flowing in her body. She wasn't used to sitting still. At home, if she wasn't working, she was doing something to stay busy, like playing with Ben, or walking Foster. She felt crazy when she was idle for too long. They were now several yards away from the trail markers. Kate turned by a large dead tree lying on its side, and then stepped between two boulders. The footing was a little tricky, and Claudia carefully watched Maryanne's step to make sure she didn't slip. They balanced against the warm rock with their hands during the narrowest pass. Once they got through, Claudia looked ahead, beyond the two women and Jackson Browne to see a gently sloping path that was relatively clear of obstacles.

"I can't say I've ever seen anything like this before," Maryanne said, looking around at the strange plant life. "Even though Texas is dry, we still have a lot more green life than you do here."

"Springtime can be very green," Kate said. "But it is only for a short while."

"What's that plant right there? It looks so soft," Maryanne

said, and veered quickly off the path toward it.

Claudia jumped when Kate stopped walking and turned to look at them. "Don't touch that or get anywhere near it! They are jumping cholla, and they will dislodge their needles into your skin if you get too close. The desert is a harsh place, and everything here evolves in order to protect itself from the elements."

"If even the plants here are mean, I wonder what the wild animals have evolved into?" Claudia muttered.

They followed Kate around a sharp bend, and then found another group of boulders.

"Maryanne, I'll help you through," Kate said.

Jackson Browne bounded onto the rocks, and then disappeared over them. He was obviously familiar with the unmarked territory. Kate climbed onto the first ledge, and then turned to help Maryanne. She offered her hand, and Claudia spotted from behind. Everyone breathed a long sigh of relief when they were all standing on smooth rock, walking through the great looming hallway of red stone.

Claudia hadn't realized how large the boulders actually were until they continued to walk through the rock canal, and the blue sky was only a small sliver above them. Claudia remembered the forts she built as a child, and how she always felt safe in that secret enclosed space. As she felt along the walls, she noticed they were so much cooler than the rocks she had touched earlier. A breeze blew through the compact space, and there was something distinctively different about the air. Her breathing came easier, and then she realized what it was: humidity. As the sunlight poured into the canal, she heard Maryanne suck in a breath of surprise before she could glimpse beyond her mother's shoulders to what lay ahead.

It was as if they had stepped into a different world. Where only minutes ago everything was dry and cracked, here it was wet and soft. Green jumped out at Claudia like a long-lost friend at a surprise party. Her shirt immediately clung to her body, and she wiped the sweat from her forehead. She must have been sweating before, but the desert air had sucked it right out of her pores before it could run down her skin. As they continued walking, the vegetation grew colorful with radiant flowers. She caught a glimpse of Jackson's tail wagging and wanted to run ahead to see everything that lay in front of them. She heard something that sounded out of place, like a symphony at a roller skating rink. It took a second for her to place the familiar sound, and then she realized it was rushing water.

The path finally cleared, and the three women were standing side by side, peering at the miracle. Jackson ran ahead and stuck his nose in the spring, lapping up the water.

Claudia walked to the water's edge. It bubbled from within and spilled out onto the slabs of rock surrounding it. She slid her backpack off her shoulders and sat down to remove her shoes. Claudia looked at Kate who was watching Maryanne's face and smiling at the tears and look of wonder there.

Microscopic mineral fairies seemed to live in the water and jumped around Claudia's toes and ankles. The sensation tickled so much that she laughed out loud.

Kate and Maryanne sat close to each other on a large flat stone not far from her. They slid off their socks and put their feet in the water alongside each other. Jackson ran over to Claudia, licked her arm and then settled next to her.

"My family has come here for over two centuries," Kate said.

"How have you all kept it a secret for so long?" Maryanne asked.

"Of course the rangers know about it and there are others. But everyone who has been invited here appreciates the sacredness and knows what would happen if the rest of the world found out."

"They'd exploit it," Claudia said.

"That's right. There has always been an unspoken pact that any guests here must be trustworthy. So far, it's worked."

"Thank you for trusting us," Maryanne said, and placed a hand on her heart.

"Did you ever bring Gram here?" Claudia blurted to Kate and then regretted it.

Kate nodded. "He was the first person I invited, outside of my family. We came here every time he visited Joshua Tree. Well, almost every time. Anyway, he loved it here."

"Who is Gram?" Maryanne asked.

"Someone from my past. One of my own wounds that

never healed."

"Oh," Maryanne said, and looked into the frothing pool. "I think I'm learning that everyone has those. Our pastor says that Jesus heals all of our wounds, but I'm beginning to wonder if they ever really go away."

Claudia looked up at Maryanne in surprise. She had never heard the slightest bit of religious doubt come from her mother's lips.

"I imagine our wounds are what make us more like Jesus," Kate said. "He came to care for the poor and the sick, right? Isn't that what it says in the Bible? How else would we know what they need if we haven't been poor and sick ourselves?"

"Huh. I've never heard anyone put it quite like that before, but I guess that makes sense."

Claudia smiled at the two women. She never would have guessed that her pale, rightwing mother would be having a friendly conversation with a pot smoking liberal Native American. How her father would laugh at the scenario—she wanted to photograph it all.

"Anyone hungry for lunch?" Kate asked.

"Starved," Claudia and Maryanne said at exactly the same time.

"See—you two occasionally sound like mother and daughter," Kate said.

She unwrapped some pita bread sandwiches stuffed with veggies, falafel, and cucumber dill sauce. Again, Claudia wondered why Kate's simple food tasted so good. Her hunger cowered in the shadow of the nourishment. She washed a large bite down with a long sip of water and kicked her feet in the bubbling spring with satisfaction.

"This is delicious," Maryanne said, wiping her mouth with the back of her hand. "I must get the recipe from you before we leave."

"Of course; it's very simple," Kate said, swallowing a mouthful. "A staple in our house, isn't it, Jackson?" she threw half of a sandwich to the drooling dog.

Claudia wondered if Maryanne thought that they were still going to Arizona. She knew this wasn't the right time to tell her that they weren't.

"Does your brother have any children?" Maryanne asked Kate.

"Yes. A son. But he's off at college. His mother and Ron split up a long time ago. Neither one of us can seem to get our partners to stick around for very long in the desert. I guess it's not for everyone."

"Were you ever married?" Maryanne asked, and Claudia flinched, afraid that her mother was poking around too close to Kate's exposed nerves.

"No. I never went down that road. I got close a couple of times, but I was always the one to run. My therapist says it's because of my abandonment issues. I think they say that to everyone, don't they?" Kate laughed.

"I will admit, I heard that once myself. A long time ago," Maryanne said.

Claudia's calves and shoulders tensed. If someone had abandoned Maryanne, and she knew how much it hurt—why would she do the same thing to her own daughter? And did this mean that Claudia could do the same thing to her children? She swished her feet around the water and closed her eyes. *Don't think about it now. You are on hallowed ground here.*

They finished the sandwiches. It was quiet, except for the bubbling of the spring. Kate hummed a low melody, and then sang the words, *"Well I've been where you're hanging and I think I can see how you're pinned, Yeah, when you're not feeling holy, your loneliness tells that you've sinned."*

"What song is that?" Maryanne asked Kate.

Claudia mumbled the answer without thinking, "'Sisters of Mercy', by Leonard Cohen."

"That's right," Kate said. "One of my favorites of his."

"You got that from your father," Maryanne said to Claudia. "A great memory for music."

"Songs are how I learned the meaning of words," Claudia said. "Some of them, anyway."

"I remembered something, sitting here—a Bible verse." Maryanne said.

Of course. When does she not think of a Bible verse?

"It's from Isaiah. I can't remember the chapter. 'Forget the former things; do not dwell on the past. See! I am doing a new thing! Now it springs up; do you not perceive it? I am making a way in the desert and streams in the wasteland.' It seems fitting for this place, doesn't it?"

Kate nodded her head and put her hands in prayer position under her chin. "Beautiful, Maryanne. Thank you."

Claudia sat and thought about the words, and how critical she was of everything that came out of her mother's mouth—how she couldn't listen without already assuming it would be bogus. If Kate had said the same thing, Claudia would have exclaimed the verse's profundity. But because it came from her mother, and the Bible, she instinctively dismissed it as trite.

"Well ladies, I'm afraid we should begin our walk back. I'm sure Ron has your car in running order by now," Kate pulled her feet out of the water, and put the trash in her backpack.

"I don't want to leave," Maryanne said and smiled.

"Thank you so much for sharing this," Claudia said, feeling that any words she offered wouldn't be enough. "I'm honored that you let us in on such a big secret."

On the way back to the truck, they walked in silence, like three nuns and a dog leaving mass.

Chapter 14

Once they got back to Kate's house, and Claudia had cell phone service again, she checked her messages.

"Uh, hello there, Miss Nichols, this is Ron. Well, we replaced the valve, but it looks like that wasn't the issue after all. I'm afraid you need a new head gasket."

Claudia called Ron back, shaking her head and biting her lip.

"So what does that mean?" she asked, her foot tapping against the leg of the coffee table.

"Well, the part isn't the problem. In fact, we have one here that will work with your model just fine. It's the labor, you see. We'll have to remove the engine, and that's a hell of a headache."

"How long does it take?"

"A day, at least. Could be longer."

Claudia sighed into the phone. "How much will it cost?"

"Including the part and the labor, around two grand."

"But the car isn't even worth that much!"

"No, it's not. You could probably only get around fifteen hundred for her. But you know what they say about Volvos, and it's true. If you put the money in her now, she'll run forever. It's your call."

"This is a nightmare. I just want to get out of here. So there is nothing else you can do to get her running—just long enough to get us home?"

"Nope. Sorry. I've tried everything else."

"Okay. Let me think for a minute. I'll call you back."

Claudia's shirt was stiff with dried sweat from the hike and the spring. Her heels were slightly blistered from wearing damp socks on the way back down. Maryanne was in the shower, and Kate was outside feeding the animals. She dialed Alex's number. He didn't answer. She called Louisa and got her voicemail. She paced Kate's living room. She thought about Ramona and chewed on her lip to stop the tears, but it didn't work. They ran down her face and under her shirt, adding another layer of salt to her already crusting skin. She knew what Alex would say, that it wasn't worth paying to have Ramona fixed. They were going to sell the Accord and get something new; that was the plan, she reminded herself. They didn't need three cars. It made her even angrier that Maryanne had ever shown up with Ramona and stirred Claudia's feelings and memories, only to have her taken away again. It felt like a mean trick.

Claudia heard Kate walk inside and wash her hands in the sink. When Kate turned around and looked at Claudia's face, she asked, "What is it, dear? What's wrong?" Claudia told her about the conversation with Ron, and as she spoke, her crying intensified which made her feel embarrassed, and the more embarrassed she felt, the more she babbled and snorted. Soon snot was pouring out of her nose and she was hiccupping with the sobs. "What is wrong with me?" she asked Kate.

"Nothing is wrong with you. You are at a crossroad in your life, in more ways than one. It is perfectly natural that you would be emotional."

"It's just a stupid car," Claudia stammered.

"No. It's obvious that Ramona is much more than a car. I'm not sure what she represents to you. Only you can figure that out. I think it might be useful for you to go and spend some time with her, try to find what it is that connects you to this car. Do you want me to take you to Ron's shop?"

Claudia nodded and wiped the tears still flowing out of her eyes. It felt good to have someone validate her feelings, as foreign and weird as they were to her. She sniffed and wiped her nose.

Ron walked out of the garage when Kate pulled up and came around to her window. She said something to him in a low voice, which Claudia couldn't hear. She felt like the one kid who had to leave summer camp because she was homesick.

"Go right ahead, take your time," Ron said.

Claudia hopped out of the truck and walked over to the garage. She opened Ramona's driver's door and sat down inside. The cushion of the chair fit her body perfectly; she had never found another car seat as comfortable.

"Why here?" Claudia asked Ramona. "Why couldn't you have waited just a little longer, 'til we got back to L.A.? I know it's not your fault, I guess that's like asking a cancer victim why they didn't pick a more benign form of the disease. It's just that, right now—this is when I need you most. I need you to take me away from all of this. You can't leave me with her; you know that was our pact. I know I'm the one who broke the promise first by leaving you behind. But I thought you would understand." Claudia leaned her head on Ramona's steering wheel and wondered if Kate and Ron had been watching her talk out loud. She didn't really care. "I'm going to figure this out," Claudia said. "You'll see." She wiped the tears from her face and smoothed her hair back. She took a deep breath and walked back to Kate's truck, where Kate was waiting patiently with Ron.

"I'll have to call you later," Claudia said to Ron.

"Okay, she'll be here," he said.

Kate drove them back to the house in silence.

"Go on to my bathroom and run a bath," Kate said, when they walked through the doors.

"Yeah, I'm a mess," Claudia laughed.

She started the water in Kate's small bathroom and adjusted the temperature. She removed her ponytail elastic and rubbed her aching head, breaking apart the stickiness of her hair. She dropped her clothes and shoes in a heap by the toilet, slid into the tub, and sank all the way under. Bubbles escaped from her nostrils and floated to the over world. She rubbed her face underwater. Just before the last bit of air in her lungs went stale, she surfaced. She thought this second baptism of the day would stop her ridiculous tears, but it didn't. They kept coming, even stronger than during the breakdown with Kate. She cried like she hadn't cried in years. She cried like she did when Jake broke her heart in the fourth grade. She cried like the time she didn't make cheerleading tryouts. She sobbed like she had in her room late at night, while her father slept alone and she wondered where her mother was and if she would ever come back.

Claudia remembered the first day she got Ramona—she drove all the way from Landry to Austin. Her dad thought she was at a birthday party for one of her classmates. Claudia contemplated driving clear out of Texas and on into California. She imagined getting her GED by mail and finding a job as a waitress in a little diner until she could save enough for beauty school. But her dad hadn't met Betsy yet, and she couldn't bear the thought of him being alone. He was the only reason she turned around that night.

Claudia wondered if she focused only on the bad

memories and didn't recognize the good. She knew there were times when the three of them were happy, moments amidst the forgotten pickup times from school, and the dark, drawn curtains blocking out the world during Maryanne's migraines. There had been trips to the beach, and rollercoaster rides—her tiny body sandwiched between Maryanne and Peter, the wind flying against their faces. But when Maryanne came back after the lost year, everything was different. Claudia and Peter were different because they had learned to live without her; and the once hermit-like Maryanne suddenly wanted to be at church every chance she got. Peter didn't share the same passion for what he called, "those fraidy cat Jesus freaks." Maryanne fought the divorce, insisting that God was against it, but still, she spent less time at home than she did in the fellowship hall of Crestview Baptist.

The water was cold, and Claudia's fingertips were shriveled. The tears had finally stopped. She wrung the water out of her hair when she stood and wrapped a large towel around her body. It felt good to be clean—of the sweat and some of the old memories. She took her time getting dressed and drying her hair. She rubbed lotion into her sore feet and all over her dry skin. No matter how much water she tried to drink, or how much moisturizer she used in this place, she still felt depleted.

She heard a muffled ring from under her dirty clothes and dug quickly to find her phone.

"Sorry I missed you earlier," Alex said as soon as she answered.

"It's so good to hear your voice," Claudia quivered, and the tears jumped to the brims of her eyes again. She leaned her head back to keep her face from getting splotchy now that she had taken the time to piece herself back together.

"Oh, babe—I know I haven't been great about calling on this trip. It's been so packed," he said.

"No. It's not that. I don't know what to do . . ."

Alex listened to her dilemma about Ramona. "Baby, this doesn't sound like you. I've never heard you so torn up over a decision before."

"You do think I should just get rid of her, right? And don't ask me if I'm getting ready to start my period."

"Okay—it's not that the two grand would completely kill us, but is it really necessary? Does this car really mean this much to you?"

"No. Yes? I don't know. Damn it, can you just tell me what to do?"

"Oh, no—absolutely not. You have to make the decision. I won't be responsible for any regrets."

Claudia loved Alex's wisdom, but right then, it also drove her crazy.

"Listen, I fly out tomorrow morning at nine. Call me when you wake up, and we'll talk about it some more, okay? Just sleep on it tonight."

"Okay. Hey, how was the play?"

"Great. I think we should go see it together next month, before it closes. We can stay at that little boutique hotel in the Meatpacking District."

"I wish I was there with you now.

Chapter 15

Mom, you need to call that shrink in Scottsdale, and tell them we definitely aren't coming," Claudia said.

"Oh. But I was thinking we could rent a car and at least spend some time with Howard tomorrow morning," Maryanne said, setting the forks and knives by the placemats for dinner.

"You're welcome to go if you want, but forget about us going together. I have enough to think about with Ramona, and I have to find a replacement for work on Tuesday. And honestly, even without all of this crap going on, I still wouldn't go with you. It was a terrible idea, and you need to drop it."

"Well, what if we just talked on the phone with him? I'm sure he would be willing to do that," Maryanne said in a high-pitched pouty tone that made Claudia want to permanently graffiti obscenities all over her mother's body. She heard the Clash, and the Sex Pistols, and the Ramones all at once, urging her on.

Claudia looked directly in Maryanne's face waited for a dramatic second, and then said in a snarl, "No. Don't ask me about it again."

Kate cleared her throat and said, "Claudia, would you mind changing Franny and Zooey's water?" she held up her hands, dripping with some kind of goo.

Claudia looked at Kate, and then Maryanne, knowing that she was the behavior-deficient child being tricked out of the room. "Sure," she said, and left the sharp chill in the kitchen for the warmth outside. She found the hose and switched on the faucet. She peered through the glass door and saw Kate with her hand on Maryanne's arm, saying something in earnest while Maryanne shrugged and dabbed her eyes. Oh please—don't let her fool you, Kate.

When had these two formed an alliance—while she was taking a bath? Kate was Claudia's cool pot-smoking buddy, not Maryanne's shoulder to weep on. She jerked the hose from its coil and stomped with it to the stable. The stream of water sloshed into the buckets, and the horses backed away from the spray. She threw the hose to the side, and tripped over it when she tried to hurry back to turn off the faucet. The fumble only added to her frustration, and she contemplated sitting down in the mud in protest. "Is everything cleared up now? Are we all good?" she asked with her hands on her hips when she entered the kitchen.

"You know, my grandmother used to say, 'When you are

in doubt, be still and wait; when doubt no longer exists for you, go forward with courage,'" Kate said.

Claudia wanted to reply with something witty and dry. She wanted to excuse Kate's irritating proverbs. But she knew that the words were true, and also that Kate saw through Claudia's defensiveness and impatience and knew it all came from a feeling of helplessness. Nothing got past the woman. It was like trying to fool a mind reader.

"Can I help with the food?" Claudia asked, noticing that her shoulders were inching up toward her ears. She lowered them back into place.

"The Eggplant Parmesan is almost ready, but you can slice the tomatoes for the salad."

Claudia nodded and picked up the serrated knife by the cutting board and sawed lightly back and forth through the red flesh, the juice and seeds running onto the white plastic. Claudia thought about the thin, tight skins that held all of the tomato guts inside, and almost felt sad for the little fruits with their mess and seeds lying exposed on the cutting board. No one ever wanted those parts.

"Perfect," Kate said, and scattered the bits of tomato flesh on the pile of greens.

"Excuse me," Maryanne said, and walked out of the room.

Kate gave Claudia a look communicating so many things at once, caution, understanding, concern. She handed Claudia a glass and filled it with wine. "Cheers," she said, clinking their glasses together.

Maryanne returned. "I talked to Howard and canceled everything," she said. "I still think we should talk to someone, Claudia, but I won't try to force it. I'll wait until you're ready."

"Good," Claudia said, and sighed. "Hey—why don't you have just one glass of wine with us, it won't kill you. You won't go to hell for it, you know."

"I can't," Maryanne said matter-of-factly.

"I don't understand anything about you," Claudia mumbled.

"Oh! It is definitely ready now!" Kate said, standing up from where she was squatting, peering into the oven. She put a mitt on her hand and slid the dish off the oven rack and onto the stovetop. "Take a look at this!"

Kate placed the dish on a trivet on the table. The breadcrumbs were crispy and brown, the cheese oozed up between the thin layers of eggplant. Claudia moved the salad bowl so there would be enough room on the table. They sat and bowed their heads, but instead of Kate's silent prayer of the previous night, Maryanne raised her voice, "Dear, gracious, Heavenly Father, thank you for your provision. Bless this food that we are about to receive, and make our bodies strong so we can serve you all the days of our lives. Amen."

It was exactly the same prayer that Maryanne prayed over the few cooked meals they shared together all those years ago. She wondered if that's all Maryanne's religion was: a list of rituals, to give her life a sense of order. God knew there hadn't been much order in her life before the religion appeared.

"I can't believe how exhausted I am," Maryanne said, stifling a yawn. "I really have to get back into aerobics class when I get back. Peggy keeps me on the email list, but I've gotten into such a rut of not responding, I can't believe she hasn't taken me off by now."

Claudia tried to picture Maryanne in the class. She had never seen her mother dance, or act silly in any way. She wondered if she had any sense of rhythm. She doubted it. "You should try Pilates," she said to Maryanne.

"Oh, I don't think we have that in Landry. That's the thing that hooks you up to all the ropes?"

"That's part of it. Surely there's a class at the Landry YMCA. It's really helped me." Claudia sat up a little straighter, remembering she hadn't been to Pilates in a month.

"Tim cancelled our membership. He never went and said it was a waste."

"Doesn't he have some kind of a heart condition—high cholesterol or something? It seems like it might help him if he exercised regularly," Claudia said, chomping on salad.

"Trust me, if I could make him take better care of himself, I would," Maryanne said, and yawned again. "I am so sorry! I better go to bed before I fall into this plate." She took her dish to the sink and rinsed the little bit of eggplant and salad that was left into the garbage disposal.

"Sleep well," Kate said and waved.

Claudia shook her head after Maryanne walked out of the room.

"What?" Kate asked.

"I just don't get it. I don't understand how we can be related. We are so different."

"You desperately want to be different from her, don't you?" Kate asked.

"But we are different! She is so closed-minded, has absolutely no sense of style and no idea what is going on in the rest of the world. She is so afraid of everything. I left Landry as soon as I could and made something of myself. I've traveled and met new people, and learned from different cultures and perspectives. Everything is so black and white in her miniscule world."

Kate laughed. "I'm sorry," she said, when Claudia shot her a look. "It's just, you sound so much like I did when I was younger."

"But you did so many cool things—I mean, hanging out with the Rolling Stones? Who gets to say they did that?"

"Claudia," Kate's voice turned grave. "Trust me when I say that I would trade all of those memories to take back the chance I once had for a family of my own." Kate leaned forward when she said this, as if she were trying to embed the words into Claudia's consciousness.

There was nothing Claudia could say to that.

Kate leaned back in her chair, suddenly lighter like a switch had flipped and said, "Would you give me a haircut? I haven't had one in ages." She swung several feet of white hair around her shoulders.

"Sure." Claudia said, glad to have something other than Maryanne or Ramona to think about.

Chapter 16

Kate came out of the bathroom with a towel turban wrapped around her head. Her face was flushed from leaning over the tub to wet her hair. She sat straight and still in the kitchen chair Claudia had pulled away from the table.

"How long has it been since you've had a cut?" Claudia asked, combing through the damp strands.

"Oh I don't know, a year—maybe longer."

"Yeah. I can see that now," Claudia said, wrestling with a stubborn tangle. "What do you want me to do?"

"Cut it all off." Kate's voice was resolute. Her eyes were closed.

"Are you sure? Have you ever had short hair before?" Claudia was always wary when someone wanted to make a drastic change. She had seen plenty of meltdowns after a transformation.

"No, I haven't. And I think it's about time. This old

woman needs a new look."

"Okay. Here we go." Claudia first felt the structure of Kate's skull to make sure there weren't any weird lumps or flat areas. Underneath all that silver hair, Kate had a nice round occipital bone, a great showcase for a short cut. Her hairline wasn't too low or jumpy, and that gave Claudia freedom to do whatever she wanted with the outline.

"Did you ever see photos of Mia Farrow with short hair?" Kate asked.

"You mean the Vidal Sassoon cut for 'Rosemary's Baby'. It's one of the most famous haircuts of all time—the five-thousand dollar haircut." Claudia sectioned off Kate's hair with barrettes Kate had provided.

"I don't want to mess with your plan, but that's kind of what I've envisioned, without the price tag, hopefully."

"We are on the same page," Claudia said. "These scissors actually aren't too bad," she said, after the first snip. A long piece of white fell to the floor.

"Oh, good. The last time I used them was to cut Franny's mane." Kate kept her eyes closed and exhaled deeply through her nose.

"Tell me more about Gram Parsons," Claudia said. She knew the best time to get a person to talk was during a haircut. Something mysterious happened during the process—the falling hair was like a roofie of truth serum.

"'*Out with the truckers and the kickers and the cowboy angels . . . a good saloon in every single town,*' that was Gram.

That song said it all."

"But I want to know about the two of you. I mean, you can't tell me that it never got romantic. I saw a picture of you then, you were stunning, and still are. Free love and all that stuff, right?"

"Then an angel appeared, she was just seventeen," Kate said.

"Was he talking about you?" Claudia let another long piece fall from Kate's head.

"Yeah, me and a lot of other women. I knew I was just his Joshua Tree port, and that he probably had one in every city. But I couldn't help being true to him. It was a terrible way to live, just waiting for him to show up. By then, he already had a serious girlfriend, whom he later married, and a child from a previous relationship. But we never talked about them. I was just one of his escapes."

Claudia started to layer Kate's hair. "I'm sorry. I've always been so intrigued by the early days of Rock and Roll—it affected everything culturally—not that I need to tell you that. You would think working with actors, I would know that behind the scenes it's a completely different story than what you see on film or in photographs."

"Well—it's true, there were plenty of exhilarating times. He flew me to France once, where he was hanging out while the Stones were recording *Exile on Main Street*. It was before he married Gretchen, although I knew that she had also been at the castle before I arrived. By then the drugs had gotten so bad—I spent most of my time, like my mom had with my dad, cleaning up after him and trying to make him behave like a civilized human. I wasn't surprised when he later told me that Keith's girlfriend eventually kicked him out after I left."

Claudia didn't want to interrupt Kate's flow of memory, but Jackson Browne was trying to eat the hair that was piling up on the floor. She nudged him away from the white heap with her foot.

"When I think about it now, I can't believe that I was only eighteen. I was just a baby." Kate held her hands turned upward on her lap, casually catching pieces of cut hair.

Claudia chuckled and said, *"'Please don't put your life in the hands of a rock and roll band, who'll throw it all away.'"*

"Who wrote that? It sounds familiar," Kate said.

"Oasis."

"Oh, one of the new groups," Kate said.

"No, they're not really new— actually they've already broken up. But don't worry about them—they stole everything they did from the Beatles and Stones, anyway. I want to hear more of your Gram story."

"There really is nothing new under the sun when it comes to music and men, is there?" Kate asked, and opened her eyes.

Claudia knew at that point that she wouldn't get anything else out of Kate. She shouldn't have interjected. She was so hungry to know where Kate and Gram stood relationally when he died. She walked around in front of Kate and finished the detail on her fringe area. The little white flecks snowed down onto Kate's dark face. Her large eyes and high cheekbones stood out even more against the frame of the short haircut. "Do you want to take a look?" she asked Kate after she dusted off her face.

Kate lifted her hands to her head and ran her fingers through the short hair. "It's perfect," she said. "It feels wonderful!" She took off the towel around her shoulders, and left it in a pile with the hair. She walked into the kitchen and removed a small canister from a drawer. Claudia could see as she opened the box that Kate was going to roll another joint. She wondered why all of her clients couldn't be like this: trust her enough to not even look in the mirror, and then throw a celebration

Chapter 17

Under the blankets and stars, Claudia and Kate sank into their high. The cool air of the desert night blew through the yard and ruffled the hair of the animals. The landscape glowed and in the distance the mountains, where the women had been earlier that day, were a fixed presence.

"I bet," Claudia said while exhaling a stream of smoke and handing the joint back to Kate, "that you weren't just like every other girl to Gram."

"Oh, it was so long ago," Kate threw her head back against the chair. "Of course I felt like we had something special—it was the first time I had been in love."

"But I mean, you were like, his beacon in the night—his anchor in the storm."

"He was certainly looking for some kind of spiritual redemption here. He had a lot of guilt, a lot of darkness passed down to him through generations. I told him about the Cahuilla's beliefs—their reverence for nature and the cycle of life. I was really just regurgitating my grandmother's chatter, but he took it all in, desperate for something he hadn't heard in the Bible Belt that could make sense of things."

Claudia looked out at the open landscape. The sky expanded like the skin of a womb; without it, she might explode into the universe. "There is definitely something spiritual about this place," she said.

"Maybe that's why I can't leave. Part of me believes that the souls of my ancestors, and Gram, are all still here."

"Yes. That makes so much sense," Claudia nodded her head up and down for emphasis. "All of your roots are here, man. I get it, for sure. If I had roots in a particular place, I would never leave. Alex—he is my root. He's like a giant, strong root of some kind—I don't know much about trees, but he goes deep."

"Joshua Trees have roots that grow up to thirty feet under the ground. Some of the trees have been here for almost two hundred years," Kate said in a calm, even tone, droning like a chant.

"That's it, then! He's like a freaking Joshua Tree root. Good—what do you call it? Symbolism?"

"Analogy, maybe. They're the same thing, really."

"That's the one—analogy. Okay, but we were getting somewhere before. I'm not going to steer off course this time, no matter how numb my eyelids feel. I was saying—I think you were Gram's root."

"Well, then, I didn't go deep enough to brace the wind for him," Kate said.

"What happened?" Claudia asked, even though she was certain she knew.

"What happens to most addicts, I guess. The darkness overcame the light. He was much too young to die. And the fact that he died here only made it worse."

"Were you here when it happened?"

"Yes. But I had cut things off a few months before," Kate's brow furrowed.

"Dear God. You never talked about it again before he. . ." Claudia put her hands to her face, partly out of empathy, and partly because her cheeks felt like they were blowing up like a chipmunk's.

"Look!" Kate said, and pointed beyond the fence.

Before Claudia could see what she was pointing to, Kate had scampered out the side gate and crouched, stretching like a mountain cat in the direction of the mountains. Claudia then saw what she was stalking: a white deer. Its eyes flickered. Its pale tail twitched. Claudia held her breath as Kate moved closer. Each inch took an hour. The deer's ears rotated, searching for sound. Claudia's eyes grew as Kate finally approached the animal, her body low, her hand outstretched—an offering. Claudia bit her lip and sat up in her chair, careful to not make any noise. Kate's fingers reached for the deer's flank. The animal skirted back, nodded once in Kate's direction, and then leapt away.

Kate watched the deer disappear into the mountains, and then sank to her knees. Her cropped white head dropped between her shoulders and rested on her chest. It was the most sacred thing Claudia had ever seen. She didn't know why, but she trembled at the holiness of it. She looked away from Kate, who was still bowed in the direction of the mountains. Such a moment deserved privacy. Claudia closed her eyes and felt the breeze against her face. It carried the scent of sage and pine. She didn't need Kate, or anyone else to explain the significance of the white deer. She knew the ghostly creature was a miracle from the second she first saw it.

When Kate stood up from her prostrate pose and walked back into the yard, Claudia could barely make out her figure in the darkness. The night was thick, and the stars were few. They wouldn't have been able to see the deer now, and Claudia wondered how it knew to come at the exact moment it did. Kate pulled the blanket up around her shoulders and sat transfixed in the chair. Tears ran down her brown face, and she let them drop into the blanket. Claudia smiled at her, and Kate smiled back, the tears continuing their journey down onto the dry ground. Perhaps something new and green would grow out of them. Neither one of the women moved. They stayed there until early morning, keeping vigil.

Chapter 18

When the light of day broke her slumber, Claudia stretched her neck and back, and found Kate doing the same.

"My bed's big enough for the both of us," Kate mumbled, and Claudia nodded and followed her through the sliding door and into her bedroom. She collapsed on the far side of the mattress and instantly fell asleep.

Hours later, when she rubbed her eyes, she found herself alone. Kate had already gotten up, and as evidenced by the steam rolling out of the bathroom, already showered. Claudia remembered the deer's face, its wide-set eyes, calm and blinking. Again, she longed for a photograph of the moment, as she had at the spring—she could forget details so easily. She took her phone out the back pocket of the jeans she was still wearing. Alex had called three hours ago. The time said—that couldn't be right. She removed the sticky substance from the corners of her eyes with the tips of her fingers. Two o'clock? She sat up and jumped off the bed.

"Hello, sleepyhead," Maryanne said when Claudia entered the kitchen. "It seems you must be pretty worn out, too."

"Yeah, more than I knew, I guess." Claudia realized that Kate had said nothing of the deer sighting to Maryanne, or else she would have already heard about it.

"I love what you did with Kate's hair," Maryanne said.

"Thanks." Claudia poured a cup of coffee and added some cream. "I think it looks great on her. She has good bones. I really need to call Alex back," she said after a large swallow, and walked a few feet away before pushing speed-dial on her phone.

"I was starting to think you'd been abducted by aliens out there," Alex said.

"I know. I couldn't wake up. Sorry. You're already home?" She took another sip of coffee.

"Almost. Just got in a cab at the airport. So did you make a decision about Ramona?"

"No. Honestly, I haven't even thought about it since we talked yesterday."

"What have you been doing?"

"I don't know. That's a good question," Claudia said and yawned.

"Well, as soon as I check on Foster, I'm heading that way."

Claudia's stomach sank, she wasn't sure why. "Oh. But I thought you said I should make a decision about Ramona on my own?" she whispered and opened the sliding glass door to go outside, suddenly feeling self-conscious about Maryanne and Kate listening to her conversation.

"And I thought you wanted my help," Alex said.

"I do. I just feel like, maybe—I don't know—maybe we got stuck here for a reason. Maybe there are some things that I'm supposed to learn from Kate. She's a pretty cool woman."

"Oh no. Remember you asked me to tell you if you were sounding like your mother?" Alex said.

Claudia laughed. "I know. It sounds nuts. There have just been a couple of things that have happened here—strange things, and maybe they are some sort of sign or something."

"Is that Kate woman giving you Kool Aid?"

"No." Claudia almost told Alex about the great weed that Kate was giving her, but decided it might not strengthen her already shaky case.

"Okay, listen, if you feel that this is something you need to sort out on your own, I understand. But if you start talking about a compound and leaders and shit, I am hightailing it out there."

"Deal," Claudia said. "So what do you have going on tonight?"

"Hmm? Damn! Sorry, a sixteen-wheeler almost ran us over. Uh, tonight—nothing. I'm staying in."

"Okay."

After she hung up with Alex, she called Theresa, a

hairstylist she had worked with several different times, and asked if she could cover for her at the studio.

"I'd be thrilled to. I just had a weeklong *Vanity Fair* shoot cancel," she said.

Claudia wondered if this could be yet another sign. When she walked back into the kitchen, Maryanne was cleaning handfuls of used gum wrappers out of her purse, and Kate was straightening the living room.

"I have a client this afternoon," Kate said, looking up at Claudia.

"So we thought maybe you and me could go into town and pick up some things Kate needed. She said there are a couple of cute little shops we could poke our heads around in," Maryanne said.

"Okay, just let me brush my teeth," Claudia still tasted the pot from the night before, combined with the bitter coffee aftertaste. Her back was stiff from sleeping in the patio chair for so long, already undoing the massage Kate had performed the other night. She bent over to stretch her hamstrings and open her vertebrae. "I'll drive," she said, grabbing the keys dangling from Kate's hand.

"If you go out of the driveway and take a left, you'll come to a stop sign about five miles later. Turn right, and it will take you in to town. Pretty much everything is on that main drive. You can't get lost," Kate said.

Claudia started the engine in Kate's truck and adjusted the mirrors. The leather seats of the old Ford truck were cracked and scraped the back of her legs like antagonistic strips of beef jerky. Maryanne fastened her seatbelt and folded her hands in her lap.

When Claudia turned onto the main road, she saw what Kate meant about not getting lost. There was a mile-long stretch of stores, and beyond that, more vacuous desert. The options were reassuringly limited.

"Oh, what is that little place?" Maryanne squealed, pointing to a small shop; the overhanging sign said, "Lucy's Looks". Claudia made a quick right and pulled into the spacious parking lot, hosting only two other cars.

The doors chimed as they walked through them. A woman, looking to be in her forties (though Claudia knew it was hard to tell here—the arid atmosphere tended to age people pre-maturely), with a mess of dreadlocked hair pulled high onto the top of her head, and wearing only a crocheted bikini top and a long bohemian skirt greeted them.

"Hello," Maryanne said, wearing a smudge of fear on her face, and turned quickly to the racks of clothing.

Claudia walked down the aisle of used articles and found a vintage sundress in her size. "What do you think?" she asked Maryanne.

"It's cute, you should try it on," Maryanne said.

"This would look good on you," Claudia held up a blouse with a wide neckline, and a subtle floral print.

Within minutes, both women amassed an armload of clothing. "Where are the dressing rooms?" Claudia asked the sales woman.

"We only have one, and it's right back there," she pointed to the back corner of the store, where Claudia and Maryanne found a small closet with no mirror and a flimsy door.

"You go first," Maryanne said.

Claudia pulled the sundress over her shorts and tank top, and came out to find a mirror. There was a foggy one behind the circular rack that said "boy scout shirts". Claudia wondered why there were so many—were the shirts from scouts who got lost on the desert trail up in the mountains and never made it back? Such a morbid thought. How did she come up with this stuff? The dress looked cute, and at ten bucks, she couldn't pass it up. A pair of old Levis worked as well, and she found some brown moccasin ankle boots that were almost like new. After she re-hung and cleared the clothes out of the dressing closet, Maryanne went inside.

"Oh, these pants don't fit at all, there's no point in me even coming out," Maryanne said.

"That's okay, try something else," Claudia watched the dreadlocked woman sway to the radio at the cash register. Ugh, she was listening to Phish.

"This blouse isn't too bad," Maryanne said.

"Let me see it," Claudia said.

Maryanne walked to the mirror and pulled at the hem of the shirt. "Oh, I don't know. I look frumpy."

"No you don't. But if you don't feel good in it, you'll act frumpy."

"There isn't much I feel good in these days," Maryanne said, and walked back behind the door.

Claudia stared at the faded diamond pattern of the carpet until the lines blurred together. "Mom?" she asked, after a few seconds. "Where did you go when you left?" She stopped and squinted her eyes shut while she waited. Where the hell did that come from? Take it back, take it back. She listened closely as Maryanne's rustling stopped, and Claudia cleared her throat to break the uncomfortable silence. She heard her mother swallow, open her mouth, and then swallow again.

"I thought your father told you, I was with a doctor for the migraines."

"Yeah, he told me that. But we never talked about it again, and you never mentioned what doctor it was, or what state you were in, or how they cured the headaches."

"I didn't think it would make much of a difference," Maryanne said.

"You didn't even come home for the holidays that year. You only called a couple of times."

"I know, Claudia. This is all a part of why I wanted us to go to a counselor together."

"So you could get up the nerve to talk to me? But I'm here now and I'm listening. We don't need someone else in the room. If you like, I could ask Lady Rasta up there to come back here as a witness, or a mediator—whatever it is you think a counselor is going to do for us."

Maryanne leaned against the back of the cube. Claudia

saw her feet underneath the door and heard her weight shift against the plywood wall. "I don't know where to start," Maryanne said.

"So it was more than migraines." Claudia's throat tightened, and she clenched her jaw to keep her stomach acid from rising past her throat.

"It was true that I had migraines. But that wasn't really the problem. It was more of a symptom, I suppose. You see—this is why they give you a script to follow at those recovery places, but of course I didn't want any part of that NA stuff, and I've forgotten it by now."

"What are you talking about?"

"Dear Lord Jesus, give me strength," Maryanne said. "Do you remember the day before I left?"

"Yes. I've replayed it a thousand times. You couldn't pick me up from ballet because you were sick, and when I got home and knocked on your bedroom door, you didn't answer. I went in your bathroom, and you were throwing up, and I asked if you were okay. You screamed at me to leave you alone."

Maryanne sniffled behind the closed door. "What you didn't know, what I had gotten very good at keeping from you and even your father—was that I was taking a handful of pills every day at that point. It started with a back injury from an old car accident—you were two. After the back problem went away, every time I tried to stop taking the pills, the migraines came back—so I would start up again.

That day you came into the bathroom, I had just swallowed an entire bottle of Percocet." Maryanne stopped.

Claudia leaned against the door, hardly breathing, not daring to make a sound. Memories of a drugged out ("tired, sad, sick" as her father had called it) Maryanne flashed in her mind, the once blurry images now clearly developed.

After a few more seconds, Maryanne started again, "I thought you and Peter would be better on your own than dealing with the pathetic excuse I had become. But the second I swallowed the last pill, I thought of you, and I immediately threw them all up. I didn't even have to stick my finger down my throat, it was just a gut reaction, you might say. And that was when you walked in. And I knew I had to go away and get help. I knew I couldn't do it on my own, and I couldn't take care of you. I couldn't even take care of myself."

Claudia slid to the floor against the closed door. "But why didn't you tell me when you came back?"

"Because you were so young and innocent. I thought I was doing what was best for you. And I had met a pastor in rehab who said that we shouldn't dwell on the past. I substituted church for a twelve step program and told myself that I was protecting you by not exposing you to the shame of having an addict for a mother."

"But all that time, I just assumed you didn't love me. That it was my fault you had so many headaches, because I was a bad kid."

A stifled hiccupping sound came from behind the door. "I am so sorry."

"Why didn't Dad tell me?" Claudia's thoughts were now flipping through twenty-nine years of memories, trying to make sense of the disjointed puzzle.

"I made him promise he wouldn't."

"I'm really pissed off," Claudia said, realizing how true the words were even as she spoke them. "Really pissed. At both of you."

"You have every right to be."

"Don't say that, it only makes it worse," Claudia said.

"I imagine there are a lot of feelings you are going to experience, and that was why I hoped a therapist could help us through it."

"How? By putting us in a time machine so we could travel back before any of it happened? To when I was two, for God's sake?"

"You have no idea how many times I've wished I could go back."

Claudia looked up from the floor to the tan sagging belly of the woman with the nappy hair who was suddenly standing over her. "Can I take some of those items for you?" she asked.

"Sure. Take all of them. I don't want anything, anymore."

"Is your friend okay in there?" the woman whispered.

"I don't know," Claudia said, and looked back to the floor, chewing on the edge of a frayed fingernail.

"Claudia?" Maryanne asked after a few seconds. "Is it okay with you if I come out now?"

Claudia moved away from the door and stood up from the ground, dusting the grime off of her shorts.

"Did you find anything that worked?" the woman asked Maryanne.

"No. Nothing worked." Maryanne handed the clothes to her.

"We should go to the grocery store," Claudia mumbled, and walked to the store's front door.

"I have the list in the car," Maryanne straightened her shirt and followed.

The sales woman waved goodbye, and the doors chimed cheerily behind them as they walked out of the store.

Chapter 19

Kate's radio hummed when they got in the truck. "You can't be serious with the freaking Crosby, Stills, and Nash right now," Claudia said under her breath, peering through the filthy windshield in search of the grocery store. She found it next to an old Laundromat, a sad little building with chipped hospital-green paint. "Teach Your Children" continued to mock the tension between the women—*"and know they love you"*.

"What about Dad? What happened with him when you came back?" Claudia pulled into a parking space.

"I think we had both been living in denial for so long. And the only way I could stay clean was to throw myself into church. He didn't feel the same, and we grew further apart." Maryanne unbuckled her seatbelt.

"Sounds like swapping one addiction for another," Claudia said. She held the grocery store door open for

Maryanne.

"Maybe it was, but it was better than what I was doing before. I know it seems fake to you, but my faith has gotten me through a lot. It is very real to me," Maryanne said, not knowing what direction to walk in.

Claudia found a cart and slowly pushed it toward the produce. Maryanne looked at the list and stopped the cart when they got to the butternut squash and onions.

"Again, I'm not saying it was right," Maryanne continued, unconcerned with the people around her as she talked and wrestled apart a plastic bag. "I should have told you sooner. Maybe when you were a little older than six—I don't know. At a certain point, it did start to feel like lying instead of protection. I knew it was a piece you were missing in your life. I could just never find the right time to tell you."

"No. I don't buy that. There were a million times you could have told me. I just don't know why Dad didn't say anything. We talked about everything else. After you two split up, I knew his loyalty was to me." Claudia filled a bag with McIntosh apples.

"I think—I don't know—maybe he wanted you to feel as normal as possible. It was bad enough that your parents were divorced. He wanted you to feel safe and didn't want you to try to take care of him because I wasn't there. One day, Claudia, you'll have a child, and you'll understand the dilemma. It's so much harder when you are the one making all of the decisions, fearing that each one will somehow destroy their lives forever. I was twenty when I had you. I had no idea how to be a parent."

The women walked to the dairy section and Maryanne handed Claudia a container of blue cheese to put in the basket.

"I'm never having kids," Claudia said.

"Don't say that. I would never—never trade you for anything. Yes, I went about things the wrong way; and I'm still trying to figure out how to talk to you—you're pretty intimidating."

"What do you mean?" Claudia asked. She assumed she was an easy person to talk to.

"You're so strong. And I love that about you. I envy it . . ." Maryanne's voice faltered. "But because you don't need me; because you learned how to take care of yourself so early—I don't know where I fit in." She dabbed under her eyes and looked up at the fluorescent lights to keep her thick mascara from running.

Claudia resisted the urge to run out of the grocery store and tried to put herself in her mother's shoes, ignoring the palpitations fluttering in her chest. She understood how someone could become an addict. She had seen enough of it to know that it wasn't always a choice in the beginning.

"Thank you for telling me the truth," she said, her hands still on the cart, her eyes uncomfortably focused on Maryanne's. "I know it must have been very hard for you after all of these years."

"I do feel like a giant weight has been lifted," Maryanne said, and shook her arms and wrists, her manicured fingernails somehow still perfect after three days in the desert. "Do you think we can try to be friends?"

"I don't know, I mean, I can't just switch gears that quickly," Claudia said. "Where do you think the organic walnuts would be?"

"Maybe over there? With the spices and oils?"

"Yeah, you might be right. We'll try that."

At the checkout line, Maryanne flipped through a gossip magazine. "Look at this," she said. "These girls are practically naked! And they wear these outfits in public?"

Claudia laughed. "That's Piper, one of the girls I work with," she said, pointing to the girl who was indeed dressed more for a strip club than an award show. "I think she was leaving the room when you came to see me at the studio?"

"Oh my Lord, that's her? She looks totally different." Maryanne said, her eyes almost as large as the apples she placed by the register.

Claudia nodded.

"Well, her hair looks great."

Claudia looked at the picture again. "Yeah, I remember this day. That jeweled comb on the side is worth twenty thousand dollars. Ridiculous, huh? She borrowed it from a famous jewelry store. Those shoes probably cost just as much."

"That's a lot of money for a bunch of nothing. She should

have gotten a real dress instead."

Claudia laughed. "It's true."

"I don't know how you do it," Maryanne said. "I would be a nervous wreck dealing with those people everyday. It'd be enough to drive me right back to the pharmacy."

Claudia burst into laughter. "Do you know what I just realized for the first time?" she said.

"What?"

"You're funny."

"Funny weird or funny ha-ha? You know what— it doesn't matter. The word fun is in there somewhere and I'll take that for all it's worth." Maryanne reapplied her lipstick using the shiny end of the tube as a mirror and smacked her lips together.

"But I'm still pissed," Claudia said as the walked through the doors.

"That's fine, honey. I'm still—'pissed' about it too." Maryanne struggled to say the word, but looked pleased after she spit it out.

Chapter 20

A wave of patchouli and peppermint greeted Claudia and Maryanne when they walked into Kate's house, but she was nowhere in sight.

Claudia detected a soft and chiming sound escape from the crack under the massage room door. "She must still be with her client."

"I'll just put these things away," Maryanne whispered back, and placed two bags on the counter in the kitchen. Claudia followed her and set the rest of the bags down. She filled a glass with water and magically made the liquid disappear. It wasn't as hot as the day before, or maybe she was just getting used to it—either way, her body was a dry sponge capable of soaking up an ocean.

Maryanne opened the refrigerator and found a home for the perishable cheese and yogurt. "I wonder where Kate keeps her kitchen scissors. The wrapper around these flowers is so tight." She picked at the plastic imprisoning the wildflowers she had insisted on buying for Kate at the store.

Claudia stood at the sliding glass door watching the sheep doze in the dirt. She was sleepy herself and swayed, contemplating last night's surreal albino deer visitation. She wondered if maybe she and Kate had hallucinated simultaneously. Maybe Kate had them smoking peyote instead of weed.

"Oh no," Maryanne said, holding her hand up to her clavicle in dismay, as Claudia turned around.

The drawer by the sink was open and so was Kate's canister.

"What is it?" Claudia asked from the other side of the room, feigning ignorance.

Maryanne held up the opened tin and sniffed it with a look of disdain. "I'm pretty sure it's marijuana. Did you know about this?" She spoke quietly, but still managed to employ the universal tone of maternal disappointment—words were nonessential.

"Mom—it's really not that big of a deal."

"Just answer the question, did you know about this? Is this what you two have been doing the past couple of nights after I went to sleep?" Maryanne's tone intensified.

"Yes, okay? I got high with Kate. So what. Can you lower your voice? She can probably hear us!" Claudia whispered.

"This is how it starts, Claudia. Sneaking around—you

are genetically disposed to addiction, you know."

"Mom, you don't get addicted to pot."

"That's what the doctors used to say about pain medication."

"You can't go around assuming that everyone is going to have the same problems that you did. It's not fair or realistic."

"This is not okay," she said, holding up the canister, the whites of her eyes flashing. "It's illegal and I can't support you doing it or us being in a house with it."

"It's practically legal in California now, and anyway, you can't make decisions for me." All of the old anger that had been temporarily bated with Maryanne's remorse that afternoon returned again like a virus with even stronger symptoms.

"You're right," Maryanne said, and then lowered her voice again, "but I can make decisions for myself. I won't stay here anymore. I'll get a room somewhere else. And you need to decide what you're going to do about Ramona—tonight."

"I'm trying to decide—but my God, it's just one thing after . . ." Claudia stopped talking when Kate walked out of the massage room, followed by a staggering man who was trying to smooth his ruffled hair.

"Now remember," Kate said in a soothing voice when they got to the front door, "drink plenty of water tonight and try to take it easy for the next couple of days. Don't hesitate to call me if you need help processing anything that came up today."

"Thank you so much," the man said, and placed a large, hairy hand on Kate's arm. "This woman is amazing, you know," he said to Claudia and Maryanne, watching from the kitchen.

Maryanne smirked, and as soon as the man walked out the front door, she cleared her throat and approached Kate with the tin box. "I wasn't looking for this, but now that I've found it, I can't ignore it," she said.

Kate remained calm and after pausing for a moment said, "I'm so sorry my lifestyle makes you uncomfortable, Maryanne."

"And I'm sorry that you find it appropriate to offer my daughter drugs. How exactly do you justify that?"

"Claudia is a grown woman. The two of you will never have a real relationship now if you don't learn to accept that."

Maryanne stared at Kate for a second before opening her mouth. "Well, I'm very grateful for your hospitality and kindness. But I can no longer stay here knowing about the kind of life you lead. And if Claudia doesn't get Ramona fixed, I will find a way to the closest airport and fly home," Maryanne said, looking at Claudia for the last part.

"Mom, don't you think you're overreacting just a little bit?" Claudia asked.

"Claudia, I've made up my mind. Now are you coming

with me or are you staying here?" Maryanne crossed her arms over her stomach.

Claudia turned to Kate and asked, "Can I borrow your truck and help her find a place to stay for the night? I'll bring it right back."

"Of course," Kate said. "But before you go, Maryanne, I want you to know that I've really enjoyed the time we've had together. It means a lot to me, and you've given me a lot to think about. We encounter every person for a reason."

Maryanne harrumphed. "Thank you for showing us the spring," she said primly and looked at the door. "I'll just get my things now."

Chapter 21

Are you sure you don't want me to look for a restaurant first—you can cool down for a bit and then see if you still want to pay for a room?" Maryanne's diatribe seemed like such a waste of time, money, and energy—a silly showcase for her self-righteousness.

"I'm sure. I think I saw a motel just a little ways from the grocery store on the opposite side of the road." Maryanne stared straight ahead at the headlight-lit road.

"Okay, I just had to ask," Claudia drove in the same direction they had been only hours ago, although it seemed like a week had already passed; so much had happened in one day. She wondered how Maryanne could snap from the vulnerable confession of her addiction back to her pious attitude so easily. She was a rubber band of conviction.

"Just right over there, I think," Maryanne pointed.

Claudia followed her finger and saw a small wooden sign

with the words "Joshua Tree Motel" carved out in front of a sad little row of rooms.

"Mom, really? Look at this place."

"I'm sure it'll be just fine," Maryanne said.

Claudia parked the car and walked with her mother to the welcome desk inside. The walls were chipped wood paneling and the carpet was a nubby orange, stained with several large ominous brown spots. A coffee table with brochures on local attractions sat between two mismatched polyester loveseats.

"I'd like a room, please," Maryanne said, clutching her purse to her side.

"Well, we're pretty full at the moment. There's a rock climbing convention starting tomorrow morning and the place is packed with those crazies. Let me see here . . ." a man, bald on the top of his head with a greasy ponytail in the back flipped through a three ring binder. "Oh. Okay. Heh. I forgot we had a cancellation for this one. It's a Queen size bed."

"That's great," Maryanne said.

"Alright, here's the key. Feel free to use the pool, and we have a continental breakfast in here until nine in the morning."

"That's lovely," Maryanne said, and smiled at Claudia. "Are you sure you don't want to stay here?" she asked, as they walked to get her bag.

"I have to take the truck back to Kate," Claudia said.

Maryanne shrugged her shoulders and shook her head.

They walked to the door adorned with a brass number eight. Maryanne unlocked it, pushed it open, and they glanced around the room of peach cinderblock walls and outdated furniture before walking through the door. After they went in, Claudia noticed an old desk and looked up at the painting hanging above it. Her stomach kicked like an angry mule into her throat. She immediately recognized the face in the portrait. It was the same man who was in the photograph with Kate and Keith Richards. It was Gram Parsons. She was instantly discombobulated and wanted to leave before Maryanne could guilt her into staying any longer. "Okay. I'll call you in the morning with a decision about Ramona," she said, tripping on loose carpet on her way to the door.

"I'd appreciate that," Maryanne replied. "And Claudia," she shuffled toward her daughter and awkwardly hugged her around the neck for a brief moment. "Despite this other stuff—I'm real glad we talked today."

"Yeah. Okay, sleep tight." When Claudia was on the other side of the closed door, she looked at it, and then turned to the landscape in the distance. She walked back inside to the welcome desk and found the ponytailed man flipping through a car magazine.

"That room my mom's in—with the painting of Gram Parsons on the wall?"

"Oh yeah. Hallowed ground, room eight is. Last place

anyone ever saw him alive. Tequila, heroine, and morphine. Don't ever try to mix 'em."

"Oh God. Don't tell my mom about what happened in there, okay? She'll probably try to hold a prayer meeting or something to cast out the evil spirits."

"Wouldn't be the first time," the man laughed.

Claudia paused and thought about asking Maryanne one more time to come back with her to Kate's house. But she knew it wouldn't do any good, so she walked away from the motel.

She got in Kate's truck and noticed the gas tank was almost on empty. There was a service station just a few buildings up. As she filled the tank, she thought about room eight and how Maryanne was probably unpacking her things now, completely unaware of the room's history and how it related to Kate. She went inside the station, paid for the gas and bought a pack of cigarettes. She had a long night of thinking ahead of her.

When Claudia returned to the house, she found Kate sitting outside with her feet propped up on a sleeping Jackson Browne. Claudia could tell she was high by the gloss in her eyes and the elongation of her vowels. "Oh, hi Claaaudia. Did Maryanne get settled in alriiight?"

"Yeah, she's fine. Sorry about all of the drama today." Claudia tapped her cigarettes against her palm to pack the tobacco.

"Oh. It's fine. I understand. Do you want—I can go get

some more . . ." Kate put an imaginary joint to her lips in a game charades; the secret word was marijuana.

"No. Thanks. I need to be clearheaded tonight," Claudia said, and lit her cigarette.

"Mmm Hmm," Kate nodded. "She's right about me, you know—your mom. But I'm too old now to change now. My crutches are the only way I can walk. I'm a pathetic cripple otherwise."

"Oh no, Kate. She was too harsh. The background of that whole conversation when we were gone—she had just told me the reason she left when I was six was because she went to rehab for a pill addiction."

"Whoa." Kate's head rolled so loosely it looked like it might fall off her neck.

"Yeah. And she has this irrational fear that I will end up addicted to something like her and ruin my life and it will be her fault."

"Yes. That's it. Fear." Kate nodded, and looked at the horses twitching their ears.

Claudia watched the distance growing in the woman's eyes as the warm breeze ruffled Kate's short silver hair like feathers on a baby bird. Suddenly she felt sorry for her. She took the smooth smoke of the lit cigarette into her lungs and blew a cloud into the navy sky.

"She would probably be about your age, maybe just a little older," Kate muttered, unblinking.

Confusion lit Claudia's face.

"I didn't tell him. There wasn't any need to. I knew what was best. Or I thought I did anyway. One of my aunts made the remedy and promised not to tell anyone. I've never been as sick as I was then. But—it was over in two days. I knew it would have been a girl."

Whatever was bubbling out of Kate had been buried for a long time in the deepest parts of her, much like the unexpected spring on the desert mountain. Her voice was different now, like it belonged to someone else. Claudia willed her onward in her mind.

"Gram already had a little girl. I was only nineteen. My father would have hunted him down and killed him, and then finished me if he knew what I had done. After it was over, I couldn't look at Gram again. He tried to contact me repeatedly to find out what was wrong, but I told him I never wanted to see him again. And then five months later . . ."

Claudia's eyes filled with tears. This was what had paralyzed Kate—the guilt that she never told Gram about his unborn child and the aching question of what the child would be like—the legacy of a man gone far too soon. She quickly wiped her eyes and tried to steady herself. She needed to be strong for Kate. She couldn't imagine living under the weight of such a crippling secret for so many years.

"To Cahuilla, the white deer is the most sacred of all the white animals. She is a messenger from the spirit realm. If she stays long enough to let you touch her, then you are right with the Great Spirits. She brings their forgiveness with an embrace."

Claudia clenched a sob in her throat and bit the inside of her mouth to stifle the sound.

"There is still unrest between me and those I've loved and lost." Kate turned to Claudia, the light of the candle burned in her dark wet eyes.

Claudia wiped the tears from her own face. "But it's just a legend. Maybe it's enough that the deer came to you at all—that you even saw it. That's pretty supernatural in itself."

"No. It is a warning." Kate looked at Claudia so intently that Claudia had to look away. Claudia was double gutted with the sadness of both Kate's story and her mother's addiction.

"I'm hungry, are you?" Kate asked casually, as if they had just been talking about the weather and quickly left Claudia to go into the kitchen.

Chapter 22

Kate returned with two glasses of wine and a plate of bread and cheese.

"Sorry we ruined dinner tonight," Claudia said.

"It's fine. I'll use the groceries tomorrow." Kate handed Claudia a glass.

"Were you angry with Gram?" Claudia asked, swallowing a mouthful of wine.

"Oh, yes—I wanted him to come back to life just so I could kill him myself, I was so furious. It wasn't just that he left me and everyone else in his life, though that was infuriating enough. It was that he threw himself away so easily. He knew his body was giving out and that it couldn't take much more, but he kept pushing it further and further. Intentional or not, he knew better after watching his dad do the same thing to his own family—only his father put an actual gun to his own head—on Christmas Eve, if you can believe it."

Claudia broke off a chunk of bread, smeared it with cheese and handed it to Kate. Then she prepared a piece for herself. She was deep in thought as they ate, her head bowed in silence for a moment.

"That was how I felt about Mom, that she wasted our lives together because she went away and never came back the same. Supposedly she was doing what she thought was best for everyone. Same as you did when you found out you were pregnant, I suppose."

"We can only carve out our true paths with the tools we've been given. Some have a compass, some a light, and others nothing but a pair of walking shoes. I empathize with Maryanne. I really do. Between the two of us, she was definitely the wiser at her crisis point."

"Do you really think that? How would you have raised a child on your own?"

"I don't know." Kate swallowed a mouthful of wine. "But kids raise kids all the time."

"Yeah, and there are a lot of messed up kids running around because of it. I'm not saying you did the right thing or the wrong thing. Who knows what that is anyway? I'm just thinking that, you know—that white deer—maybe what she really wants is for you to forgive yourself?"

Kate turned her head away from Claudia and looked toward the mountains again. "It's so much easier to forgive other people than it is ourselves." Her words came slowly, one at a time. "I forgave Gram—after I got done hating him. I understood his darkness. It's hard and dangerous to be an artist. You're always walking so close to the edge, it's easy to fall into the abyss. Me—I've always been the caretaker. Except for this one time—the most important time—I failed."

"But what would you tell me if I was in your place?" Claudia tore off another piece of bread.

"I would say that your guilt is toxic. That it will poison your body and your relationships until you learn to let go of it." Kate smiled and then threw her silver head back and laughed. "I know—it's easy, right? Remember, those who can't do, teach."

Claudia laughed. "Yeah, I guess that's true." She looked over at Jackson Browne lying on his side in the dirt, his rib-cage rising and falling with loud snores. "I suppose Mom is doing the best she can right now."

Kate nodded her head. "It'd be a whole lot easier if the woman would lighten up about the weed," she smiled and rolled her eyes, "but yeah—you're right. She's trying, that much is obvious."

Claudia leaned her head back over the back of the chair and sighed, looking up at the stars. "I think it's also pretty obvious that we broke down here for a reason. Maybe Ramona knew—or someone did."

Kate also looked up and said, "I've been the Wizard hiding behind the screen, trying to act like I have the whole well-being thing in aces. Truth is, I'm just as unwell as everyone else. And to make it even worse, I'm old and stuck in my ways. You're still young. Anything is possible. In a year, I might crawl an inch toward recovery, but you—you can move mountains with your youth and vigor. You'll see."

"I guess some people never get the chance to do this—reassess things—think about what kind of person they want to be."

"That's true. Most people don't take the time to do it. Everyone's rushing off but going nowhere. Oh look, I'm on empty. I'll be right back." Kate stepped inside, and Jackson raised his head, but then dropped it sleepily to the ground when he saw Kate return in seconds.

"That's okay, I'm good," Claudia said, holding a hand over her glass.

"See what I mean? You're already skipping ahead of me. Next year, you'll be building hospitals in Rwanda and stuff."

"Oh, come on. Don't go and set an impossible standard for me—baby steps."

"Okay, we'll start with a charitable carwash or something," Kate said.

"Ugh," Claudia groaned. "Cars—I need to—hang on, who's this?" Claudia looked at her phone and answered. "Hey, Mom. How's the motel treating you?"

Maryanne was silent and then sniffled into the phone. Her breathing was uneven. "Claudia. I need to go to a hospital."

"What? Why? What's wrong?" Claudia asked and stood up. The knee-jerk reaction was programmed into the fibers of her being: something's wrong with Mom, drop everything; act fast.

"Just please come get me," Maryanne answered, her voice quivering.

"We have to go," Claudia said to Kate, and ran to the truck.

Kate followed without asking questions and threw the keys to Claudia. They didn't speak. Claudia chewed the nails of her left hand and steered with her right. They pulled into the motel and Claudia circled around to Maryanne's room.

"I'll be right back," Claudia said unbuckling her seatbelt and watched the color drain from Kate's face when they parked directly in front of room number eight. Kate nodded slowly, still staring at the faded brass eight. "I'm sorry, Kate. I know you never wanted to come here." Claudia jumped out of the truck and knocked on the door. Maryanne opened it, her purse in hand, tears streaming down her face. "Are you okay?" Claudia asked her.

Maryanne wiped her nose with a balled-up tissue and walked straight to the truck without answering the question.

Claudia peeled out of the parking lot, and following Kate's directions, was in front of the small Joshua Tree County Hospital within five minutes. Claudia jumped down from the truck and helped Maryanne out, walking her through the automatic doors while Kate parked. They approached the front desk. "Fill these out please," a woman wearing large red-framed glasses said in a tired voice. Claudia easily found a place for them to sit and looked around the mostly empty waiting room. At least they would be able to see a doctor quickly. Maryanne put on her bifocals and answered the questions on the sheet of paper.

"I'll take it up for you," Claudia said when she finished.

"That's okay, I'll go." Maryanne walked the clipboard to the woman and returned to her seat.

Kate walked into the waiting room, glanced around at the few people and spotted Claudia and Maryanne. She sat down on the other side of Maryanne. All three women looked directly ahead, perched on the edge of their seats like three birds on a wire.

"Excuse me, Mrs. Uh, Maryanne Hastings? How many weeks?"

Maryanne cleared her throat, looked at the woman and muttered, "Ten".

"I'm sorry, I couldn't hear you?" the woman asked loudly, holding her hand up to her ear.

"Ten," Maryanne said again, embarrassment in her voice.

Claudia tried to think what this could mean. Ten weeks of what? Cancer? Lou Gehrig's Disease? Then she understood. It all clicked into place. "Mom, you're—pregnant?"

Maryanne nodded and looked down; she licked her lips and then looked up again at Claudia. "I'm sorry. I was going to tell you—I just wanted to clear up the other part first. I didn't want you to think—and now I'm spotting—" she whispered to Claudia and covered her mouth with her hand.

Claudia's jaw fell open. Nothing came out. She wanted to snap her fingers and wake up in her bed at home with Alex and Foster.

"You can come with me, Maryanne," a nurse standing at the open door said. "We will let you know of any developments," she said to Claudia and Kate.

Claudia watched Maryanne walk slowly away with the nurse.

"I was wondering when she was going to tell you," Kate said.

"What? You knew? She told you, but not me?" Claudia glanced around the room, thinking that perhaps these strangers in the room knew too and she was the last person on the planet kept in the dark. At this point, nothing would surprise her.

"No. She didn't tell me. I saw it the minute the two of you got in the truck after Ramona broke down. That wasn't carsickness on her face. And then the extreme fatigue every night—I wasn't pregnant for very long, but I have worked and lived with plenty of women who were. And I could tell that you didn't know. You would have been more careful with her."

"But she's so old!"

"How old is she?"

"Um, let's see—she was twenty when she had me, so—forty-nine, I guess?"

"That isn't too old. Many women don't go through menopause until their mid-fifties."

"So that's what everything was about—her coming to L.A., Ramona as a peace offering, the counseling scam—it was all about the baby, not because she wanted to be with me. She just wants a clean slate so she can start over—a free pass." Claudia's eyes circled the room again as she thought about all of the details that added up to yet another one of Maryanne's shattering lies. She was dizzy and sick.

"Claudia—is it really so bad that she wants a clean slate? Isn't that what we all want?"

Claudia opened her mouth to tell Kate to shut up and mind her own business. Her forehead wrinkled between her brows as the shadow of a headache descended. Instead of speaking, she leaned forward and sifted through the magazines on the coffee table. She flipped the pages of *Cooking for Diabetics*, not even stopping to look at the photos. She tried unsuccessfully to concentrate to make the spinning stop.

"I feel like they should be telling us something by now," Claudia said after twenty minutes of torturous silence. She stood up and peered around the desk.

Kate smiled. "They will. Most of the waiting at hospitals is because of all the legality crap—signing papers and that kind of thing."

"Do you know if she's going to be okay? If the baby—I mean, do you have one of your premonitions or whatever you get about it?" Claudia tapped her toes on the faded carpet.

"I'm sorry, I don't," Kate said, and put her hand on Claudia's knee.

"I feel like I'm in the Twilight Zone. I really do. Like we've fallen down a freaking rabbit hole or something." Claudia's legs now bounced up and down. Her throat was dry.

"I have to admit, I haven't had this much excitement in a long, long time, before you two showed up—I was beginning to think that my life was headed toward 'normalcy', whatever that means."

It was enough to make Claudia laugh a little. "I don't think you will ever have to worry about leading an ordinary life."

"We can only hope," Kate said and nodded.

"Why can't they ever have good magazines in waiting rooms?" Claudia asked, and again pushed through the stack on the table in front of them.

"Maybe they're just trying to keep everyone's heart rate down. Nothing too exciting or thought provoking allowed. We all know that can be risky business," Kate said.

"I suppose that's why they have so many bridal magazines—booooorrrring," Claudia held up a cover with a bride in a full, long-trained gown, a bouquet of crimson roses in her hand.

"I take it you don't want all of that," Kate said.

"I don't know why. I'm supposed to want it. I guess I just feel more comfortable prepping other people for the spotlight than being in it myself."

"But you deserve to have your day too. Just think of it as your one chance to be the demanding, bitchy client that you probably have to deal with all the time in your line of work. I have them too, and they wear me out. You might resent it later if you don't take the opportunity to play the part."

Claudia didn't answer but nodded, wondering if Piper had made the new stylist cry yet, as she continued to flip through the magazine pages.

"Is there a Miss Nichols?" the nurse called.

"That's me," Claudia stood up from her chair.

"Your mother would like to see you," the nurse said.

Claudia followed the nurse through the doors and down the hall to a small area separated from the others by thin sheets hanging from the ceiling. She stepped into the space as the nurse held back the drape. Maryanne was lying on the bed in a hospital gown, crying.

"Oh no, Mom. What did they say?" Claudia reached for Maryanne's hand. Maryanne cried even harder and covered her squinting eyes with her other hand, the hospital bracelet circling her wrist.

"They said so far, everything is okay," Maryanne cried. "The heartbeat is strong—bleeding just sometimes happens. They don't know why. I'm supposed to stay on bed rest for a few days."

"Okay. That's good—that's really good," Claudia said and squeezed Maryanne's hand.

"Thank you for not being upset with me," Maryanne licked the salt off her lips and looked at Claudia.

"I just want you to be okay. And I'm okay. You don't have to worry about me," Claudia smiled. She paused at the familiarity of the old sentiment, wondering how many times she had said or thought it. "I can't believe you're pregnant!" she laughed. "Old Tim must be pretty potent, huh!"

"Claudia!" Maryanne said, and turned red.

"So, do you have to stay here tonight or what?"

"No. They're just finishing up the paperwork and then we can leave."

"You aren't going to stay at the motel, are you?" Claudia said.

"Definitely not. That place smells like old pee and cigarettes."

"Yeah," Claudia couldn't help but picture what else had been spilled in the room the night Gram died. She pushed the thought out of her head.

When the doctor returned with the paperwork, Claudia stepped through the curtains so Maryanne could change. She waited outside and then they went to find Kate in the waiting room.

"We just need to make a quick stop at the motel to get

her things," Claudia whispered to Kate. "Is that okay."

"It's fine," Kate said.

"Okay," Claudia was relieved, thinking there are too many fragile women and too many painful memories to try to keep straight at the moment.

The dust swirled about the tires as they drove into the motel's parking lot. Claudia looked at Kate when she parked in front of room eight. The outdoor lighting revealed the deep creases between her brows.

"Mom, you stay here. I'll get your bag," Claudia turned to Maryanne. Her eyes grew big when she saw Kate undo her seatbelt and follow her out the door on the driver's side.

"It's time," Kate said.

"Okay," Claudia answered, as they walked up to the room. She unlocked the door and pushed it open. Kate walked through, hanging several feet behind. Claudia went directly into the bathroom and gathered Maryanne's wide variety of toiletries. She placed everything in the carefully organized but over-packed suitcase. She watched as Kate took a deep breath in and looked around the room, scanning the peach walls, the tacky polyester bedspread, the old Naugahyde and wood laminate furniture. Her eyes finally rested on the portrait of Gram and instantly filled with tears. "What a cheesy painting," she said. "They could have at least found a decent artist." Kate exhaled and closed her eyes. She put her palms together beneath her lips. She swayed back and forth a bit and then opened her eyes.

"Oh Gram. You son of a bitch," she said.

Claudia placed a hand on her friend's shoulder. She couldn't imagine walking into a room where Alex had died such a terrible, thoughtless death. Claudia watched Kate take one last look at the painting of Gram before she turned and then walked out of the room. Claudia grabbed the suitcase and closed the door behind them.

When they got back to the house and situated Maryanne in the guestroom, Claudia stepped outside to call Alex. She needed a centering voice of reason. He didn't answer. She left him a voicemail saying, "It's been another crazy day here in the desert of denial. Call me." She stared at her phone for a minute, thinking perhaps he would call her right back. She heard the sliding glass door behind her and turned to see Kate walking outside.

"I'm going for a ride," Kate said.

"Right now? Claudia asked, looking out into the darkness.

"Yes, now. Are you coming or not?"

Claudia looked back at the house, thought about Maryanne sleeping soundly, and said, "Sure, yeah."

She followed Kate to the stable where Franny and Zooey were tied.

"Have you ever ridden before?" Kate asked.

"Once, when I was little. But it was just one of those dumb trail rides they take church camp kids on."

"Yeah, I know the ones. They box those old horses up in tiny stalls and make them walk the same path out in the heat over and over, never letting them roam free. Anyway, this will be good for both of us then."

Claudia stood in front of the stable and watched closely as Kate bridled and saddled the horses. "I'm going to put you on Franny because she's a little more mellow than Zooey over here. He can take off pretty fast if he gets excited."

"Good idea," Claudia said.

Kate led Franny out into the yard. "First rule is, always mount a horse from the left."

Claudia followed Kate's directions, put her foot in the stirrup, and swung her weight over. She settled into the saddle and took the reins in her hand.

Kate walked Claudia and Franny through the gate and then led Zooey out; whom she mounted after the gate was securely closed behind them. Claudia watched her fasten something around her head and then switch on a headlamp. She had been wondering how they were going to see through the shroud of darkness, but had resigned herself to follow blindly along. How often did one get the opportunity to go horseback riding after midnight? She was relieved when the light beamed from Kate's forehead onto the ground, lighting what lay before them, which was mostly small cacti and brush.

There was a gentle rhythm in the beats of the horse's hooves, and Claudia was proud of how comfortable she felt in the saddle, steering Franny this way and that, following Kate and Zooey's lead.

"Do you go riding at night often?" Claudia asked.

"No. Hardly ever," Kate said.

"Was it being in the motel room?" Claudia asked, as Kate slowed Zooey's pace so they were beside each other.

Kate waited, and then answered with one of her roundabout proverbs, "Life has a crazy way of reminding you of its cycle and how you're just a small, fleeting blip in it. You and I were sitting there, talking about what happened all those years ago—and bam! The present and future come crashing through, as if to say, 'Get off your ass and stop thinking about your self all the damn time, old lady'. All of this," Kate motioned to the expanse of dry land around and in front of them, "barren as it seems, perpetuates itself year after year after year. It never just holes up and says, 'Nope, I've had it. I'm sick of rationing water and waiting for the next rain. Let's just all shrivel up and die'. Your mom has a new life in her—full of possibilities and second chances. It's the same with everything out here. Just when it looks like something is about to die, it cycles through again."

Claudia jumped when something scurried across their path. It was so dark; she couldn't tell what it was.

"I thought I was honoring Gram by never moving on. Really I was just giving up."

Claudia wasn't sure she followed everything Kate was saying, but she was glad that she was with her and that Kate was continuing whatever kind of catharsis had bubbled up inside of her. A dry wind blew against them and tickled the small hairs on the back of Claudia's neck beneath her dirty ponytail.

"I guess we should turn around," Kate said. "The mountain lions sometimes pay us a visit this time of year."

"Oh—yeah, guess we should then." Claudia quickly pulled on the left rein to turn Franny around and rubbed her hand down the side of the horse.

Once they were safely in Kate's fenced yard, Claudia swung herself off Franny and walked her around to the stable.

"You go on in and get ready for bed," Kate said. "It's been a long day. I'll put the tackle up—won't take but a minute."

"Okay. Thanks for doing this with me," Claudia said.

"For what? Chewing your ear off? Anytime," Kate said.

Chapter 23

"Mom, do you want coffee?" Claudia asked, rubbing her eyes when she walked into the guestroom, her thighs sore from the horseback ride the night before.

"I probably shouldn't right now after reading that pamphlet they gave me at the hospital. Everything is so different than when I was pregnant with you. I had a martini almost every night back then."

"And see how well I turned out?" Claudia yawned and laughed. "I can't even picture you with a martini in your hand."

"Well, I drank 'em, trust me. Now I'm supposed to limit my caffeine intake, not eat deli meat or certain cheeses—it says even some fish is bad." Maryanne sat up against the pillow behind her.

"What about orange juice, is that okay?"

Maryanne nodded and smiled.

When Claudia returned with a glass of fresh orange juice and a plate of buttered toast, Maryanne was on the phone. "Yes hon, they said everything should be fine. They just want me to rest for a few days as a precaution, that's all. No—no I don't need you to come out here, but that's sweet. Thank you. Claudia is taking real good care of me," she looked up at Claudia and smiled. "Okay. I love you too."

"Is he excited about the baby?" Claudia asked, when Maryanne hung up the phone.

"He's ecstatic. He never thought he'd have one of his own after getting married at such a late age and all so he is being a little over-protective, but it's sweet. It was such a nightmare convincing him to let me come see you though. Finally, I just got in Ramona and left. Wasn't until I was ten hours away that he called and apologized for throwing a tantrum. He was just worried. He's a good man, Claudia. I hope you can get to know him."

"He needs to do something about that awful toupee," Claudia said. She traced the stitching of the quilt with her finger. She had no desire whatsoever to know Tim.

Maryanne laughed through a mouthful of toast. "Good Lord, I know. Maybe you could give him some options."

"Well, I guess that's a little further down the list of priorities right now. We need to make sure you and this baby are going to be okay first."

Maryanne reached out for Claudia's hand and grabbed it. "I couldn't ask for anything more right now," she said.

Even as she squirmed inwardly at her mother's touch, Claudia squeezed Maryanne's hand. "Not even a counseling session with Howard?"

"Howard couldn't have done this. I know you hate to hear it, but this is all the work of the Lord." Maryanne raised her eyebrows and nodded with assurance.

"Hmmm. Well, I suppose it is pretty miraculous that we are speaking to each other at all. I'm going to check on Kate," Claudia said. There was nowhere else for her to go in the conversation or in the room that was closing in tightly around her.

The sun pierced the windows in the kitchen and reflected off the glasses in the sink and the stainless steel appliances. Jackson Browne jumped up from his cushion on the floor and licked Claudia's ankles. She found Kate outside, collecting eggs from the chicken coup.

"What can I do?" Claudia asked. "I need a job."

"Just change the water in the buckets and spread some of that hay."

Claudia found a bale by the side of the house and wrestled off a big chunk. She sprinkled some on the ground near the sheep, and then in the horses' feed buckets. She felt a new affinity for the animals after their adventure and rubbed their suede muzzles. The water in all of the buckets was a murky pink from the red dust that randomly blew through the stable. She rinsed them with the hose and filled them with clean, sparkling water. She inhaled the fresh dry air and then exhaled it forcefully. Letting go of her issues with Maryanne was easy in theory, but so hard to practice. She reminded herself of what her Pilates instructor would say when an exercise was particularly difficult: breathe into the place where it hurts.

Kate came near with a basket holding four eggs. "Beautiful, aren't they?"

Claudia smiled at the four perfect tan treasures.

"Today my intuition tells me that there is a goat cheese omelet in our near future," Kate said.

Claudia followed her inside and washed her hands in the sink. Kate cracked the eggs into a bowl and whipped them with a whisk. "I thought you might like to run some errands with me later," she said, beating the yolks and whites into a frothy light yellow.

"Yeah, sure. I guess Mom will be okay for a few hours." Claudia's shoulders tightened. She remembered a time before Maryanne left. Her dad had a meeting after dinner and he said, "Make sure to check in on your mother before you go to bed. She's sleeping now, but if you need me for any reason at all, I will be at Gordon's Steak House." He handed her a small pad of paper with the number written on it. "You remember how to dial a phone number, right? And what is our address again?" Claudia realized now that her dad was scared to leave her alone with Maryanne. He must have lived with the constant fear that one day she would forget to turn off the stove, or would drive into oncoming traffic, or worse—just wouldn't wake up. Here Claudia was again making sure that Maryanne would survive. She had to remind herself that it was different now; Maryanne was no longer an addict, she was just pregnant.

"Grab a plate, would you?" Kate asked, spatula in hand.

Claudia passed her one from the mismatched stack in the cupboard. She watched Kate slide the bubbling omelet out of the pan and then sprinkle some chopped parsley over the top. Even Louisa didn't seem to enjoy cooking as much as Kate did. Claudia had never known a woman take so much care with each meal. She had heard about these kinds of women when she was in school, but never witnessed it. Most of her friends' moms had to work and relied on frozen dinners at night. Kate was like a liberated Mrs. Cleaver, without the family of course.

They sat on the bed with Maryanne and all three ate from the same plate.

"You like movies?" Kate asked Maryanne.

"Some movies. Not horror movies. Or too-sad movies." Maryanne grimaced and shook her head.

"What about Cary Grant?"

Maryanne nodded, and her thickly mascaraed eyes brightened.

"Hitchcock?"

"Oh, I love old Hitchcock movies." Claudia jumped in, her posture straightening.

"Yes, but not *Psycho* or *Vertigo*," Maryanne added.

"Okay, the light ones, I got it" Kate said. "I have a friend with an extra T.V. and DVD player. Claudia and I are going to get them today."

"That's so kind of you," Maryanne's face brightened. "I know you have lots of books, but I'm not the biggest reader in the world. I think the book club at church puts up with me because I always bring a bucket of fried chicken from Sally's meat and three."

"And I guess there are only so many times you can paint your nails," Claudia said, still wondering how Maryanne's nails weren't chipped at all—she must have been painting them every morning before Claudia got up along with strategically teasing her bouffant hair.

Maryanne ignored the comment and finished the last bite of the omelet. "I think I might have to take a little snooze while you ladies are gone." She covered a small yawn and fluffed the pillow behind her.

Claudia stood and carried the plate into the kitchen. She turned on the faucet and exhaled as the water rinsed away bits of uneaten parsley and unwelcome memories. Breathe into the place where it hurts.

"Are you okay?" Kate asked, coming up from behind.

"Yeah. Just having a hard time forgetting the past today." Claudia dried her hands on a towel. Then she quickly looked up, embarrassed and confused by the tears that jumped to her eyes without warning and tried to stop them from spilling over the edge by rolling her eyes to the ceiling.

"Well, you know I'm quite familiar with those kind of days," Kate said. "Come on, getting out will do us good."

Chapter 24

Kate pulled out of the driveway and sang with Neil Young on the radio: *I've been to Hollywood, I've been to Redwood.*

His voice always reminded Claudia of the drunk guys playing their guitars and howling for cash on the Promenade. She knew she was supposed to like him, because he was an important member of Rock and Roll's elite, but he always sounded so whiny. She couldn't change her taste no matter how hard she tried, though she smiled as Kate and Neil sang together.

Claudia turned her face to the wind coming through the window and closed her eyes to shield them from the dust. She glanced down at the phone in her lap. It had been more than twenty-four hours now since she'd last talked to Alex. No texts, and no missed calls, her compassionless phone revealed.

"And I'm getting old," Kate sang. She drove in the

opposite direction of the main street and shops. Her brown arm sat on the edge of the truck's open window.

Claudia slid down in her seat and watched the occasional puff of a small cloud fly past. The Joshua Trees became sparse the further they drove, their fingers still pointed heavenward, patiently waiting for a drop of rain.

"I think Alex is getting sick of me," Claudia said.

"What do you mean?" Kate asked.

"He's not calling me back. I think he's realized that I'm a mess." Claudia looked to Kate for some kind of reassurance.

"Maybe he already knew that. Maybe you're just now realizing that you're a mess—that's okay, you know."

"But he always calls me back."

Kate steered around a curving road into a dirt driveway. A beat-up trailer sat ten yards away surrounded by assorted junk: children's tricycles, spare tires, a rusted ceramic sink.

"And these people can spare a television and DVD player?" Claudia asked, wondering if they even had enough to eat.

"Sure. I don't know where all the stuff comes from, but they're always trying to get rid of something. Come on."

Claudia followed Kate to the trailer, stepping over the blade of an old fan. Or was it a boat rudder?

A woman with long mousy hair, wearing faded overalls over nothing but a stained satin bra and holding a young boy stained worse than the undergarment, stepped aside from the open door to let them enter the trailer.

"Julie, this is my friend Claudia," Kate said.

"Hi," the woman said, glancing only briefly at Claudia. "Tom left the stuff over there," she nodded in the direction of a couch with the padding coming out of the cushions.

A small TV and DVD player sat at the foot of the couch along with a four year old girl playing with a headless Barbie and a screwdriver.

"Do you mind grabbing those?" Kate asked Claudia, nodding to the electronics.

Before Claudia turned in compliance, she saw Kate reach into her tote and pull out a Ziploc baggie full of pot.

"We'll have cash next week," the mother said.

Claudia's ears pricked. She looked at the little girl on the ground acting out a conversation between the disconnected Barbie and the screwdriver. She seemed unaware of everything around her; she had constructed an imaginary world of inanimate objects that was safer than the real one of people who said and did confusing, bad things. Dolls and tools and bikes and cars—those things can't hurt you the way people can. Claudia picked up the DVD player and the television and walked out to the truck.

"I'm right behind you," Kate said.

A couple of minutes later, Kate joined her. Claudia was silent and chewed her lip. The television and DVD player were on the seat between her and Kate. Her stomach was flipped upside down; the nausea crawled up into her throat. "So, uh—you're like a drug dealer?" She looked out the window as she asked the question.

Kate started the truck and put it in reverse. "You sound a lot like your mom right now, you know."

"That's a cheap shot," Claudia said.

"You think I can live on what I make doing massage in this place?"

Claudia cleared her throat and paused. "I don't want to judge you, I just—you could move. Or get another job. It's not like you don't have a choice," Claudia said.

"You'll see. That's easy to say when you're twenty-nine. I told you it's too late for me now."

Claudia shook her head in disbelief. "But don't you feel bad knowing that woman is probably getting high in front of her kids? I mean, smoking a little every night is one thing, but selling? That's like a whole different playing field."

"Her husband has a stomach ulcer. They use it medicinally," Kate said.

Claudia gave her a who-do-you-think-you're-bullshitting look. "Then why don't they get a med card for it? I'm just asking because I—I saw the blank stare on that little girl's face, and I know what it means," Claudia said.

"Oh yeah? What?" Kate braked at a stop sign and glared at Claudia with narrowed eyes.

"She's lonely," Claudia said. Her eyes brightened with hot tears. Her toes curled up in her shoes and her knuckles grew pale from gripping her knees. She looked straight ahead at the dusty road. Kate said nothing in return. Claudia rested her burning head in her hand. *That little girl is so lonely.*

For a while, the only sounds to come out of the truck were that of the Velvet Underground, *"Stephanie says that she wants to know, why she's given half her life to people she hates now."*

Chapter 25

Are you coming in?" Kate asked Claudia, parking in front of a small video rental store with a neon sign that said, "Movies" in cursive, except the M and the E were burnt out so it just read, "ovis".

"I guess," Claudia said. Maybe it was that she, like Maryanne, was prudish at heart, but something just didn't sit quite right with her about being a sidekick for a drug dealer. But she also didn't want to burn to a crisp in the scorching sun; it was a lose/lose situation.

"We're looking for some oldies today, Artie," Kate said to the man on the traction ladder stocking the shelves.

"I'm gonna need a little more information than that," he said smiling, and climbed down off the ladder, all five feet of him.

"She likes Cary Grant," Claudia spoke up.

"I always took you for more of a Steve McQueen kind of

girl," Artie said, looking at Kate.

"No, not her. My mom. That is why we're here, right?" Claudia asked Kate.

"Of course it is. Do you have *Charade* and *The Philadelphia Story*?" Kate asked.

"You ladies kick back. I'll set you up." He climbed onto the ladder again and pushed himself across the room and back, grabbing a disk from one side and two from the other like a flying acrobat. Soon, he held an armful. "This should about do it," he said, and handed Kate the stack before climbing down.

"Perfect," Kate said, walking the discs to the counter.

Claudia stepped up and said, "I'll cover these," reaching for her wallet.

"Oh no, no," Artie said. "Miss Kate has a tab here."

Kate smiled at Claudia's confusion and reached into her bag. Claudia cut her eyes to the man in the back of the store looking at comedies. Kate plopped a plump green baggie down on the counter like it was a wholesome stack of homemade cookies from a bake sale.

Claudia swallowed and inched slowly backwards to the door.

"You ladies have a wonderful night," Artie smiled wide, and put the baggie in the pocket of his short pants.

"Who doesn't buy weed from you in this town?" Claudia asked, opening the truck door. She liked things much better when Kate was just the casual midnight toker.

"I've lived here my whole life, remember sweetie? Loyalty still means something here."

"What about the cops? Surely they know? It's such a small place."

"The local cops don't worry about me. It's the freaks that roll in for the music festivals with the coke and the smack they keep track of. You said you wanted to live during the sixties, but I gotta say sister, I don't think you would have made it. Listen, the secret is to keep things small enough . . ."

Claudia put her hands up to her ears. "La la la la la la. Don't tell me anything else. I don't want to know anything. God, those people saw me with you today!"

Kate laughed and rested her right hand on Claudia's shoulder while keeping her eyes on the road. "You. Must. Relax."

Claudia let out a skeptical chortle and ran her hands through her hair while the wind blew it in different directions. "Ha! Yes. Relax, that must be my problem. I'm stuck in this hellhole with a broken down car, my knocked up mom, and a drug dealer in her fifties. Why wouldn't I relax? Thank you for this illumination, oh wise one. I don't know what I was waiting for. I mean it certainly doesn't look like my prince charming is coming to save me. Might as well relax." Claudia's voice was near yelling as she waved her hands frantically in the air.

Kate recoiled at Claudia's reaction, but kept her mouth

shut and her eyes on the road. Claudia sighed loudly and tried to steady the flurry of activity in her brain and her heart. She looked over at Kate and said, "I'm sorry. I'm just—"

"You just have a lot of shit going on," Kate said. "I can handle it, but before you go spinning things in that clever head of yours, listen: I'm not some desperate, evil drug lord, okay?"

Claudia nodded and rechecked the call history for any sign of Alex before dialing Ron's number. "Hey, Ron. Sorry I haven't called you back before now—what's that? Yes. Yes, I have made a decision. Go ahead and fix her. I need to get home as soon as possible. You do take credit cards, right? Otherwise, I'm screwed. Good. Okay, thanks."

"What about Maryanne?" Kate asked, turning into her driveway.

"What about her? Ron said it would be the day after tomorrow before Ramona's ready. Mom should be off bed rest by then."

Kate didn't reply. After she put the truck in park in her driveway, she lifted the television and DVD player and carried them to the front door. Claudia took the stack of movies inside.

Claudia tiptoed into the guest room and found Maryanne still sleeping, like she was enjoying an afternoon siesta on vacation or something.

Claudia didn't feel like talking to Kate anymore—she

needed a break, so she went outside and found a small area of shade on the patio. She dialed Louisa's number. When the voicemail beep sounded, she could barely refrain from sobbing.

"Lou, I really wish I could talk to you right now. I think I'm losing it. Things are becoming way too complicated here. But Ramona will be ready really soon, and I'll be home the day after tomorrow if I don't implode before then. Call me back. Oh, and have you talked to Alex? Call me. Bye."

She looked at her stubby fingernails. So much for getting that French manicure to go with her new engagement ring. She tore at a hangnail and looked at her phone again, willing it to ring. Someone outside of this God-forsaken place had to give her perspective, or she was going to end up just as crazy as Kate or worse, Maryanne. She dialed another number, hoping the entire world hadn't forsaken her.

"Dad?"

"Hey, there. I was wondering how things went for you two. How was the spa?"

"Dad—why didn't you tell me why Mom really left?" It wasn't what Claudia meant to say, it just came out, like what had happened in the car with Kate. Her censor had gone kaput.

"What?" Her dad sounded shocked.

"Dad, Please."

Claudia heard Peter sigh hard into the receiver.

"Never mind," Claudia said. "It's done and in the past. I

just—in some ways, things were easier when I thought she left because she didn't want us. It was cleaner that way. Now I don't know how to feel about her. One minute I feel sorry for her, and the next I think she's completely insane and I want to get as far away as possible."

"I think you answered your own question. But we both know it wouldn't have been easy whatever her reasons were for leaving."

"I'm scared for her new kid."

"Huh?"

"Oh, Dad. I'm in so far over my head." Claudia's voice fell to an exhausted whine.

"Okay, first of all, what can I do to help? And second of all, your mother is pregnant?"

"There's nothing you can do right now—unfortunately, this is one of those times I have to just do it on my own. And yes, can you believe it? Another Maryanne junior will be joining the human race. I'll be thirty years older than my half-sibling. God, it makes my head ache."

"Well, if it's any consolation, I don't think you're crazy. You might be one of the sanest people I know."

Tears swallowed Claudia's eyes, and the sheep eating hay blurred into two fuzzy white clouds that had lost their way and landed on the ground. "Thanks. You don't know how much that means when everything looks completely upside down."

Chapter 26

Oh, there you are," Kate said. Maryanne's awake now and I'm making black bean burgers with polenta for dinner." Kate smiled when Claudia came inside, like nothing disagreeable had happened that day. She was chopping an onion with all of the Barefoot Contessa's skilled efficiency.

Claudia barely glanced at Kate and walked past her into the guestroom. "How are you feeling?" she asked Maryanne, trying to sound genuine.

"Oh hi. Fine. I can't believe I slept for so long." Maryanne stretched her hands over her head and yawned. "Claudia, your eyes look real red. Is everything okay?"

"Yep," Claudia said with the same efficiency as Kate's knife. Because as much as she wanted to collapse onto someone right now and say how not okay everything was, she knew her mother couldn't be that person. Maryanne would never be that person for Claudia. Claudia looked at the dresser facing the foot of the bed. "I'll be right back," she said, her eyes threatening to flood again. She walked into the kitchen and retrieved the pawned television and player.

She set the television on top of the dresser and found a nearby electrical outlet. She fiddled with the cords attached to the back of the DVD player. Let's see—if this one goes here, and that one—oh wait. Over there, I guess? Okay, that looks right. She pushed the buttons on the front of the television and the player. She laughed when they both came on. "No way! Okay, let's try a movie," she said to Maryanne. The blue screen with the warning of copy and licensing appeared. "It works!" Alex always MacGyvered everything electronic in their house, carefully reading the fine print of the manuals and making sense of what seemed like Greek to Claudia. She just didn't have the patience for that kind of minute detail.

"Oh great!" Maryanne said, clapping her hands together in front of her chest. "What are we going to watch?"

Claudia read off the titles of the movies that were stacked on the dresser.

"Oooh, *Rear Window*, have you seen that one?" Maryanne said.

"I don't think so," Claudia said.

"Claudia?" Kate called from the kitchen. "Could you come here for a minute?" Claudia walked into the hallway.

"I'm in here," Kate said, her voice coming from the room next to the massage studio, the one that had the lock box on it.

Claudia pushed open the cracked door and then immediately wished she hadn't. Kate was sitting at a table with a scale and a heap of marijuana. On one side of the room was a wide array of interesting Native American artifacts, which must have been keepsakes from Kate's family. On the other side of the small room, was a row of plants under fluorescent lights. Claudia closed the door behind her. "What are you doing? I don't want to see this! I'm leaving," she whispered harshly.

"Fine, but I need for you to plate the food. You guys go ahead and eat. I've got work to do tonight." She looked up at Claudia over a pair of bifocals, some tweezers, and the thick bud she was deseeding. Claudia shook her head and closed the door behind her.

Claudia took two plates out of the pantry and placed them on the counter. She opened the lid of a saucepan and found the polenta, steaming and firm. The burgers were in the oven on low. *One day, I will look back on all of this, and if I ever straighten myself out enough to have a kid, I'll tell her about this and she'll look at Alex and say, 'Daddy, is that true Mommy and Gran stayed with a drug dealer that one time?' And he'll laugh and say, 'Yes, sweetie, isn't that funny.' This is all assuming, of course, I ever see Alex again long enough to become impregnated. Assuming he isn't dead, or in jail, or abducted by aliens.* Claudia realized that she was furiously heaping way too much polenta onto the plate and scooped half of it out and onto the other plate.

"Claudia!" Maryanne called. "Can you bring me some water?"

"I'll be right there!" Claudia said, and with as much kindness as she could muster, found a tray and carefully balanced the plates, glasses, and silverware while she walked into the guestroom.

"That smells fantastic!" Maryanne said. "Where is Kate?"

"She's— sorting some things out. She said for us to go ahead without her." Claudia was so tired of secrets popping up like moles beneath shallow soil that she almost blurted out, "Mom! There's a room full of marijuana plants and probably pounds of the stuff! Kate is a full-on drug dealer!" But she didn't for the sake of Kate, who would most certainly be visited by the police within moments of Maryanne hearing the news, and also for the sake of her innocent brother or sister still held captive within the ever-excitable Maryanne, who was subject to rocketing blood pressure. "Want to start the movie?" she asked calmly instead.

Maryanne nodded with a mouth full of food. Claudia stood up from the edge of the bed and pushed play.

She took a small bite of polenta, thinking that she couldn't keep much down, her stomach still up in arms. But, as with all of Kate's food, it was delicious, and she couldn't stop eating once she started.

"Can you imagine having a giant cast on your leg like that?" Maryanne asked, looking at Jimmy Stewart on the screen. "I'm already getting antsy being in bed for a couple of days, but that would be absolutely miserable. The heat and the itching!" She shivered and then opened her mouth widely for another bite.

The longer Claudia watched Jimmy Stewart sitting in the same chair, staring out the same window, the more her hands perspired and feet clenched. But when Grace Kelly appeared like a golden angel sent down from heaven to make all things new, Claudia exhaled and settled back against the headboard next to Maryanne. There was something transcendent about Grace Kelly. She was so beautiful and graceful—and nurturing. Her voice sounded like a river bubbling along smooth pebbles. Claudia watched the goddess float across the screen and care for Jimmy Stewart. Claudia knew Grace would have been the perfect mom. She would have packed lunches with sandwiches that had the crusts cut off, delicious homemade brownies without nuts, and carrots cut in those perfect little rectangles.

"Do you mind getting me some more water," Maryanne asked, while clearing her throat, breaking Claudia's reverie.

"Sure, no problem." Claudia imagined herself as Grace Kelly and straightened her posture while smiling close-mouthed. She gently secured each item on the tray and carefully placed the napkins over the finished plates. If only she had been wearing one of those gorgeous full-skirted dresses and it had been Jimmy Stewart in the bed instead of her forty-nine year old pregnant mother, the scene would have been quite perfect.

The fluorescent light poured out of the partially opened door of Kate's miniature greenhouse when Claudia stepped out of the bedroom. Claudia continued on into the kitchen and set the tray of dirty dishes on the counter. She refilled Maryanne's glass and found an unopened bottle of wine. It looked expensive, the kind Kate might have been saving for a special occasion.

Claudia didn't hesitate; she opened the bottle, filled a wine glass nearly to the rim, and swallowed a giant gulp before returning to Maryanne. She walked to the side of the bed in the guestroom, handed Maryanne her glass of water, sat down on the bed and leaned back against the headboard with her wine. She waited for Maryanne to make a comment, but apparently she was so enraptured by the movie, the woman didn't even notice that Claudia was drinking in the middle of the day.

"Truly, I've forgotten what happens here! Did that man with the ugly glasses really kill his wife or not? Oh, it's so suspenseful!" Maryanne said, her eyes still on the screen.

"I have no idea what's going on. I must have missed a pretty important piece of the story," Claudia said. "Imagine that."

Chapter 27

Hey, it's me. Again. I'm starting to worry, babe. I really need to talk to you." Claudia drained the bottom of her wine glass and sank into the pillow on the couch. She could hear Maryanne snoring from the guestroom. Kate still hadn't left her office of iniquity and was silently working away, even though it had been dark outside for a while. Claudia was half-thinking about asking her for a joint, when her phone rang.

"Hello?" she said without looking at the number.

"Hey you," Louisa said.

"Thank God. Lou, I'm losing my mind. You have to help me."

"Why? What happened?

"You know what? It doesn't matter. It's so ridiculous I can't even muster up the energy to attempt to explain it right now. Just talk to me, please. How's Ben? How's Charles?

Have you guys seen Alex? Because I haven't heard from him in, oh—going on thirty-six hours now, and I just wanted to make sure that he hasn't joined the Scientologists and been deprogrammed and forgotten that he has a fiancé or anything you know, weird like that."

"Wow. Slow down there. Um, the boys are great, thanks for asking. And Claude—I haven't known what to do about this, and it's been driving me crazy, so just hang tight with me, okay?"

"What? What! Tell me." Claudia's breathing quickened, and she put her feet on the ground beneath the couch to steady herself.

"Uh, okay—here goes. Charles saw Alex out the other night. And it was probably nothing, but you're my best friend, and I really feel like the right thing to do is tell you."

"Then tell me, damn it! What is it?"

"He was with a woman—in a booth away from the rest of the restaurant. Charles said they were sitting close, talking about something that looked private and very serious. And that Alex had his hand over hers. That was all he saw. Charles didn't recognize the woman. You know, it was probably nothing at all—I mean—maybe it wasn't even Alex. I've been telling Charles he needs to get his eyes checked. I just thought I needed to tell you. But really, let's wait until we hear the whole story to jump to any kind of conclusions, okay?"

"Oh my God, I think I'm going to puke. Wha—why

didn't Charles say something to Alex? Ask who she was? Or just say hello to see his reaction?"

"Claudia, you have to understand it was an awkward situation for Charles. He didn't know what to do."

"What? Awkward for him? What about me? Wait. Louisa, he must have thought something was definitely going on between the two of them if he said something to you about it. That's not like Charles to get all girly and gossipy about things he usually wouldn't even notice."

"He said he wasn't sure, he just had a strange feeling about it."

"What did she look like?" Claudia refilled her glass with the bottle of wine on the coffee table. She was already buzzed and starting to slur her words.

"Claudia—"

"What. Did. She. Look like, Louisa?"

"Charles said she was tall and blonde." Louisa sighed loudly into the phone. "Okay, okay, I'm just going to say it: he said she was really hot—tan, boobs, heels, short black dress, the whole thing."

"Fuck." Claudia scrounged in the dark in the living room for her pack of cigarettes and found the near empty box in her purse on the armchair. She walked outside, cigarette in mouth, wineglass and lighter in hand, the phone between her head and shoulder.

"I know. That's exactly what I said," Louisa said.

"I guess it all makes sense now—him always showing up

late, the never-ending phone calls. God, I'm an idiot, aren't I?"

"Whoa, whoa, whoa. Slow down. We don't know anything for sure yet."

"Whatever," Claudia snorted. "Everyone always leaves at some point. At least with me they do."

"Claudia—stop. That's not true. I mean, I haven't left you—," Louisa said. "And also, not to sound like a bitch here, but it seems like you're usually the first person to leave."

"Just beating them to the chase. And thank you for being the exception to the rule, I won't run off on you," Claudia said, and inhaled smoke again. She couldn't fill her lungs fast enough.

"Just don't worry about Alex right now. Take some time, come home, and then you can approach it with a clear head."

"Mmm hmm," Claudia said, exhaling a cloud. "Clear head. Wait until then. I'll be waiting forever. I've got to go," she said.

"Clau—" Louisa was saying as Claudia hung up the phone.

Claudia already had a headache and her throat was dry from the wine, but she smoked the rest of the cigarette down to the stub and then lit the last one. She heard the sliding glass door behind her.

"Everything okay?" Kate asked.

"Oh yeah. Everything is wonderful." Claudia's voice was

expressionless. She didn't even turn around to see Kate.

"Look, I know you are disappointed with me. You wanted me to be safe enough for you to understand, but wild enough that I was different from your mother. But just as there are many different kinds of animals, there are many different kinds of people. You can't change anyone, you can only decide who you want to be."

"Thanks for another giant helping of your bullshit wisdom," Claudia said. Her mouth was going numb and the landscape tilted like a ride she wanted to get off of immediately.

"My ancestors used to make tools out of buffalo shit. In times of famine, they also sometimes ate it. So maybe you can find something useful to do with my bullshit."

Claudia heard the glass door slide open, and then close again. She shut her eyes to stop the spinning. She felt like she was going to fall off her chair and keep tilting with the world until she slid off the edge. *If I can just make it to the couch, I can pass out and I'll be fine.* She tentatively stood, her eyes still closed. *Nope, not going to work.* She ran to the side of the yard and vomited. When she was done retching, her eyes ran with tears, a physical reaction to the involuntary convulsion of her stomach. But the tears quickly changed course and came from a different place, though the force was just as strong and unstoppable as the vomiting had been. She sobbed from a heart that was broken many years ago and had never healed. And now it was breaking open again with the thought of Alex wanting someone else more than he wanted her.

Chapter 28

Claudia felt something wet and squishy on her face and pushed it away with the back of her hand. The next time it came at her she recognized the bumpy texture of Jackson's tongue and moaned, "Go away," without opening her eyes. He nudged her foot falling off the couch with his black nose.

"Good morning, sunshine!" Kate sang in a tone entirely too loud and too high-pitched for Claudia's hangover. "How about some fresh orange juice?" she said from the kitchen only yards away.

"No," Claudia groaned, and wrapped the pillow around her head, searching for the courage to view the light of day.

"Well then, you can try this instead." Kate walked over to the couch and set something on the coffee table. Claudia cracked her eyes to find a plate of crispy golden potatoes and a glass of something dark and bubbling, most likely a witchy brew that Kate concocted.

"What's that?" Claudia nodded at the glass.

"Coca-Cola, of course. Isn't that what everyone drinks when they're hungover?"

The right side of Claudia's mouth lifted just enough to qualify as a half-smile. She inched her body to an upright position and rested her head in her hands before taking a small sip of the Coke. "How's Mom?"

"She's okay, but she already called the preacher of her church and Al Anon. She's pretty upset about what you did last night."

"What? You didn't tell her, did you?" Claudia looked at Kate.

"No, of course not. So did you finally talk to your man last night?" Kate asked, glancing at Claudia's phone on the coffee table.

Claudia stared into her glass and said nothing.

"Guess not. Guess you don't want to talk about it either."

"Good guess," Claudia said, and lay down again, closing her eyes. "Can someone just make this all go away?" she mumbled and waved her hand. "Just let me wake up on an island somewhere with a cabana boy to peel grapes and serve me iced glasses of—oh no, no, no—no alcohol. I'm never drinking again. He can serve me fruit smoothies and lobster sushi and massage my poor feet. And maybe he could play a tasteful medley of songs on his acoustic guitar. But no Jimmy Buffet or Steve Miller."

"Shhhh!" Kate said, and ran to the sliding glass door. Claudia heard the door open and close behind Kate, but laid her head on the pillow and tried to go back to sleep. Then she heard something above her—someone was walking on the roof, and they sounded like they might come crashing through any minute. She carefully pulled herself to a sitting position again and inched off the couch. She walked to the sliding glass door, looking down to shield her eyes from the flood of light. She couldn't find Kate anywhere and heard the rustling again on the roof. She walked over to the side of the house where a long steel ladder was fully extended and resting against the structure. She shielded her eyes from the sun and looked up at Kate who was peering out onto the mountains. "What do you know? It's coming," Kate said. She climbed down from the ladder and stood next to Claudia. "Do you feel it?" she asked. It wasn't until that moment that Claudia noticed the strength of the breeze. She finally dared to look up at the mountains even though it wracked her head to do so. She saw a thick, dark covering of clouds approaching them quickly, devouring the blue sky in huge, greedy bites. The temperature had dropped. "Should we go inside?" Claudia asked over the thunder.

"Are you kidding?" Kate said. "No way."

Within minutes, the clouds were over them and released determined raindrops that broke open on Kate and Claudia's skin, and then instantly disappeared into the earth, like the ground had opened its mouth to swallow them all in one gulp. The sheep lifted their noses to the sky and scooted under the scaffolding of the stable where Franny and Zooey were neighing. Claudia stood in the stream, letting it run over every part of her, hoping it would sink in through her skin and into her heart. Kate laughed and shook her head back and forth, reflecting drops in every direction. They both turned when they heard the sliding glass door open and saw Maryanne standing under the patio covering. "What are you two doing?" she yelled.

"Come on!" Claudia said. "It feels great!"

"Y'all are crazy. I'm not coming out there! What if you get struck by lightning?"

"Do you see any lightning?" Claudia said.

Kate just laughed and spun back and forth in the shower.

The dark sky lightened. And just as fast as they had come, the clouds passed and it was blue and bright again. Everything now sparkled like it had been covered in diamonds, dripping with prisms of light that would momentarily disappear.

"Wow," Claudia said to Kate.

"I'm glad you guys got to see it. It was a short one. Occasionally it will monsoon for days. We take whatever we can get."

"I'm going to clean up," Claudia said, and went inside. She had forgotten about her headache while standing in the rain, but now realized that the excitement had only made it worse. She rubbed her temples in the warm shower, and then dried off without looking in the mirror. All of her clothes were dirty, as she hadn't thought to wash any of them. So she put on her jeans that were crumpled in a ball even though they still had red smudges on them from the horseback ride. She was just about to brush her teeth when she heard a shrill scream coming from the hallway. She quickly opened the door and found Maryanne and Kate standing next to each other.

"Oh dear. I must have left the door cracked," Kate said, glancing into the doorway of the greenroom, which Maryanne was looking in, her mouth agape.

"Perfect," Claudia said, and rubbed her head.

Claudia and Kate looked at Maryanne calmly, blinking, and waited for her to say something

"Shouldn't you be lying down," Claudia finally asked.

Maryanne was silent and stared at the women.

"Here, at least sit down on the couch," Kate said. "You're probably dizzy after not being on your feet for so long and now all this excitement of the storm and—everything. You really need to take it slow, you know."

Maryanne sat down on the couch next to Claudia. "Do you know what's in that room?" she said slowly, in an unnaturally even tone.

"I didn't until last night. Pretty crazy, huh? Uh-oh. Can't talk anymore. Head will explode. Everyone just keep the volume down." Claudia closed her eyes.

"I—I have to call the police," Maryanne said, in an even

louder tone.

"No, you really don't have to do that," Kate said. "Why don't we all just sit here and relax and try to think about the big picture. Is this a life or death situation? No. Is anyone really being hurt in any way here? I hope not. I don't think so. Just try to think about it clearly, Maryanne. I know this is way beyond your spectrum of normalcy, but that doesn't mean you need to feel afraid."

"I'm going to call my lawyer and ask him what I should do," Maryanne said, and walked back to the guestroom. Her floral nightgown fluttered behind her.

"This is great. Really great," Claudia said, and buried her wet head again in the pillow on the couch.

"Ah, it's nothing. When you've seen as many raids as I have, a threat from a scared pregnant woman is par for the course," Kate said, and waved her hand at the insignificance.

But Claudia could see in Kate's eyes and the shaky way she picked up the uneaten breakfast plate that she was in fact nervous.

"Why don't you go in there and try to calm her down? I'm sure if you talked to her, she would understand that it's not worth her trouble to call the police." Kate said.

"Didn't you say the cops know about you and don't care? That they only care about the hard drug dealers who come into town from other places?" Claudia rubbed her temples, still lying down.

"Yes, they probably know I sell to a few people in town.

I've never had an actual conversation with any of them about it, but I have a feeling. But growing without a permit is an entirely different thing, and I'm breeding a new strain that could make me very comfortable for the rest of my life. I'm talking—small castle in France comfortable for the rest of my life. Yes, it's true that they would probably just take the plants and leave me alone—legalization bills are on the brink of passing in California, but that's my future in there. It's all I've got. Just talk to your mother, would you?" she looked at Claudia with pleading eyes.

"Kate, I'm not doing anything. You deal with it. It's your mess." Claudia closed her eyes again. *I am on the beach, drinking a fruit smoothie. Oh look, sweet attractive cabana boy: there's a dolphin playing in the clear waves over there! Everything is so peaceful here. I never want to leave.*

"But she doesn't trust me anymore," Kate said.

Claudia ignored her voice. *And over there, a sailboat with sane, happy people laughing and singing. What's that? You want to rub oil on my back? Well, sure. I think I'll have some chocolate-dipped strawberries when you're done with that.*

"Claudia, please? I'm begging you."

"Please just stop talking. I need headache medicine. Do you have anything here?"

"Pills? No. But you know what always helps me?"

"Ah, I'm sure I can guess. Never mind. I'll go to the store. May I borrow your truck, please?"

"I could go for you."

"No, I'd really like to get out for a while by myself."

"If you'd just pop your head in to check on her, I'd feel so much better about giving you the keys," Kate said, with a fox-like expression on her face.

"Oh, I see how it is. You're all about the even trade in your business, aren't you? Well, you win because I have to get the hell out of here." Claudia walked to the guestroom and pushed the door open. Maryanne was sitting on the bed with her jaw askance in thought.

"Look, this is the deal: Ramona will be ready tomorrow afternoon. Then we can leave and forget that any of this madness ever happened. Please, Mom, don't do anything right now. You don't have to talk to Kate. You can completely ignore her, that's fine. But I just want to leave as soon and as easily as possible, and I think that you do too, right?"

Maryanne nodded.

"I'm going out for a little bit. Do you need anything?"

Maryanne shook her head and looked down at the bedspread mournfully, her bottom lip protruding.

Claudia thought she had seen Oscars won for worse performances.

"Well—" Maryanne said just as Claudia was turning to leave.

"Yes?"

"Maybe you could bring me a little juice with some ice and put in one of the movies for me?"

"Sure."

Claudia walked slowly into the kitchen telling herself to stay calm and that very soon she would have Ramona and be on her way. Each step she took felt like a hammer blow to her head. Kate was waiting at the counter. "She's chilled out. But don't do anything to set her off. I wouldn't even go in there if I were you. She'll find a way to start the argument again," Claudia said, closing the refrigerator door and holding the glass of juice.

"Thank you. Take as long as you like," Kate said, handing her the keys.

Claudia was almost as happy as when her dad first handed her the keys to Ramona, liberated, if only for a little while. She put on her sunglasses and started the engine, her head still pulsing with pain. The radio was not an option at the moment. Silence, free of Kate and Maryanne's squawking voices was the most perfect song she could imagine. She pulled into the small grocery store parking lot and found a spot near the entrance under the shade of the roof. The pharmacy, where she grasped at a bottle of Excedrin, was right up front, and she easily located some electrolyte-enhanced water nearby. She opened both bottles before she got in line and managed to swallow several pills down her acidic throat. *Small sips and I should be able to keep this down.* Why is that woman with the bad perm staring at me like that? Claudia took her sunglasses off the top of her head and nonchalantly looked at her reflection in the shiny plastic of the lenses. Her hair was in a wet knot on the top of her head and she could see the mascara she put on the day before was in dark streaks all over her face from the rain and the shower and not redoing her makeup. She looked like Alice Cooper after a particularly sweaty show. She pulled her sunglasses on again to cover her eyes and quickly paid for the items before practically sprinting to the bathroom.

She splashed cold water on her face and washed away the black rivulets beneath her eyes. She combed her damp hair the best she could with her fingers and pulled it back again in a bun. She looked closely at herself—the dark circles of exhaustion under her eyes and the red splotches on her face. "It's hopeless. I am beyond touching up at this point—beyond Photoshop. I need serious repair," she muttered into the glass.

Claudia left the grocery store and started driving. Not in the direction of Kate's house, but toward the freeway. The air conditioner wicked pieces of drying hair away from her face and the Excedrin was starting to kick in. She turned the knob on the radio and laughed when "Second Hand News" came on. It was a kind of bedroom joke between she and Alex, but then she felt another wave of nausea thinking about Alex, which grew even worse when she thought about the irony of the lyrics and had to turn the station. There was nothing but fuzz. She kept searching until she picked up a college radio station playing The Dead Weather. She turned up the volume a bit, but not too loud so as to protect her still fragile head, and listened to "Treat Me Like Your Mother," a song that Maryanne most definitely would not approve of, if for no other reason than the angry guitars. Claudia maniacally tapped out the drumbeat on Kate's steering wheel. Her headache was now only a fading shadow behind her eyes, though the acid still rose in her throat. She chased it down again with the electrolyte water. *Play dumb, play dead, trying to manipulate.* Kate, Maryanne, Alex, she was sick of them all. Sick of bouncing around between them like a silver ball in a pinball machine just trying to keep from falling down the hole, each demand chiming loudly in her head.

Claudia exited at Palm Springs. Several miles down the road, she saw a large mall surrounded by expensive looking hotels. She drove Kate's rain-washed truck up to the most extravagant looking one and pulled through to the valet.

"There's a spa here, I assume?" Claudia said, when the uniformed young man came to the truck's opened window.

"Yes, ma'am. A very popular one, in fact."

Claudia put the truck in park and left the keys in the ignition. The valet struggled to open the driver's door for her. "It sticks a little," Claudia said, giving it a push from the inside.

He handed her a ticket while she scrounged in her purse for some cash and handed him a waded up five-dollar bill.

She walked through the translucent doors into a foyer of fountains and gilded chandeliers. It looked like a bad replica of Caesar's Palace in Vegas. A group of older women with faces pulled into permanent expressions of terror and lips that might explode with sudden pressure changes stared at her over their lunchtime cocktails. They all looked like fish waiting to be caught on a fisherman's line. Claudia was again aware of her dingy white v-neck and her dirty jeans.

"Can I help you," an over-tanned woman with dark hair and haltingly red lipstick asked from behind a desk.

Claudia cleared her throat. "Yes, the spa. I'd like to book an appointment."

"You're welcome to check our availability, though we stay pretty booked. It's right down this hallway. Would you like me to accompany you?" The woman said with a cautious glare at Claudia's attire.

"No, I can find it, thanks." Claudia felt the woman staring after her when she walked down the sconce lit hall. She found the spa doors and stepped aside as a man in white opened them for her.

"Hello," whispered the receptionist, over the sound of gently bubbling water that must have been coming from a nature sounds CD because there wasn't a fountain in sight. "What can we do for you today?"

"I need a cut and color—and a pedicure and manicure if you have anything available." She couldn't even remember the last time she had paid someone to make her look good.

"Okay, let me see . . . ah! Good news! Brian can get you in right now for your hair, and by the time he is done, we should have some openings for your other services."

"Perfect." Claudia knew that she was taking a chance with a stylist who could see her immediately because it usually meant one of several things: either he was new and hadn't built a clientele, was terrible and had a bad reputation, or in the best possible scenario, was usually busy, but had a last minute cancellation. At that moment, she didn't care if he had just stepped out of beauty school or fried his last client's hair off her head. She just wanted to sit and have someone else take care of her, even if the end result wasn't stellar.

Brian appeared and Claudia was surprised to find a stylish, yet understated guy probably close to her age. "Follow me," he said with a pleasant smile.

Claudia took a seat in the chair, melting into the cushion with gratitude.

"What are we doing today?" Brian asked, and put a black cape around Claudia's neck so all she could see were her tired eyes and her dirty tangled hair. "Um, I don't know."

"Well, why don't you tell me a little about your lifestyle—do you spend a lot of time on your hair or not very much? Do you need something low maintenance?"

Claudia laughed and said, "I'm pretty sure you can see the answer to that question. I definitely haven't been able to spend much time on myself lately."

Brian spun the chair around to face him instead of looking at her in the mirror and said in a low, confidential tone, "Why don't you tell me why you're really here and that will help me know what to do."

Claudia looked down at her hands in her lap.

"That's a very pretty ring," Brian said, nodding to her hand.

Claudia touched it and moved it around on her finger. "I think my fiancé is cheating on me. And on top of that, I might accidentally kill my mother." She let out an exhausted laugh.

"Got it. You don't need to say another word. Reinvention is the best revenge," he said, and spun her around again to face the mirror.

Claudia closed her eyes. How had she become one of those over-emotional women who break down in the chair? She pitied those women—they were weak and needy. She felt the cool squish of color against her scalp as Brian applied it in careful sections. For all she knew, he was turning her into a flaming redhead or worse, a blond. Maybe he was planning on buzzing it all off. She didn't care. As long as she looked like a different person than when she came in, she would be happy—or at least not quite as depressed.

Chapter 29

While Claudia's color was processing, she moved to a different chair where each nail on her fingers and toes was individually filed, buffed, and painted.

"Hmmm, there's not much for me to work with here," the manicurist said holding Claudia's gnawed-on fingers. "We could always do artificial nails"

"No. Just do the best you can. Try to make me look human again." Claudia sipped a glass of white wine; her resolve to quit drinking disappeared along with her headache.

"Careful, they're still wet," the manicurist said, as the shampoo tech led Claudia to the shampoo bowl.

Claudia almost fell asleep while her hair was being washed. When she felt the towel being wrapped around her head, she gave herself a little shake to regain consciousness. She closed her eyes again after sitting in the styling chair before Brian removed the towel and started combing out her hair. She didn't want to see anything until the transformation was complete.

Brian sectioned off the hair and started cutting. Claudia's nerves fluttered when she felt length fall to the floor and her head get lighter. She reminded herself of what she always said to her clients, "Change is good", and took a deep breath.

"I'm really excited about this. You're going to look great," Brian said.

Claudia knew that what Brian said was either sincere or compensation for the fact that he was nervous her hair was going to look like crap and she was going to freak out.

"I'm excited too," she said, and tried not to moan with pleasure from the mild tension at her scalp with each stroke of Brian's comb. It was better than a massage, better than sex, someone messing with her hair. Her head felt lighter and lighter with each snip of the scissors. Brian shook the loose strands out of her hair. Claudia heard him put down the scissors and comb and pick up the hair dryer. He sprayed some product in her hair and used his hands to move the hair back and forth in the hot stream of air. Claudia's head wobbled loosely like one of those chintzy bobble-head characters on people's dashboards, and she reminded herself how this drove her crazy when her clients did this as she had to chase their heads all over the place. She stiffened up again, still keeping her eyes closed.

"You know what would be great?" Brian said loudly over

the dryer. "Christine could do your makeup and make the look complete. What do you think?"

"Sure!" Claudia shouted. Anything so people could keep touching her.

The dryer went off and Brian spun her in the opposite direction, away from the mirror, she guessed. "Be right back," he said, and she heard him walk away.

The woman in the chair next to her said to the other stylist, "Oh, her hair looks great! Maybe we should do something like that with mine?"

"But your hair is curly," the other stylist said. "I don't think that would work for you at all."

Claudia smiled to herself, encouraged by the compliment and also for the other stylist—knowing how annoying it was when clients wanted you to do something impossible with their hair.

"Hi there," a friendly voice in front of Claudia said. "You can open your eyes now, there are no mirrors in front of you. Oh look, you have great green eyes. This will be fun!"

Claudia mindlessly took direction from Christine with the flawless skin and sexy beauty mark above her lip: "Look up for me, open your mouth a little, close your eyes . . .do you mind if I pluck your eyebrows some? Okay, we're done! Ready to take a look?"

Claudia nodded at Christine and Brian smiling at her with excitement. Brian spun the chair around slowly and took off the cape. Claudia took a deep breath and looked up into the mirror.

"Oh my God, is that me?" Her skin was even and fresh, her eyes looked so much larger the way Christine had framed them with a light shadow and liner. Her lips shined and her cheeks glowed. And her hair—she couldn't stop touching it and moving it around. It was perfect. Almost exactly what she would have done if someone with her length came in to her for a change: very choppy and texturized with pieces that brushed her collarbone. The front swept sexily over her right eye. The color was slightly darker than it was before, with subtle golden pieces painted around her face. Brian and Christine stood behind her and beamed at her satisfaction and their own. "Now you just need to go shopping and get rid of the Indigo Girls outfit," Brian said and grimaced in a friendly way at her stretched, faded jeans and baggy white t-shirt.

"You are definitely right about that," Claudia laughed and stood up. "Thanks so much, guys. Really. You have no idea how important this was."

"Here's my card if you're ever back in town," Brian said.

"Great, here's mine if you're ever in L.A.," Claudia handed him her card with the words "freelance hairstylist" printed under her name.

"You sneaky little minx!" Brian said, and turned red.

She waved to both of them and walked to the receptionist to pay the bill.

"That will be five-hundred and fifty dollars," the salon

manager said.

Claudia handed her the credit card. She would have to pick up some extra work when she got home to pay for the extravagance—plus there would also be Ramona's repairs. But if the goal was to enjoy herself, she might as well go all the way. She left generous tips for Brian, Christine, and the manicurist and walked out the door with a mission to complete her reinvention.

Chapter 30

Claudia stood in front of an enormous three-way mirror in the boutique checking out a slim cut pair of dark jeans and a black top she had just put on in the dressing room. She was surprised that even with all of Kate's delicious cooking, she had dropped a size—the upside of stress.

"Those look fantastic on you," the salesgirl said. "You should try on these wedges to make sure the jeans are the right length for going out at night. What size do you wear?"

"Eight." Claudia slid her newly manicured toes into the shoes. "Wow, they're actually pretty comfortable."

"I know. I bought two pairs myself, one in each color. Yep, the jeans are perfect with those."

"You're a smart woman. Now I have to get these too."

"Well, it takes one to know one. You should look at this dress we just got in."

By the time Claudia left the store, she had bought three

tops, two pairs of jeans, a dress, a jacket, and two pairs of shoes. She decided she should wear heels more often because of the way they lifted her butt—or at least the way they made her butt look in that mirror. Her credit card now boasted another eight hundred dollars of debt. Forget about working extra, Alex is paying for all of this—and everything else he's put me through. Claudia chased him out of her thoughts because it chipped away at the pyramid of confidence she was spending so much time and money building in this Mecca of retired dreams and plastic reinforcements. A Radiohead earworm wriggled its way into her brain: *But gravity always wins . . .*

The heat came off the cracked leather seat of Kate's truck through the cotton of Claudia's new jeans. She didn't want to go back to Joshua Tree, but she couldn't think of anywhere else to go. She felt faint and realized she hadn't eaten anything since the small bites of potato that morning and stopped at an In-N-Out Burger. Some ketchup dripped on her leg, and she quickly wiped it away. The good thing about dark jeans was that nothing showed up against them.

The sun was sloping in the sky. She crammed a few fries in her mouth and drove toward the freeway. Her new hair moved about wildly in the air, and she tucked it behind her ears to keep it out of her eyes. The thirty-minute drive didn't seem long enough. She wanted to keep driving; she didn't care where. She just didn't want to have to stop; but she saw the gas tank and knew she was going to have to pull over close to Joshua Tree for gas anyway. And, no matter how tempting it was, she couldn't bring herself to desert Maryanne.

She got out of the truck at the same gas station where she bought the pack of cigarettes two days before. After she pumped the gas, she went inside to pay. "Yeah, that's me over on pump five. Might as well give me a pack of American Spirit Lights while you're at it," she told the attendant. So much for only smoking one pack a year.

Claudia looked down and noticed a cardboard box next to some shot glasses with bad illustrations of Joshua Trees printed on the side. "Two dollars", the piece of paper taped to the side of the cardboard box said. She pushed through the pile of cassette tapes: Linda Ronstadt, Waylon Jennings, Michael Jackson—wow, Gram Parsons and Emmylou Harris's *Grievous Angel.*

"I'll take this too," Claudia said handing the tape to the guy at the register, and jumped when she heard a voice close behind her.

"Are you a Parsons fan?"

She turned around, and her face changed from frightened to friendly when she saw an attractive guy in his early twenties with longish brown hair and a body-skimming Kings of Leon t-shirt smiling at her.

"Yeah, sort of. I don't really know his music though," Claudia said.

"But you're in Joshua Tree so you're curious, right?" his

southern drawl reminded her of Texas.

"Something like that."

"You even own a cassette player?" he asked. He had a dimple in his right cheek that only showed up when he smiled.

"Actually, yeah, there's one in the truck I'm driving. And believe it or not, also in my car, but it's in the shop right now." She wasn't sure why she mentioned her car being in the shop and grimaced awkwardly.

"Damn. I'm a sucker for a pretty girl with an old soul."

Claudia's cheeks grew warm and she glanced away smiling. She felt like she did when little Danny in first grade asked her to hold his hand.

"Wanna share a beer and listen to some Gram?" he asked.

Claudia thought for a brief moment. "No, I should get back."

"You probably have a boyfriend waiting for you at home, I'm sure," the guy said with a defeated smile.

Claudia smiled back and said nothing, but thought of what was and wasn't waiting for her back at Kate's.

They each paid for their items. The guy opened the door for her as they walked out together.

"Well, it was nice seeing you," he said, starting off in the other direction.

"Yeah, you too." Claudia paused. "You know what? I'll take you up on that beer."

"Really?" he said, and smiled wide, that dimple popping

up making her want to reach out and pinch his cheek.

"So do you live here?" Claudia asked him, walking to Kate's truck as he followed behind.

"No. My band played here last night. They went on home, but I wanted to check out the place. You know, some spiritual peace and quiet."

"Yeah," Claudia said, and started the truck. She unwrapped the plastic around the tape's case, and then pushed the cassette into the deck. "I guess I'll just pull over there away from the gas pump," she said, putting the shift in gear.

The jangly guitars of the band started, and Claudia parked by the telephone booth, several yards from the lights of the gas pumps. When she heard Gram's voice for the first time, she thought it was like finally having a telephone conversation with someone you've become friends with over email. Was it what she expected? Not really—he kind of sounded like he was trying out for a part in a country musical, his southern accent was laid on too thick to sound real. She had thought his voice would have more of a gravel tone, be a bit more whiskey-soaked than sweet and chorus-boyish. But when Emmylou joined him, something magical happened, and Gram sounded confident and soulful. Claudia heard the pain she knew was in his heart. He was just one of those people who wasn't meant to sing alone.

"This place truly is amazing, isn't it?" the guy said, handing her an opened beer.

"Yeah, I love gas stations," Claudia said. "I'm actually

touring the country and collecting as many gas station Polaroids as I can."

"You're funny," he said, laughing and almost spitting out a mouthful of beer. "I meant Joshua Tree, of course."

"Yeah, it is. The telephone poles and gas pumps don't quite fit the soundtrack, do they? I have an idea." Claudia put the beer between her knees and drove out of the parking lot. She thought for a second before turning left toward Kate's house. "There's a park entrance just a little ways up here," she said. "It's really pretty there; there's nothing in the way of the sky."

"Oh great. I'm still finding my way around here," he said, and leaned back against the seat, taking a swig off his beer. "I don't know about you, but sometimes I get scared that we're going to run out of places like this. One day there'll be nothing but skyscrapers."

"That's so depressing."

"I know. Okay, new rule: we won't talk about anything depressing tonight. Is it a deal?"

"Deal." Claudia smiled, and turned on the road leading up to the park.

"Oh, this one's really good," he said, and reached to turn up the volume. He sang along to the words, *Once we were as sweet and warm, as the golden morning sun . . .*

Claudia noticed a tattoo on the inside of his forearm. It was a Bettie Page type pinup girl in a red bikini with a sailor hat and patent leather high heels. Claudia had always wanted a tattoo, but couldn't decide what she might live with forever and not regret.

She pulled up to the place where Kate parked the truck several days before —well, before so much had happened: the revelation of Maryanne's addiction and pregnancy, Kate's green pharmaceutical company, Alex's—whatever was happening with Alex. And she had thought things were complicated back then.

"Mind if we sit in the back for a better view?" he asked.

"Nope, I don't mind at all." It was so nice to be with someone who didn't need to have a heavy conversation about one thing or the other. Claudia turned the volume up even louder and left the door open. The truck's headlights shone against the climb of mountain in front of them. Otherwise, there was no other light except for the stars and a crescent moon. She took his hand to climb into the truck bed where he had hopped up. His hair fell into his face when he leaned down to reach for her. She held on to her beer with her other hand.

"Now this is the way Gram is supposed to be heard," he said, scooting back to lean against the rear window, looking up at the sky.

Claudia took off her new shoes, sat cross-legged and scanned the stars. It was like a bad case of chickenpox up there, not a square inch without spots. Some stars seemed so close she could almost scratch them, and some were so distant, they shone faint as a scar that no longer hurt except for the odd twitch of memory. She didn't really like beer, but she drank it down fast wondering what exactly she was doing in the back of the truck with a random guy and trying to ignore the slight tug on her conscience.

"Here you go," he said, opening another beer for her.

"Thanks." The faster she drank, the less she noticed the bitter taste. She felt like she was in eighth grade again trying to impress the football team.

Out with the truckers and the kickers and the cowboy angels, Gram sang, and Claudia recognized the lyrics Kate had mentioned before.

"This might sound kinda weird, but you've got some really pretty feet," he said.

Claudia giggled, buzzed and embarrassingly said, "Thanks. Just had them done today," and wiggled her toes. "You might not have thought they were so pretty before." She wondered if the mystery girl at the restaurant with Alex had nice feet. She finished her second beer and so did her new friend. She felt him looking at her and she liked it. He didn't know anything about her, and that meant she could be whomever she wanted to with him—anyone in the world, he wouldn't know the difference.

"You know what?" she said, biting her bottom lip coyly. "I've got to pee." She took another giant gulp of beer, no longer noticing the taste.

He laughed. "You know I do too? I was just sitting here wondering how long I was going to be able to hold it."

"There's a flashlight in the glove compartment. I'll go first and then you can go."

"I can go with you, I mean—that sounded weird, didn't it? Well don't go far, there're probably bears and shit."

"I've been here before. There's a bend right around there," she pointed. "If you hear me scream, you better come running fast."

"Okay. But hurry because I'm kind of a wuss and to be honest, I don't like sitting around here by myself."

She laughed, swallowed an impressive amount of beer, put on her inappropriate shoes and grabbed the flashlight. Several yards away from the glow of the headlights, she realized how dark it really was. She could only see what the flashlight illuminated directly in front of her. As soon as she was sure she could no longer be seen, she unzipped her jeans and situated herself in a crouching position that hopefully wouldn't drench her pants or her feet. She thought of the many ways it would be easier to be a boy than a girl.

She smiled walking back when she saw him looking eagerly for her. "No beers, I mean bears," she said, and laughed. "I think you'll be safe."

He took the flashlight from her and jumped over the side of the truck. "I'm sorry, but I'm not going all the way over there," he said. "You're just going to have to turn your head. I try to be a gentleman most of the time, but I'm going to have to pass right now I'm afraid."

Claudia opened another beer and closed her eyes, waving

him away with her other hand. "Go on, sissy." She heard the zipper on his pants, and then the sound of a stream hitting the ground. She laughed through her nose at the childishness of it all.

"Much better," he said, climbing back into the truck.

"Oh, I guess the tape flips over automatically," Claudia said when the first song played again.

"I expect you to learn all of these songs tonight backward and forward. You can sing Emmylou's part and I'll take Gram's. Unless, of course, you want to switch. I have no problem singing like a girl."

"I have a better idea," Claudia said, officially lit with the impulsive enthusiasm of her buzz. "Let's go for a hike!"

"What? Are you crazy, woman?"

"Come on, it'll be fun. I know the way!"

"I'll go, but for the record in case we get eaten alive by a wild animal, this was all your idea."

"My idea. Noted." Claudia nodded.

"You can't go in those shoes."

"No, of course not silly. I'm not that crazy." Claudia retrieved the dusty Pumas she had worn earlier in the day from her bag and replaced the more attractive new ones with the tennis shoes. She glanced at her phone sitting in her purse, tempted to see what calls, if any, she had missed; but decided she would only feel worse knowing that another full day had gone by without Alex calling again. It was better to wonder than know for sure that he was forgetting about her. She turned off the truck and put the keys in her back pocket.

"Okay, this way!" she said, taking hold of the flashlight.

"You think Gram's ghost is still lurking around this place?" the guy asked.

"Are you trying to freak me out talking about ghosts or what?" she tapped him on his arm.

"No, I'm serious. You know his road manager burned his body around here somewhere," he said.

"What? That's disgusting."

"The guy said it was what Gram wanted—told him so at a mutual friend's funeral or something. But the body didn't burn all the way and Gram's step-dad, who no one in the family liked, took what was left of him and buried it somewhere else."

"What a screwed up family. And I thought mine was weird, geez. Oh! Don't touch that!" Claudia yelled, seeing him reach for the jumping cholla off to the right of the path. It'll stick you."

"Oh. Thanks," he said.

They passed over the first boulder.

"I think we should stop and smoke a cigarette," he said.

"What? No! We have to keep going, you'll never believe what lies ahead," Claudia said.

"My lungs need to refuel—with nicotine."

"Fine," she said. "There's a flat area right up here."

They leaned against a rock and he took out his pack of

cigarettes. Claudia flashed the surrounding area with light, catching a prairie dog scampering away. "There's your scary wild beast," she said, and took out her own cigarettes. He lit it for her.

It was quiet while they smoked.

He put out his stub on the side of the rock and reached up to push Claudia's hair away from her face and tucked it behind her ear. His hand rested gently against her neck. She tried not to tense and put out the rest of her cigarette. She swallowed and turned to face him, still unsure. He pulled her toward him and kissed her. It was strange to feel someone else's lips on hers after being only with Alex for so long. There was suddenly a tongue in her mouth other than her own and a body pressing her firmly into the rock. "Ouch!" she said, half-laughing. "Slow down, buddy!" But he only pressed harder, and then sloppily kissed her neck. "Hey!" she said, trying to move her arms, but he had her pinned and was a lot stronger than she would have guessed from his lanky frame. No, no, no, no. This isn't what I wanted. "Get off of me!" He clawed at her jeans and scratched her stomach as he undid the button.

"You've made this so easy it almost isn't even fun anymore," he said in a voice completely different from the southern accent he used before.

She managed to get one hand free and reached for the flashlight, but couldn't find it. He pushed an elbow into her side and she coughed.

"That's right, fight me. It makes it so much better for me," he said, and wrestled to get her pants down.

She could only hear her rapid heartbeat in her ears.

"You're not going to give up now, are you?" he growled through his teeth, reaching for his belt buckle.

She looked up at him blankly, and in the split second that he looked down at the stubborn buckle, she fulcrumed her knee against his crotch. He withdrew into a wincing ball. "Fucking bitch!" he said.

She wriggled free of him, and tripping over a rock, ran blindly to the path. She heard him running behind her. It was so dark without the flashlight. She wished she had left the truck headlights on down below. He was close behind her, and then she noticed that he had found the flashlight when the plants and rubble at her feet shone so bright in such a jerking motion that she had to look away. Everything was bouncing and sliding and falling along with her, down into the unknown. His hand was suddenly on her shoulder as she slid down the path. Her shirt pulled up and her back scraped raw on the rocks. They were tumbling over one another. He slid past her; now she was behind and above him. She saw the flashlight in his hand and scrambled toward it. He was crouching to get up when she stepped on his wrist and grabbed the light. He pulled away, stood up, and came at her again. She held the flashlight above her and then smashed it hard against his head. It was enough to make him stumble back, but didn't knock him to the ground. She turned to go off the path to the other side, but he grabbed her ankle and was quickly on top of her again. She couldn't see anything, but held tightly to the flashlight. She turned beneath him onto her side, and then squirmed onto her knees. He was behind her grabbing at the unbuttoned waistband of her jeans. She kicked wildly, looking for some kind of contact between her foot and his body. The keys fell out of her pocket, and he jumped off her body to search for them. She kicked him in the chest, holding the light away from his reach, searching for the keys. She saw them directly next to his right hand and so did he. He grabbed the keys, stood over her, and then punted her jaw for the win.

Claudia fell back. Lying on the ground with the flashlight next to her, she fixed her blurry eyes only long enough to see his boots scrambling away from her down the hill. Then, as everything went black, she heard the sound of Kate's truck driving away.

Chapter 31

She had no idea how long she had been lying in the darkness when she came to. The first clear thought that formed in her mind was Gracie's small voice when they were sitting in the car, singing "Do You Believe In Magic". Claudia had no clue why this particular memory woke her from the blackout or how she could remember the made up words Gracie had put into the song, but it was enough to bring her back from unconsciousness and into the present, as she slowly felt the rocky ground beneath her hands and face. She crawled slowly onto all fours and spit out a mouthful of blood, the rest ran down her throat and gagged her. When she coughed, her entire upper body reeled in pain. It was still black outside and the flashlight next to her was flickering with a dying battery. She reached her hand behind her and slowly balanced herself in an upright sitting position without falling over. She had first located the pain in her jaw and the inability to open it more than a couple of centimeters when she'd spit; but then the pain spread up into her head and down her neck and shoulders. When she took in air, her right side tightened in pain like a metal corset was crunching her bones. She could only take in small breaths without losing the ability to breathe at all. Her right eye was swollen. She scooted to the side of a boulder and guided her way up. Her feet and ankles seemed to be okay—nothing sprained or broken.

She found her way back to the path and judiciously watched each step in the beam of the flashlight. The last thing she needed was another fall. She tasted blood again. She tried to move her tongue, but it was fat and stiff in her mouth. She never thought swallowing could be so difficult or painful. Her foot slid in a loose pile of dust, but she caught herself. Every muscle screamed after her body braced itself against the fall. It seemed like an impossible feat to make it down the hill without blacking out again. She was so tired.

"Okay God, I'm not one to pray often. Alright, ever. Sorry I've given Mom such a hard time about you." Her eyes stung when the tears came, but her broken skin burned more when they spilled over. "I guess I thought she was weak and you were just a crutch." She continued to inch down the hill, her tears making it even more difficult to see. "But I could really, really use a crutch right now. Please let me get back alive." She stood still and waited for the tears to stop until she could focus her eyes again.

The flashlight's aura was fading. She tried to hurry, but knew that it was more important to watch her step. The slope of the hill eventually began to even out, and when she finally got to the parking lot (after what seemed like hours), the black horizon had begun to change from black to purple.

The flashlight died just as she realized she could now see in front of her without it. There was nothing she could do but continue to walk as long as she was able. It was slow, painful work. She couldn't think about how far she had to go, she just had to keep moving, one foot in front of the other.

The purple sky morphed to pink, the crooked Joshua trees formidable silhouettes in the infantile light of dawn. Claudia moved steadily down the side of the road, her right eye swelling completely shut now. Something black and large flew overhead. Vultures, just waiting for me to fall into a heap of flesh. She squinted at something just ahead lying close to her on the ground. It was a long, smooth stick. She slowly leaned down to pick it up, her arm wrapped around her aching side, and then stood up straight, with the stick on end. It was almost her height, several inches in diameter, and it went ahead of her with each step, taking enough weight off of her feet to make the balancing act a little easier. With small breaths and small steps, she continued onward.

She gripped the stick tighter in her shaking hand when she first saw the headlights coming around the dark bend of the road. Though there was a soft light spreading throughout the sky now, she only had the use of one eye and the lights of the approaching car blurred together. She was afraid that perhaps her attacker had returned to finish what he had first set out to do on the mountain. But then she realized it was a small car coming her way and not Kate's truck because the headlights were low to the ground. She continued walking as the car drove steadily toward her. When it got close enough for her to make out a blurry outline, it stopped, and a door opened. She slowed her pace even more in trepidation of who was standing in front of her, but she kept walking. She wanted to yell for help, unsure if the driver had seen her, but she didn't have the strength or enough breath in her lungs. She stood for a moment and waved her stick in the air as a sign of her surrender.

"Hello?" a voice called out from the shadowed silhouette of a woman. It was a familiar voice, one she had never been so happy to hear. Nothing else could have torn away her instinct to survive, like a wounded animal snarling at anyone who comes near. Her body melted with release. Tears and saliva poured down her face. For the first time in a long while, she knew everything was going to be okay.

"Mom?" she called as loudly as she could, and then recoiled from the pain in her side. She was laughing and crying without air, relief and shame and exhaustion choking up inside of her. She leaned into the stick to steady her steps, trying to walk faster, but Maryanne ran to her side before she could get any further. She put her arm around her and led her daughter to Ramona where Claudia collapsed against the seat.

"What happened?" Maryanne asked.

"He got away. Took Kate's—"

"Shhh. You're safe now."

Chapter 32

The stretch of time from when she first sat down in Ramona to when they were settled in a hospital room was a foggy series of underdeveloped images in Claudia's memory. She remembered walking through the hospital doors while leaning on Maryanne, the weight of a heavy vest on her throbbing body and the flash of an x-ray machine, the relief of lying down in a bed, and the prick of a needle on the back of her hand.

"Are you warm enough?" a young nurse asked her.

Claudia nodded in a fuzzy haze. The pain medication was finally taking affect. Apparently they hadn't been able to give her anything until they finished taking the x-rays. She was now hooked up to fluids and a drip of Dilaudid because the state of her jaw made it impossible to swallow pills.

"Thank you," Maryanne said to the nurse, who scribbled

something on Claudia's chart, and then left the room.

There was a sharp knock on the door. Maryanne stood up from the end of Claudia's bed where she had been attentively sitting since they got to the room.

Claudia heard whispering and then saw Kate. She tried to smile, but her face was too numb and wonky to obey.

"Hey there, little runaway," Kate said, and came to the side of the bed. Claudia didn't realize how bad she looked until Kate unsuccessfully tried to hide her surprise upon seeing her wounded face. Claudia reached for her hand. "What an asshole," Kate said. "We're going to find him."

Claudia nodded sleepily. "Kaay, youa truck," she mumbled.

Kate shook the words away, closing her eyes. "You need to focus on healing right now. I have some special oils that we'll use tomorrow after you've slept. And we'll do massage wherever you're skin isn't broken. But right now, just let your mama take care of you." Kate placed her hand lightly on the back of Claudia's head, and then looked at Maryanne.

Claudia nodded and tried smiling again, a pitiful drooling, half-cocked grimace. The fatigue conquered her resolve, and she told herself she would sleep for just a minute or two.

A doctor walked in the room and peered at the three women over thick black eyeglass frames. "Well ladies, it looks like Miss Claudia here has two broken ribs. Fortunately, nothing in the face or skull was fractured. The jaw is not dislocated as I'd feared, just badly bruised—

it will be a long while before she's chomping into any big cheeseburgers, okay? The best we can do is keep her here overnight, push the liquids, keep the pain down, and see how she's feeling tomorrow. Now there's the question of the police . . ."

"She can't answer any questions now," Maryanne said, and laid her hand on Claudia's shin. "We'll deal with that whenever she feels up to it."

Even through the meds, the abrupt insurgence of maternal reflexes in Maryanne surprised Claudia. She was like a mama bear guarding her cub.

"Are you sure about that? The sooner they get a statement . . ."

"I'm sure," Maryanne said firmly. "Right now she needs to rest."

Claudia's one eyelid that wasn't already swollen shut weighed heavy, and she could no longer keep it open, nor felt the need to. Maryanne would take care of any questions or concerns that might arise. She gave in to the strong pull of unconsciousness she had been fighting since she woke from the blackout on the mountain. Just as everything in the room started to fade away and a blank slate of sleep appeared, she heard Maryanne say, "Is everything okay at the house?" And then Kate answered, (or at least this is what Claudia heard) "The walruses are fine, but the spandex is not happy."

Several hours later, Claudia woke to someone screaming

and then realized it was her own voice breaking the silence of her sleep. Maryanne jumped off the armchair in the corner and ran to her side.

"What is it? Are you okay? Is it the pain?"

"I don't know. I don't remember. . ." Claudia scratched at the back of her hand before she became aware that the IV needle was still under her skin with a long tube attached to it. She looked around the room. "I'm so sorry, Mom. This is all my fault." Her face hurt again when the tears started.

"No, no. Whatever happened was not your fault."

"But I drove him up there. I was going to show him the spring that Kate took us to. Even though it was supposed to be a secret." Claudia's eyes widened and the whites glowed in the dark, lit only by the blinking monitors and the hallway light creeping under the door.

"Why?" Maryanne asked, her forehead wrinkled and her eyes full of tears. "Why would you share something that special with a stranger?"

"I don't know. I thought—I just wanted to feel—new with someone. It was so stupid. I'm so ashamed." Claudia covered her face. "Mom," she moaned. "— I really have to pee. I don't know if I can do it by myself."

Maryanne took hold of the IV pole on the other side of the bed. Claudia grabbed her arm and scooted to the edge. They inched the several feet to the bathroom. Claudia blinked in the bright light and eased her way onto the toilet.

"It makes sense," Maryanne said. "What you said before."

Maryanne looked at the bathroom door when she said this. "You've been taking care of almost everything except yourself since we've been here."

"Yeah. Geez, they must have pumped gallons of this stuff into me," Claudia said and laughed. She sounded like a faucet left running.

Maryanne laughed too.

Claudia almost nodded off again before she could even flush.

"Come on, sweetheart, up you go." Maryanne led Claudia back to the hospital bed.

"Mom?" Claudia said, sliding her legs under the covers.

"Yes, baby?"

"Ron already fixed Ramona?"

"Yes, he said he tried to call you yesterday morning to let you know she was ready early. We tried like crazy to get a hold of you all day. I must have called every thirty minutes."

"What? You did?"

"You didn't hear your phone?"

"No. Mom?"

"Uh-huh?"

"Is that stick I found on the road still in Ramona?"

"Yeah, in the backseat. Why?" Maryanne said.

"I don't know—just wondering. You know what I just remembered? I never charged my phone the night before . . ." Claudia instantly fell asleep again, hearing Maryanne say, "It's okay, baby."

Hours later, she sat up with a start and every muscle in her body recoiled from the sudden movement. She coughed weakly and blinked at Maryanne in the chair across the room talking on the phone.

"Claudia, are you awake? It's your dad. Do you feel like saying a quick hello?"

Claudia nodded, and with great effort, pulled herself up a little further in the bed.

"Hey," she said quietly.

"Baby. I am so glad you're okay. I was so scared when your mother called."

Claudia could only say, "Mmm hmmm," trying hard not to start crying again, her head rolling drowsily back onto the pillow.

"It's okay," Peter said. "Your mother told me your jaw's pretty bad. Don't say anything else. I just had to tell you how much I love you and I'm so, so glad you're all right." Claudia heard Betsy shouting in the background, "We love you Claudia! Get better!"

"Thanks Dad," Claudia whispered. "Love."

Chapter 33

Good morning," a too-cheerful voice standing over Claudia said. Before she could even see where it came from, a thermometer wrapped in a small plastic condom slid under her sticky tongue and she almost gagged in surprise. Within seconds, the thing beeped and she jumped a little, still not completely awake. "Mmm hmm, that's good. Ninety-eight point seven. We'll take it." The nurse unsheathed the thermometer and threw the plastic in the trashcan next to the bed. Claudia blinked at Maryanne sleepily straightening herself under a blanket in the armchair at the foot of the bed. The nurse wrapped a Velcro cuff around Claudia's arm. "Well, your blood pressure's a little high, but that's to be expected, with the pain and . . . everything."

Claudia turned and nodded over at Maryanne. "Maybe you should check her blood pressure too. She shouldn't be under any stress because she's pregnant, and now I've gone and blown everything up."

The nurse glanced at Maryanne with a question mark on her face.

"Don't listen to her. I am fine and the baby is fine. Don't worry one second about me Claudia, do you hear? We just need to get you back to—"

The door opened and Claudia abruptly came out of her fog, the IV tube pulling against the skin of her hand. She lifted the sheet to her chin and instantly thought about pulling it over her head when she saw her visitor. She quickly tucked her hair behind her ears and straightened her pastel hospital gown.

Alex stood in the door, out of breath and staring at her, his eyes filling with tears. Maryanne rose and crossed the room to greet him.

"I know you said to wait Maryanne, but I just couldn't do it any longer." He went to the side of Claudia's bed. "I had to see you."

Again, she became aware of how terrible she looked when his glazed eyes rested on her face. "If you hadn't been okay. . ." he said stopped and shook his head. "You are okay, aren't you?"

Claudia nodded. She wanted to kiss him and slap him all at the same time.

"Where were you when I called?" she asked him.

"Really long story short—I was trying to salvage my clients at the agency. I should have called you, but I swear I didn't even stop to pee. Bob decided to leave the group and called everyone before I even knew what was happening. He jumped on every client I've signed. It was a mad dash—one meeting after the next, non-stop survival mode."

"But Louisa said—"

"I know. They're at Kate's right now. I was meeting with Helen, and yes, I can see how it might have looked bad. Helen's dad died the day before, and I was trying to convince her to stay with me instead of going with Bob—you know, show her that I care about her more than just a client who pays my bills. But what Charles saw that night—my hand on hers; that was the full extent of it. Nothing else happened. It was just incredibly bad timing and a scene completely out of context."

"But Louisa said Charles didn't recognize her," Claudia said.

"It was dark and you know Charles, he was probably just staring at her legs."

"Yeah, I guess that's true." Claudia laughed as much as her broken ribs would allow.

The doctor and nurse walked into the room, which was quickly becoming cramped. "Well, your vitals look good and there isn't much we can do about the ribs. You'll just have to take it easy for the next few weeks. Looks like you have plenty of people to help you with that," he said, looking at Maryanne and Alex. "You're free to go," he said monotonously. "Mom, can I have a quick word with you?"

Maryanne walked out of the room with the doctor, and through the closed door Claudia could hear her saying, "Mmm hmm. Yes. Yes, I understand. We'll do that."

Claudia looked up at Alex. "We have a lot of things to talk about."

"Yeah, I think that's fair to say," Alex rolled his eyes and nodded. "I definitely have a few questions—but right now we need to make sure you're resting and not getting stressed about anything."

Claudia nodded.

"I called the studio and told them you had an accident out here. They were great about it, very concerned, and said they would cover everything until you were able to come back." Alex said.

"Thank you. What about you? Do you still have a job after the whole thing with Bob?"

"I guess you could say I've been demoted, but I have a few loyal clients who are willing to stick it out with me. It's going to be okay."

"Do you promise?" Claudia asked, referring to so much more than the fate of Alex's career.

"I promise."

Maryanne walked back in the room. She handed a couple of small slips of paper to Alex. "These are Claudia's prescriptions. They're better off in your hands, trust me."

Claudia let out a weak laugh. Alex looked confused, but said, "Okay, I'll take them right now. Is there a particular drugstore in town I should use?"

"There's only one." Claudia and Maryanne said at the same time.

"Oh wow. Welcome to Mayberry, huh?" Alex said

"You have no idea," Claudia said.

Chapter 34

Sitting in the passenger seat of Ramona, Claudia leaned back against the headrest while Maryanne drove slowly over the speed bumps, trying to make the ride back to Kate's as smooth as possible.

"So you're not mad at me?" Claudia asked, her words slightly slurring into one another. "For going and doing something so stupid?"

Maryanne sighed and then looked at Claudia. "No. I'm not mad at you. I'm so thankful that nothing worse happened. I can't even think about the alternative. When you were gone—I realized that I've ended up making a lot of this about me again and that you haven't had a chance to really tell me how you felt during everything—even now, having a half-sibling on the way—I know it must be strange. It's hard for me to hear how I've hurt you, but I want to listen and for you to tell me."

Claudia blinked, not knowing what to say. "Before you showed up in the park, I really thought that I might not make it back alive. All I wanted was to see you and Alex, to know that everything was okay between us. I'm not great at saying how I feel—sometimes I don't even know. I got pretty good at shutting it off when I was a kid."

"I'm sure. I hate that," Maryanne said.

"I have never needed you as much as when I was coming down off the mountain. And there you were, without me asking for your help. All of the other times you couldn't be there for me disappeared into the past. I don't want to hang on to the anger anymore. It's too heavy for me to carry around and we both have new lives ahead of us."

Maryanne looked at Claudia and let the black tears stream down her face without wiping them away. "Thank you," she said.

Claudia nodded. "Thank you for showing up—I mean—both back in L.A. and also last night. I know it must have been terrifying not knowing how I would react."

"Well you definitely made me fight for it, but I wouldn't have expected anything else. It's part of your strength. I'm sure that you don't remember this," Maryanne said, "And I don't even know why I just remembered it, but when you were really little, probably two, maybe three—we were walking down our street and there was a patch of wildflowers off the side of the road. You dragged me over to it with such determination and you stuck your face right up in the colorful blooms. But then you suddenly jumped back and wailed like something had bit your nose off. A mean old bee had stung you right on your sweet little lip. Your lip got so fat, I thought for sure you were having an allergic reaction and took you to the hospital immediately. The doctor assured me that you were okay, but I didn't believe him, and we waited a couple of more hours until I was convinced you weren't going to stop breathing."

"Huh. No, I don't remember that at all," Claudia said.

"And then we went to get ice cream to make you feel better, but you could barely swallow any of it because your lip was so big. It just ran all over your face, but you were happy and didn't care; I'm sure the cold numbed your lip and made it feel better. Everyone in the shop looked at us like I was crazy for leaving you in such a mess, but I didn't want to clean you up because I was scared I would hurt you by touching your lip. You started to feel self-conscious about all of the people staring and pointing at us, so I smeared some ice cream over my mouth to distract you and you laughed and laughed."

"I wish we had a picture of that, the two of us with ice cream all over our faces," Claudia said. "It sounds like we had fun despite the bee sting."

"We did. If I could draw it for you, I would. It's one of my favorite memories of us together."

"Will you tell me more things like that story, things that we did together when I was little—just, whenever you think of them?"

"Yes, I will," Maryanne said. "And I hope we can make new fun memories too."

"When did you call Alex?" Claudia asked, after a few moments of silence in the car.

"He called me actually. He said he'd been trying your phone all day and you wouldn't answer. I guess we know why none of us could get a hold of you now, with your battery being dead. As soon as I told him we didn't know where you were, he said he was coming. And when he showed up, Charles and Louisa were with him too."

"They were all at the house last night before you found me at the park?"

"Yeah," Maryanne nodded. "Kate was out on one of the horses looking for you and everyone else waited at her house in case you showed up."

Claudia closed her eyes and rubbed her forehead. "I can't believe how stupid I was. I could have avoided this whole thing if I had just come back like I was supposed to."

"Well, that's true, darlin'. But it won't do any good now to worry about coulda shoulda. Trust me, I learned that the hard way. I'm still learning it. Sometimes I want to beat myself up about the choices I made, but it won't change anything. There's only one direction you can go from here and it's forward, not backward."

"What does everyone think happened to me last night?"

"The truth, baby. That you were attacked by a crazy

stranger and that by the grace of God, you got away."

"So you didn't tell them about me willingly going up there with the guy yet?"

"No, I didn't. I think everyone is just relieved you're okay."

"But I have to tell Alex the truth, right?"

"I can't make that decision for you. Obviously, I haven't exactly been the best model of honesty."

"It would be so much easier to not tell him. I don't want to hurt him—or lose him."

Maryanne pulled into Kate's driveway and parked next to Alex's car. She took the long stick out of the backseat, walked around to open Claudia's door and handed it to her.

Claudia took the stick and leaned into it with her battered body and her bruised conscience. She stood in front of Kate's door, her stomach churning over all the things she needed to say to Alex. She stepped over the threshold, left the stick leaning against the wall in the foyer and followed Maryanne into the living room. Jackson Browne ran up to her, wagging his tail ferociously and licked her hands.

When she saw the cop sitting on the couch with Kate, Alex sitting directly across from them, and Charles and Louisa sitting at the kitchen table, Claudia almost turned around and walked back out the door. She had no idea that she would be facing not only Alex, but also the police. Louisa ran up to her and gently put her arms around Claudia's shoulders. "Am I hurting you? Is this okay?" her friend asked, and Claudia felt a little safer in the room full of questioning faces.

"Yes, it's fine," Claudia said, leaning onto Louisa, whose shoulders came just to Claudia's armpits.

"Alex told you about the restaurant thing? I am so stupid. I shouldn't have opened my big mouth, " Louisa said.

"No, it's fine. You were just trying to protect me. I would've done the same thing for you," Claudia told her.

"Look, we all know that I'm the idiot here," Charles said, standing up from the table. He had been sitting behind an enormous arrangement of flowers. "I can't believe I didn't recognize Helen. She's only on the biggest billboard on Sunset Boulevard. I guess I overreact if I think someone is messing with our girl—even if it's Alex. Don't even get me started on what I'll do if I come across the worm who did this to you," Charles said.

Claudia smiled and then coughed and had to sit down because her sides were aching with each wheeze.

"Hello," Maryanne said to the police officer who stood up from the couch and offered her his hand, though not his name. "I assume you are here for Claudia's statement?"

"Yes Ma'am. And everyone else's here."

Kate looked at Maryanne, worry lines covering her usually calm face. Maryanne looked at Claudia with raised eyebrows. Claudia felt like she was going to throw up.

"Whoa, this is heavy. Why do you need to talk to us?"

Charles asked. "It's not that I mind, I'm just interested in how these things go down. I've never seen something like this except for on *CSI*." Claudia looked weakly at Louisa who shook her head at Charles's inopportune levity.

"First of all, those shows are crap," the cop said, "They have nothing to do with the way the law really works, so don't get all excited about imaginary drama. The real deal is, Miss Kate here has the tiniest bit of a reputation in our little Joshua Tree. Unfortunately, that makes what happened with Miss Nichols last night a little more complicated. I need to make sure that there aren't any connections between the events last night and the people in this room. Just routine investigative stuff."

Claudia looked over at Alex, who looked completely overwhelmed and exhausted. He's never going to want me now when he hears the truth.

"Why don't we start with you and get this over with," the officer said to Claudia.

"Could we go somewhere private," she asked. "I'm having a hard enough time concentrating as it is with all this medication and everything."

"Sure. Is there a room we could use Kate? And then we can just move down the line of fire, so to speak. It shouldn't take too long. You all just hang tight," the officer said, looking at everyone else in the room.

"Of course," Kate said, and rubbed her palms down the length of her long skirt before standing up. "There are a couple of chairs in the massage room and it's certainly quiet in there. I'll just go and move the table." She walked in the direction of the hallway.

"That's okay. You stay put. I'll move anything I need to. After you," he said motioning to Claudia.

Claudia opened the door of the small room and smelled the incense lingering on the walls. She turned on a lamp next to a houseplant, and then lowered herself onto a chair. The officer sat across from her.

"Are you comfortable?" he asked.

Claudia nodded, though she wondered how comfortable one could be when they've made the worst mistake of their life.

"How long have you been in town?"

"Almost a week."

"How do you know Kate? Why were you driving her truck? Where did you go? Who saw you at the gas station? Is this the first time you encountered this man? Why did you let him get in the truck with you? What happened next?"

The questions were like ammunition shooting at her from a paintball gun. She was dodging them left and right, trying to say the right things, but still she was hit and splattered with the mess. After a few minutes of carefully sorting through her answers she said, "Okay, okay! I admit it! I wanted him to kiss me. I never even asked his name! I just wanted to feel good for one measly second. I thought everyone else in my life was moving on without me. There? Are you happy? Now you know the truth."

The cop leaned back in his chair, blinked his eyes several times and then leaned forward and said, "Miss—it doesn't matter one bit if you wanted him to kiss you or not. That's not the issue here. I don't care if you stripped down naked and told him that you liked it rough. This was obviously not a consensual situation. From everything you've told me and from the way all of your injuries line up in this medical report: the broken ribs, the scratches on your stomach, the torn skin on your back, and the massive blow to your face—" he pointed to the folder in his lap. "You are lucky to be alive and not because of some dumb mistake anyone else could have made, but because this guy is a monster. Do you understand me? Listen, we got a call early this morning that a body of a woman your age was found in Tucson. She was raped and then her skull was crushed in with the heel of a boot. Her friends last saw her get into a blue truck. Of course no one got the license plate number, but the description matches Kate's Ford."

Claudia nodded her head, looking around the room for something to quell the dizziness that was washing over her body like thick mud. Sobs gurgled up into her throat. She wrapped her arms around her middle and rocked back and forth, trying to process the information she had just heard.

"You're a brave girl. I can only hope that my daughter will have half the survivor instincts you have if she ever finds herself in a situation. Why don't you go lie down and rest? Send that big-mouthed guy and his tiny wife in here."

She stood up and then turned around to face the cop, placing her hand on the inside of her forearm. "He had a tattoo, here. "It was a dark-haired pinup girl."

"Thanks, that's very helpful. And not surprising as both you and the girl who was murdered both have brown hair."

Claudia wanted to get out of the claustrophobic darkness as quickly as possible. She went and sat down in a chair next to Alex after Charles and Louisa followed the officer into the massage/interrogation room. There should have been a single bare light bulb hanging from the ceiling, swinging and casting ominous shadows on the faces while they answered the cop's questions.

"Baby," Claudia said to Alex, "I have to get this over with. I didn't mean to, but I made up a whole crazy scenario in my head when I didn't hear from you for so long."

"You weren't the only one. We have some very imaginative friends," Alex sighed.

"But the story kept getting bigger and bigger in my head, and I somehow forgot who you really were, I mean, are—and I made you out to be an asshole who was sleeping with people behind my back. I couldn't deal with the thought of it, and I wanted to get back at you—hurt you for something you didn't even do."

"So that's why you cut off all your hair?"

"Yeah, but that was a good thing. I needed to do that. But the bad thing—I went off with that guy—I took him up into the park. I wanted his attention. I know, it was an awful thing to do and I nearly died because of it."

"Oh." Alex looked away from Claudia and down at his shoes. His knees, where his elbows rested, bounced up and down.

"It was like I was a lost kid. You know how they say kidnappers always recognize a certain type of child they know they can lure? The lonely, vulnerable ones wear some kind of sign or something—."

"Shit, Claudia."

"It was the stupidest thing I've ever done. I don't know how you can forgive me or think of me the same again." She waited and looked at him. He sat for a few long seconds and then met her eyes. "I'll never do anything like that again," she said. Please say something—please don't leave me.

"Come here," he pulled Claudia's chair closer to his. "Don't you ever, ever doubt that I love you. I'm not going anywhere. If you can't believe that now, I don't think you ever will."

"I believe you," Claudia said, and she meant it.

"Listen. Forget about the wedding; forget about our families. If it all scares you so much, we don't have to do any of it," Alex said.

"Really? You're okay with that?"

"Yeah, really. My parents will get over it, and anyway, the wedding shouldn't be about them, it's about us."

Charles and Louisa walked out of the room, and the

officer called for Alex.

"That dude is super-cool!" Charles said, a huge grin on his face. Louisa rolled her eyes at Claudia and Alex. "Claudia, did he tell you that he moved here from Brooklyn after he got involved in one of the John Gotti Jr. trials? That's script material right there. I've gotta tell Robbie about this guy. He'd have a field day asking questions for that mafia show he's pitching to NBC. I think you're up, man." Charles said to Alex. "Seriously, ask him about the Laundromat cover. That is some crazy stuff!"

Now that Claudia had stared—no kissed, a real psychopath in the face, she knew things were hardly ever what they seemed. Kate selling a little pot now and then seemed like a white lie compared to the monster she had narrowly escaped. She crumpled onto the couch and heard Kate scrubbing dishes in the kitchen, turning the garbage disposal on and off, making a racket.

"You think she's okay?" Louisa said, motioning back to Kate.

"Yeah, she's just a little odd sometimes. She's a good person though," Claudia said.

"Ouch!" Kate yelled from the sink, "Hot!"

Alex came out of the room and the officer asked for Maryanne.

"I told you, didn't I," Charles said, "Bad. Ass."

"Yeah, he's pretty tough," Alex said. "I'm glad we don't have some idiot looking for this asshole." Alex's face was red and his shirt was wrinkled. He put his arm around Claudia and whispered, "I really don't know what I would have done . . ."

She leaned her head against his and closed her eyes. She wished she could explain everything to him, how the week had been a collision of all her fear and doubt. She looked up into his eyes and smiled. "I need you," she whispered. "You know that's what scares me so much."

He kissed the top of her head. "I know. But I need you to need me, so we should be okay."

"Well," Charles said, I'm going to call Mom and check on Ben. You wanna come with, Lou?"

"Of course. I want to hear straight from your mother's mouth exactly how much sugar she's pumping into our child."

"Like she's going to tell you."

Maryanne returned to the living room and passed the torch to Kate, who was still messing with something in the sink. "Just a second," she said, and then dried her hands on a towel.

Claudia motioned Maryanne to come over to the couch. "Did you tell him?" she asked.

"About what?" Maryanne said.

"Oh please," Claudia said. "About Kate's greenroom."

"I just answered everything the man asked. No more, no less."

"Mom—you were going to call the police before. Just tell

me what you told him," Claudia said.

Maryanne stood up. "I'm going to make a sandwich. This baby is getting hungrier and hungrier." Maryanne rubbed her stomach. "Anyone else want one?" she asked, walking into the kitchen.

"Baby?" Alex asked.

Claudia just looked at him and shrugged with a well-you-didn't-answer-your-phone look. "I'm going to be a big sister," she said.

"Wow. You two will not be taking any trips without me in the future. You are a strange, dangerous combo." Alex shook his head in disbelief.

Claudia curled into a ball on the couch and scooted closer to him. "I'll remind you of that," she said. "Because I don't want to go anywhere without you."

"Me either," he said.

The room became silent until they heard Kate's argumentative voice coming out of the closed room

"Uh-oh. That doesn't sound good at all," Claudia said.

Chapter 35

It seemed to take hours, but Kate and the officer finally came out and rejoined the gang in the living room.

"Well, I guess that about does it," the officer said. Then he paused, and looked back over his shoulder at the hallway they had just left, specifically at the door next to the massage room. He turned around so he could get a better look. "That's a little odd. Now why in the world would you put a coded lock on a door in your own house, Kate?"

"It's just my personal space. You can never be too careful with your valuables. You know, the Native American museum in town has been after me for years about some of my grandparents' things. I like to know they're somewhere safe."

"Oh. That makes sense, I guess. Well, I'm just going to grab a glass of water from the tap and I'll be on my way."

"I'll get it for you," Kate said, jumping ahead of him.

"No, no. I'll get it." He gave Kate a stern look. She backed away.

"These are nice cabinets," he said, opening one and closing it again.

"Thanks, Ron put them in for me. The glasses are to your right," Kate said.

The officer looked around like he hadn't heard a word Kate said.

"Real nice, lots of space," he casually slid the drawer open where Kate's pot canister lived.

Claudia held her breath and looked over at Maryanne, waiting for her to jump up and scream everything she knew about Kate's illegal part-time job, which apparently she had not done yet.

He closed the drawer, walked away, took a glass down from the cabinet, went to the faucet and turned on the tap. "Looks like your sink's a little backed-up," he said, and flipped on the garbage disposal, which made a pathetic buzzing sound. "Might want to have a plumber come take a look at that."

"Yeah, I'll do that first thing tomorrow," Kate said. "Well, it has been a long day for all of us here. And I imagine your family is waiting to see you. Those boys of yours are getting so big."

He drained the rest of the water in his glass in one long swallow. "They really are great," he said. "You know Tommy made the California junior all-star baseball team? Thanks for the drink." He set the glass on the counter, walked over to the kitchen table and picked up his hat. "Don't forget about your promise," he said to Kate.

"I won't," she said.

"You know, I think I'd like to see some of your grandparents' things before I leave. Why don't you show me some of the stuff the museum is so hot to get their hands on?"

Claudia swallowed; her jaw smarted with pain and reminded her it was time to take her meds again. She looked at Maryanne, who in return tilted her head and raised her eyebrows as if to say Kate deserved whatever she got. Claudia remembered that she had felt the same about Kate only days before, but now things were different, and she didn't want to see anything bad happen to Kate.

"Is that an order?" Kate asked the officer.

"Well, if you want to get into labels . . ." he said. "Sure."

Kate sighed and walked to the door. She punched four numbers into the lock-box and pushed open the door. "There you go," she said, standing aside for the officer.

After he walked into the room, Claudia sat up on the couch and leaned over to see what was happening, even though it pained every wounded inch of her body. She couldn't see much because the officer blocked the door to the room, and she could only hear pieces of what they were saying.

"Mom!" she whispered. "Go see what's happening!"

"Oh, I think we should just mind our own business,

Claudia," Maryanne said. "It's out of our hands now."

Claudia glanced at Alex, who looked completely lost, and said, "Don't worry, I'll catch you up on the whole thing later," she whispered.

"Thanks," Alex said, shaking his head.

Kate and the officer walked back into the living room, and he said, "I can see how the museum would want some of those baskets. The detail is fascinating. And that buffalo hide must be worth thousands."

"Don't go spilling my secrets," Kate said.

"As long as you behave, you won't have to worry about that. I'll be checking in on you soon. And Miss Claudia, I might be calling you for a few more questions down the road. Of course if this guy turns up, we will need you to testify in court, but don't worry about that right now." He looked at Alex and said, "Take care of this one," nodding at Claudia.

Kate closed the door behind him and peered out the peephole for a few seconds. "And he tried to trick me by parking down the street instead of the driveway, ha!"

"Okay, will you please tell me what is going on?" Claudia nearly yelled at Kate.

Kate laughed and pushed her short hair away from her face. She sighed and fell onto the couch next to Claudia. "Your mom told you that you scared the shit out of us the other night, right?"

Claudia nodded.

"Good, because I hope you'll never do that again to anyone, including yourself. Did she tell you about our fight?"

Claudia shook her head.

"You've never seen two old hens go at it like we did. We blamed each other for you not showing up, we imagined ridiculous possibilities. Of course as it turns out, they weren't all that ridiculous—compared to what actually happened. We paced the house like baboons. It was the closest I've ever felt to being a mother."

Maryanne smiled. "And then she took off on that horse, and I realized it didn't matter anymore what she did for a living or how illegal it was, it just mattered that she cared about finding you as much as I did."

Kate continued, "When your mom called me from the hospital and told me that you were okay, I broke down in tears. I was a sad sack of potatoes out there in the park, wandering around on Zooey looking aimlessly for you. I told Maryanne what you said when we went to get the TV and you saw the little girl. I promised I would stop being responsible for people not living their lives—and for me not getting on with my own," Kate said.

"But," Maryanne chimed in, "I told her I understood how important this particular strain of plant was that she had been working on and all the time and research that went into it—and that it could help sick people," Maryanne added.

Claudia's eyes widened, and if her jaw hadn't been wound

so tight with pain, it would have dropped to the floor.

Alex cleared his throat. "And here we were, just sitting here while they were fighting back and forth—I was pulling my hair out wondering if you were okay and Charles was eavesdropping on Kate and Maryanne, and then he started bouncing around like a kid in a candy store when he realized that Kate sold pot."

"Whoa, whoa, whoa? Slow down," Claudia said. "So you guys all knew about the weed the whole time the cop was here? Did he ask any of you about it?"

Alex, Charles, Louisa, and Maryanne all looked around at each other and shook their heads. "No," they said collectively, in surprise.

"After you were settled in at the hospital and the doctor mentioned the police, I called Kate and told her she should be ready when they came." Maryanne said. "Which of course, she had already considered like any good drug dealer would, I suppose and was trying to figure out what to do."

Charles spoke up loudly and said, "So after your mom called, I told Kate I would help her do whatever she needed if she would just give me a tiny sample of the new weed first," he said this like it was the logical thing that anyone in their right mind would do.

Claudia shook her head and looked at Louisa, who was also shaking hers. "You're kidding, right Charles?" Claudia said.

"No way. She was going to have to get rid of most of it, and it didn't need to all go to waste. And let me tell you, the stuff is chronically magic, totally dro" he said. "It's like the best white widow without any of the side effects. No dry mouth, no paranoia, no munchies, nothing. Just bliss. The woman should make millions for this breed."

"You talk like you're such a connoisseur," Louisa said, elbowing her husband. "Have you ever even smoked 'white widow' before?"

"Well—no—but I've heard about it. I like to keep it street—you know that, babe," Charles said.

"Was that the same stuff we smoked?" Claudia asked Kate.

"No. I wasn't going to let anyone try it for a while longer, but I was in a tough spot," Kate said. "The clock was ticking, and I wasn't coming up with a plan on my own. I just couldn't think of a place where I could move everything fast enough."

Alex looked at Claudia. "So at this point, Charles is high and tearfully reminiscing about the day Ben was born and basically no use to us whatsoever," he said. "And we knew that the cops would be coming soon. So we got busy moving plants. For me, it was just a relief to have something to do until I knew you were stable enough to visit. It was like, 'Hi Kate, nice to meet you, can I help you hide your drug cartel?' And I thought I did crazy things for my actors—this is definitely a new standard, Kate."

"So where'd you put the plants? Apparently you got everything out of the greenroom because the officer didn't notice them, right?" Claudia said.

"Ever heard of hiding something in plain sight?" Kate said and bared her fox-like smile. Claudia looked at everyone grinning widely at her, except for Maryanne who looked just as confused as Claudia felt.

Claudia pushed herself off the couch and stood up, looked around the room and up at the ceiling. "I don't get it," she said. She walked into the kitchen and scanned the counter. She turned around and her eyes fell on the massive floral arrangement on the kitchen table. She walked over to it and inspected it closely. Mixed in with the tall blooms and bountiful greenery were Kate's prized sprouts. Then she remembered the plant next to the lamp in the massage room she hadn't seen before and looked up at the fern hanging by the bookshelf. "Brilliant," she said. "You guys are better than the Usual Suspects."

"I didn't notice them either," Maryanne said. "I was mopping the sweat off my forehead the whole time you were in the greenroom with the policeman, Kate."

"I thought it best if we didn't tell you where they were," Kate said. "Just in case he questioned you."

Maryanne nodded in relief. "I'm glad you didn't," she said.

"But this isn't everything you had," Claudia said, looking at the plants. "Where did the rest go?"

"Unfortunately, straight down the garbage disposal. Most of it was gone before the cop got here, but then I remembered the canister in the kitchen drawer and a small stash left in my bedroom. I was getting rid of the last of it just before he questioned me. He said they found a dime bag of weed on the girl's body in Tucson and thought maybe I had sold to the asshole that attacked you and killed that poor girl. I told him he knew me better than that—I've never sold to just any freak who rolls into town since the seventies, and that anyway, I had quit the business. Which at that moment, of course, was the truth—a new truth . . . but still. I admit, when he was messing with the sink, I was pretty nervous . . ." Kate shivered. "If he had just stuck his hand down the drain, he would have come up with a whole mess of wet, ruined hash."

"Well, I'm sure all of this has certainly cemented your decision to stop selling," Maryanne said to Kate.

"Ah, there's the Maryanne we all know. I was beginning to wonder if she had disappeared completely," Claudia said.

"All I need is to get these beauties to Oakland, hope for a huge sale at The Plant and my hands are clean once and for all."

Claudia desperately wanted to lie down and go to sleep. She felt like her body couldn't catch up to her mind and now that the officer had left and the danger had passed, she needed to retreat inside of herself. She laid her head against Alex's shoulder, and he lifted his arm around her so that she would be more comfortable on his chest.

"What are you going to do with all of your time when you're not selling anymore?" Louisa asked Kate.

"I don't know. Guess I'll have to figure that out." Kate walked into the kitchen, removed a tray of something from the freezer and slid it into the oven.

Chapter 36

I'm sorry, sweetie, I need to get this," Alex said, glancing at his phone. He shifted the dozing Claudia off his chest and onto a pillow, stood up, and walked outside.

"Claude, Charles booked us a room at some motel in town for the night. Do you guys know anything about it?" Louisa asked Claudia when she saw her eyes were open.

Claudia looked over sleepily at Maryanne with a knowing frown.

"Really? It's that bad?" Louisa noted the exchange.

"No, it's not bad, it's just . . ." Maryanne said.

"Just don't stay in room eight," Kate said from the kitchen.

"What is it about room eight?" Charles asked eagerly.

Claudia sighed loudly and said, "Louisa, will you bring me my pills? They're in my purse. Charles, just leave it. Not everything needs to be dissected." She felt grumpy and couldn't stand to listen to the tragic Gram story again. She wished they could all just be quiet and let her brain sort through all of the events.

"Geez, somebody needs a nap," Charles said out of the side of his mouth, motioning to Claudia. He then looked at Louisa's expression as she glared at him and said, "I'm sorry. I shouldn't have said that. You know me; I just get a little ADHD. Pay no attention to the silly man in the corner."

"You can get a med card for that now, you know," Kate said from the kitchen.

Claudia watched Louisa shoot daggers at Kate. "Don't put that idea in his head! He doesn't need to smoke weed to stay focused; that would only make it worse. He just needs to cut back on the caffeine and start exercising again."

"Unfortunately, she's right," Charles said, and rubbed his belly.

Alex came back through the sliding glass doors. His hair was standing on end like he had been caught in a tornado.

"Everything okay?" Claudia asked him.

"Yeah, yeah," he said, and looked around the room. "Mmm, something smells delicious," he said, changing the subject.

"Do you want to help me with the salad, Alex?" Kate asked.

"Sure."

Louisa walked back to Claudia and handed her two pills and a glass of water with a straw.

Claudia sat up and turned to watch Alex and Kate in

the kitchen, remembering that this was how she first got to know Kate, following her prep-cook orders.

"I need to call Tim," Maryanne said, sounding like she dreaded rather than anticipated the conversation. Claudia watched her walk into the guestroom.

Louisa sat down next to Claudia on the couch and both women leaned their tired heads into the cushions and looked at each other, saying in their smiles that this whole thing was just going to deepen a friendship that had already survived major life-changes.

"Are you going back home tomorrow?" Claudia asked Louisa, her voice coming out in a tired, hoarse whisper.

"Yeah. I need to see my baby and of course there's work. I haven't talked to Alex about how it will all pan out, though. I guess we should have brought our own car."

"I'm sure Alex won't mind taking you guys back."

"It just sucks he has to take us and then turn around again. But I know you need to stay here and rest and it would be awfully cramped," Louisa said.

"We'll figure it out," Claudia said.

"Lou and Charles, you guys want some wine?" Alex called from the kitchen.

They all turned to look at Alex and burst into laughter. He was wearing a gingham apron and chopping vegetables on the cutting board like he was auditioning for a Food Network show. Claudia loved that he had so little ego.

"I'll get it, buddy," Charles said. "Looks like you have

your dainty little hands full."

"You know you only want to come in here so you can stand closer to me, Charles. Admit it, you're a little turned on by me right now—it's okay, your tendencies don't frighten me, I can handle it, big boy."

"Well, I think you look hot in an apron, babe," Claudia said. "And what about me, by the way? Why did you only offer Charles and Louisa wine?"

"I'm pretty sure that if you had any wine on top of all those pills you'd pass out straight away. But be my guest, I'll hold your head up and spoon feed you every single bite of your smoothie dinner."

"Sheah, I guess you're right," Claudia said. "I'm gonna half the dosage tomorrow. The doctor said I could switch to Ibuprofen when it felt manageable. I'd rather have my glass of wine and a tiny bit of pain than feel spaced out all day like this anyway. And the pain will remind me that one: I'm lucky to be alive, and two: just because someone wears a Kings of Leon t-shirt and knows about Gram Parsons does not make them a good person or a kindred spirit. I mean, it doesn't make them a bad person, but you just never know with anyone these days, do you? It's so hard to find the line between what's real about a person and what isn't, you know?" Claudia looked at Louisa's confused face and said, "I'm rambling, aren't I?"

"Yeah, but it's okay," Louisa patted her on the knee.

"Ouch!" Claudia said, and drew her scabbing knee up

into her chest.

"Oh. Sorry," Louisa winced. "I feel like we should wrap you in a cocoon of cotton so I don't keep hurting you."

"Naw, I'm tough," Claudia moaned. "The real damage has already been done, it's just a little sensitive while it heals," Claudia said.

"Here you go, gorgeous," Charles said, handing Louisa a glass of deep scarlet liquid.

Louisa held up her glass to Claudia's glass of water and they clinked them together. "Here's to starting anew," Louisa said.

"Here, here!" Kate said from the kitchen, and raised her glass.

Claudia sipped her water through the straw.

"My gracious, that man can talk," Maryanne said, walking into the living room. "But he's getting better. It's taken a long time, but I think he finally realizes that I can actually handle myself in difficult situations."

"I think I'm finally realizing that about you too," Claudia said.

"Okay!" Kate called. "We're ready! The table is set outside. Bring your glasses with you."

Maryanne went to fill a glass with water and Louisa helped Claudia off the couch. Claudia leaned slightly on Louisa as they walked through the sliding glass doors.

A bubbling pan of lasagna sat on the table along with a colorful salad, which Alex stood proudly by, and a plate of buttered garlic bread.

"Oh this is ridiculous. You can't expect me to only eat a smoothie when this all looks so amazing. I'm at least eating the lasagna, even if I can only suck on the noodles," Claudia said. "Give me a sip of that," she took Alex's glass of wine and tilted it back in her parted lips.

"Please, sit down," Kate said to Charles, Louisa and Alex who were eating at her table for the first time.

"May I ask a blessing?" Maryanne said, looking around the table.

"Of course," Kate said.

"Father—" Maryanne said, and paused. Claudia looked up at her mom over her folded hands. Maryanne took a deep breath and resumed: "I feel like I have more questions about you now than I ever have before; why you allow some things, and stop others—but I want to thank you for protecting my daughter and for giving her such a wonderful family of friends to care for her and for bringing her back to us." She paused and then added, "Amen."

"Amen," the chorus echoed, and began passing their plates to be filled with food.

After Kate handed her a plate of lasagna, Claudia lifted a little bit of the melting cheese and soft noodles in her fork and blew on it gently. She could barely open her mouth wide enough to squeeze it in, but she succeeded even though half of it stayed on her chin. She mushed the food with her tongue against the roof of her mouth and managed to swallow. "Oh, this is so worth the pain," she said, wiping her chin and preparing another bite.

"And this is vegetarian?" Charles asked, with half a noodle hanging out of his mouth.

"Yep. I use soy-sage instead of beef," Kate said.

"This cheese on the top is so fluffy," Louisa said.

"It's a really great ricotta from the farmer's market in Santa Monica. I stock up on it every month and keep it in the freezer," Kate said, and closed her eyes after putting a forkful of the lasagna in her mouth. "I never get tired of it."

"Wow," Charles said. "We should serve this at the bar, don't you think, Lou? I mean, right now we only do sandwiches and fries and wings, but this would do great. Would you give us the recipe for our cook? I'll name it after you, I promise," Charles beamed boyishly at Kate.

Kate laughed. "Sure, I'll give you the recipe."

Claudia smiled at the table, but noticed that Maryanne's face was somber.

"What's wrong? Do you feel okay?" she asked.

"Hmm? Oh yeah, I'm fine. I just wish we lived closer to each other," Maryanne said to Claudia.

"I know," Claudia said. And for the first time since she was very small, Claudia did want to be closer to her mom.

"We'll definitely be visiting you in Texas," Alex offered. "And you're welcome at our place anytime."

"Thanks dear," Maryanne said, "I'll take you up on that," and lifted her glass of water dripping with condensation.

Kate threw a piece of garlic bread to Jackson Browne and he gobbled it up without chewing.

Claudia again looked around the table. She was content with the little circle; it felt complete. "This is going to sound cheesy," she said, "but everyone here is in my tribe."

"Like the 10,000 Maniacs record?" Charles asked with a mouthful of lasagna, his third helping.

"Exactly. And I hope I'm in all of yours," Claudia said. She looked up at the sky and a small shiver ran up her spine as the stars began to appear. She remembered the other night on the mountain when the stars seemed to be the closest thing that could save her, yet they were so far away. But looking around the table again at her tribe, she returned to the present and in that moment, knew she was safe and that there was nothing to run from.

Chapter 37

Louisa cleared the table with Maryanne and Kate, and Claudia watched Alex and Charles argue over what needed to be done to repair the garbage disposal. Between the two of them, Charles was the better handy man after years of experience of working on his motorcycle and also the occasional odd repair at the bar. Alex finally relinquished his opinions and accepted the job of flipping the disposal switch every time Charles called out, "try it now". After several rounds of this, the disposal made a frightening metal chomping sound, but then eased into a rhythmic churning.

"There goes the very last of the weed down the drain," Charles said, peering into the disposal. "It's such a shame really."

"Well," Alex said, wiping his hands on his jeans, "Whenever you guys are ready, I'll take you over to the motel." Claudia could tell he was exhausted and ready to crash.

"I'm going with you," Claudia said to Alex.

Louisa finished putting the last glass in the washer, turned around and said, "I'm ready."

Maryanne walked over to Louisa and gave her a hug. "We'll see you in the morning before you leave I hope." Charles hovered over the two women and hugged Maryanne as she let go of Louisa. "Bye, Mama Maryanne," he said. "You can stay with us anytime in Smell-A."

Maryanne chuckled.

The four of them walked out to Alex's car. Claudia strapped on her seatbelt while Charles put Louisa's bag in the trunk and Louisa settled into the back seat. Alex got in and started the engine. Mazzy Starr's "Fade Into You" played. Claudia glanced down at the handwritten cover of her compilation sitting in the little groove by the emergency break.

"You got this out of the Accord before you left?" Claudia asked Alex.

"Yeah, I brought all of them. When we were driving here, it made me feel like you were with us." He put the car in reverse after Charles hopped in the backseat and backed out of Kate's driveway.

"We totally used to do it to this song," Charles said. "In that tiny apartment where our bed was in the kitchen."

"You're such a romantic," Louisa said. "I remember."

Alex followed Claudia's directions down the street of shops and pulled into the motel parking lot.

"Wow, fancy," Louisa said.

"I know, right? You'd think they'd do a makeover or something. Maybe you should call HGTV and help them out," Claudia said.

"Want us to wait while you check in?" Alex asked.

"Naw man, I think we've got it covered, thanks. But I'll call you if I need someone to wipe my butt later."

"Douche bag," Alex said, and popped the trunk.

"See ya tomorrow, kids," Charles said. "But seriously," he said, leaning his head into the car, "I'm really glad you're okay Claudia—I love you guys." He walked around to the open trunk, pulled out Louisa's bag, and slammed the door in his not-so-suave Charles style.

Louisa waved goodbye and Alex and Claudia watched them walk into the reception area.

"All right, so here's the deal with room eight," Claudia told Alex a highlighted version of the tale.

"You realize I know plenty of screenwriters who would love to get their hands on this story—I mean Kate's involvement with musicians in the sixties, what she's been up to now—this whole thing" he said, and laughed in disbelief.

"Too bad," Claudia said, and yawned. "It's our story—for us to keep. I don't think Kate wants to share it with the rest of the world, and I've already put her at enough risk." She turned to Alex and looked at him for a couple of seconds. He looked distracted; he was watching the road, but clearly thinking of something else.

"What's going on in there?" she asked.

"Oh, you know—just work stuff. I'm trying to see the silver lining in starting over but I'm having a hard time doing it. The thing is—two of my three clients live in New York, and Helen's probably moving there now that her father has passed and she's been so successful on Broadway."

"So you go and visit, like you always have," Claudia said.

"I don't know . . .I used to stay at Bob's apartment. It could get really expensive flying there and back all the time, paying for a hotel—not to mention it's a long flight. I'm nervous that Bob will use it as an opportunity to grab these few who have been loyal to me so far."

"So what are you saying?" Claudia asked, even though she knew. Out of everything that had happened in the last week, this surprised her the most. She never would have guessed that Alex would want to move to New York. He always complained about how noisy and dirty it was and how he couldn't wait to get home.

"I can't do it alone," he said, stopping at a stop sign.

"I feel like I'm just getting to know Mom—the thought of leaving Charles and Louisa and Ben makes me want to cry—"

"I know, sweetheart, the timing is awful."

"When do you have to make a decision?"

"It's not really my decision to make," Alex said. "It's your decision."

Claudia turned and looked at the road ahead of her. She knew she could get work in New York and that it was the right thing for Alex's career. She thought about everyone and realized as close as she felt to them, soon they would all have to go back to their own lives. They couldn't stay in this little commune forever. Maryanne had Tim to go back to and the new baby to prepare for, Charles and Louisa had Ben and the bar and Louisa's needy clients. Kate—well who knew what she would be doing in the next months. Claudia certainly couldn't count on Kate to stay in one place.

"We should do it," she said.

"Really?" Alex asked.

"Yeah," Claudia nodded, encouraged by the relief and excitement on Alex's face.

When they got back to Kate's house, both Maryanne and Kate had already gone to bed. Claudia and Alex removed the cushions from the couch, and pulled out the bed. They spread out the stack of sheets Kate had left on the armchair and tucked the corners in under the old mattress. When she laid her head on his chest, Claudia thought about what all moving to New York would entail. She had barely just begun to feel settled with everything in her life, and now it was all about to change again. It wasn't that she was scared to move to a new city alone with Alex. After everything that had happened, she couldn't be more confident now that he was the right person for her. It was that these other people had played such a role in her coming to that conclusion, she couldn't imagine not having them around.

"This is going to sound crazy," Claudia said to Alex.

"I'm listening," he said.

Chapter 38

Yes, I know it's early," Claudia said to Louisa, "but Alex is heading over there right now to pick you guys up, so get your butts out of bed." She listened to Louisa moan and say, "okay" before she hung up the phone. She heard a knock on the guest room door, where she had taken over.

"Come in," she called.

"I don't know what you think of this, but if you want it, it's yours. I never knew why I hung onto it until now, it certainly hasn't fit me for over a decade," Kate said, handing a flowing, antique-white dress to Claudia.

Claudia took the hanger from Kate and looked closely at the dress. It was from the sixties, with flutter sleeves meant to hang off the shoulders and a skirt of tiered, sheer material.

"It's perfect," Claudia said. "People would pay hundreds of dollars for this in vintage shops in L.A."

"Just wait until someone calls your clothes 'vintage'," Kate said. "It's too surreal."

Claudia laughed. "Sorry. Will you ask Mom to come in here?"

"Are you kidding? She's probably still standing at the door trying to listen to our conversation. She's been pacing back and forth in excitement since you woke us."

Within seconds, Maryanne was in the room.

Claudia had just pulled the dress over her head. "Zip me up?" she asked.

Maryanne immediately teared up, sniffled loudly, and pulled the zipper on the back of Kate's old, now Claudia's new dress.

"You look so beautiful," Maryanne said.

"Except for these bruises on the side of my face."

"Oh! I have the perfect thing for that. Remember my friend Julie who sells the Arbonne? She gave me the most amazing concealer!"

"I don't know Mom, I'd rather look bruised than like I'm wearing a pound of makeup. I mean, no offense or anything, it's just not my style."

"None taken, honey. I know you like the natural look. Just let me try okay, and if you hate it, we can always wash it off and you can start over."

Claudia nodded, thinking that she would humor Maryanne, but knew she would have to redo it all.

"Just let me drape this towel around you so we don't get

anything on the dress . . . there, that's better. Come over here in the bathroom where there's more light."

Claudia followed her mom and closed her eyes after she sat down because she knew her facial expressions would betray her anxiety if she watched Maryanne dip a sponge into a vat of pancake foundation. The last thing she wanted on this day was an argument between the two of them. She winced a little as Maryanne patted the sore area of her face with a sponge. After a minute or two, she relaxed and enjoyed the touch of her mother's fingertips on her skin. When she didn't think about the glop that was going on her skin, the experience was calming and soothing.

"Do you mind if I put on just a touch of blush and eye shadow?" Maryanne asked.

Claudia smiled and feeling like she was sealing her fate, said, "Sure. Why not?"

The brushes lightly tickled her skin, and when Maryanne said, "Okay, take a look," she wanted her to keep going because it felt so good, and also because she was scared to look in the mirror.

She opened one eye and then the other, discovering the revelation slowly so she wouldn't go into shock, but she was surprised to find that her face looked nothing at all like the beauty-pageant queen she'd expected. The foundation actually matched her skin tone, unlike the orangey way it appeared on Maryanne. She hardly noticed the blush or eye shadow; they were more of a subtle shimmer than a gaudy smear of color. The bruises on her face were almost completely invisible to anyone who didn't know they were there.

"Wow. Good job, Mom. I just need some mascara and lip gloss and I'm done."

Maryanne sniffled and dabbed under her eyes with the edge of a tissue. "I'm going to give you some privacy, or I'll make a mess out of both of us," Maryanne said, turning to leave the room.

Claudia swiped her eyelashes with the mascara wand and gently dabbed her lips with a light gloss. She left her hair wavy and swept it into a low, messy bun off to the side. She'd find a flower somewhere to stick in it, maybe from the gigantic floral arrangement on the kitchen table. She didn't have any shoes that went with the dress—everything she had bought in Palm Springs except for the pair of jeans she had worn out of the store was left in Kate's absent truck. So she left the room barefoot, which was what she preferred anyway.

Alex wore a white dress shirt tucked into his jeans. Claudia still hadn't cut his hair, but he shaved that morning. Charles and Louisa were in their comfortable traveling clothes and were shocked when Claudia made her entrance.

"Are you serious?" Louisa shot up off the couch and jumped up and down.

Claudia nodded and wrinkled her nose, unable to suppress her giggling.

"Kate, when is the minister going to arrive?" Maryanne asked.

"Hmmm," Kate said, looking at the door, and then an imaginary watch on her wrist. She feigned an expression of sudden remembrance. "Oh, that's right! She's already here!" Kate said.

"Huh?" Maryanne said.

"Mom, don't freak out, but I asked Kate to perform the service."

"But—" Maryanne said, and then stopped. "Okay, but you guys will make this official as soon as you get home, right?"

Claudia and Alex nodded furtively at Maryanne.

"Okay," Maryanne said, and cleared her throat. "Well, in any case, I'm just glad that you're doing this now and that I am here for it," she sighed.

"Shall we get started?" Kate asked, while Louisa pinned a bloom into her best friend's hair.

They all walked outside under a rare parade of white clouds marching their way across the sky. Even though the heat was steadily climbing with the sun, it wasn't unbearable. Maryanne fanned herself to keep the tears from spilling out of her eyes.

Kate asked Alex and Claudia what they wanted to promise to each other. Neither one of them had prepared anything—their words were not as eloquent as if they had been written and memorized, but their vows to each other couldn't have been more honest or more intimate. The animals stood in the background, adding to the small group of witnesses. There were no rings except for Claudia's ruby. "I promise," Alex said, "to always get ice cream whenever you want, even if it's in the middle of the night. I promise to memorize every Rolling Stones song. I will always confide in you first. I will listen when you tell me I've hurt your feelings, and I'll do my best to make it right. I will be faithful to you, both physically and emotionally."

Claudia said, "I promise to trust you, wherever you may be. I won't complain about you watching the game or try to deliberately distract you during the most important play. I will bear your children and do everything within my power to make sure they always feel loved. I will not doubt you when you tell me you love me, and I will never climb into trucks with strangers."

The spectators smiled as Alex carefully leaned Claudia back and kissed her tenderly, but deeply on the mouth.

Chapter 39

As soon as Kate heard the news early that morning, she worked fast to throw together a celebratory brunch. There was fresh fruit and a cheese frittata and cinnamon rolls oozing a stream of icing. Pitchers of Mimosas rested on the table, and Claudia gladly partook, now that she was off the meds.

"I'd like to make a toast," Maryanne said, holding up a glass of orange juice. "To my beautiful and courageous daughter. I was the one who should have taught you what those things mean, but it turns out that you've been an example to me. And Alex—I know that you see and love my daughter for who she really is, even when she's not sure who she is. Because of that, I know you'll always want what's best for her. Cheers."

Claudia wondered why there was never happiness without a touch of sadness mixed in when everyone clinked their glasses together.

"But I would like to add that I wish y'all wouldn't move so far away," Maryanne added, apparently thinking along the same lines as Claudia.

"What?" Charles and Louisa said at the same time, finishing gulps of the Mimosas they had just toasted.

Claudia gave Maryanne a look-what-you-did-now glance. "We don't know exactly when—but Alex needs to be in New York for work."

Louisa looked into her glass, her smile fading.

"That's why it was so important to do this now because we are all here together. Can we please just enjoy the rest of this party? We just got married! We need some music, Kate." Claudia, tired and short of breath, sat down on the couch.

Kate walked over to her old record player and flipped through the stack of vinyl. Everyone could see she was having a difficult time making a decision, so Charles downed the rest of his drink and walked over to cast his vote. Claudia saw him point to something and nod. Kate turned so that her back was to Claudia, hiding the album art as she slid the record carefully into her hands and then onto the turntable. Claudia loved the soft cracklings of old vinyl spinning before the music started and hated that the sound could never be duplicated by tape or disc. Then she heard the piano chords, followed by the drums and guitar, and goose bumps pricked her skin. "Ahhh! Perfect!"

Louisa sat next to her on the couch and Alex sat on the arm where Claudia leaned against him. Maryanne stood near Charles, swaying to a song she had never heard. When the chorus came in, everyone (except Maryanne, who merely smiled and clapped along) sang, *Ch-ch-ch-ch-Changes.* Kate closed her eyes and spun while Charles grabbed a surprised Maryanne at the waist and danced her around the room.

Claudia sang along with every word of the song and played air drums with passion, thoroughly entertaining Louisa and Alex. Maryanne was ecstatic, with flushed cheeks and a wide smile, spinning in Charles's arms. During the last verse, Kate turned to Claudia and they sang to each other with dramatic emphasis, *Oh, look out, you rock and rollers . . .Pretty soon you're gonna get a little older.* The song ended with a trailing saxophone solo, and as "Oh You Pretty Things" started, Louisa said, "We need to get pictures!" They all filed outside, refilled glasses in hand and their skin dewy with perspiration. The only cameras around were those on their phones, but they all snapped as Claudia and Alex posed standing close together and kissed on cue. Claudia's bare feet were covered in red dust and her hair was falling slightly out of the bun.

Get some with the animals!" Charles yelled. Next, there was the endless variety of cheesy photo ops—Claudia and Alex with Maryanne, Charles and Louisa with Claudia and Alex, Kate and Maryanne with Claudia—"Oh what about Alex and Charles?" Maryanne called out.

"Okay, but we're all getting hot so this is the last one!" Claudia said. The only photo that really mattered to Claudia was the only one she couldn't have: a shot of everyone together.

When they finally went inside, quiet fell over the group from the exhaustion and the knowledge that the party was ending.

"I feel terrible, taking your groom away from you so soon," Louisa said.

"No, it's fine. This will give the three of us ladies a chance to spend a little more time together, now that no one is fighting or threatening to call the police," Claudia said, looking up at Maryanne and Kate.

"See? She already wants a break from me and we've only been married oh—what—two hours now," Alex said and laughed.

"Hush," Claudia said.

"Okay, let's not make a huge thing of this," Charles said to Louisa, and went to hug Maryanne and then Kate. "And you," he said pointing to Claudia, "I'll see you in a few. You gotta come see the little man pronto."

"Tell him I'll be there in the next couple of days," Claudia smiled.

She stood up and hugged Louisa, and then said to Alex, "Take your time, okay? Sorry you have to drive so much."

"It's okay, I have your CDs to keep me company," Alex said and kissed her.

The three of them waved goodbye again as they walked out the front door. After it closed, Jackson Browne sat with his nose to the door, wagging his tail like he expected them all to return any minute.

Chapter 40

Kate and Maryanne joined Claudia on the couch. She stretched her legs out over them, her wedding dress a soft white veil shrouding all three women.

"What do we do now?" Kate asked.

"Let's just sit here a minute," Maryanne said.

"Fine with me," Claudia said.

Maryanne and Kate both leaned their heads back and closed their eyes. Claudia sighed and sank deeper into the back cushion of the couch, surprised with contentment.

Thirty minutes went by before anyone said a word. "Ugh. I need to use the ladies' room," Maryanne finally said. "I forgot about this part of pregnancy."

Claudia lifted her legs so Maryanne could escape.

Kate's phone rang and she stood up to answer it. "Yes?" There was a long pause as she listened. "Oh—okay," she sighed. "Well, thanks for letting us know." Kate walked back to the couch and plopped down next to Claudia. She ran her fingers through her hair and said, "They found my truck."

"Really? That's great!" Claudia said.

"It's totaled. Driven off a cliff in Utah."

"Oh Kate, I'm so sorry. Did you happen to have any insurance at all?"

"No," Kate said. "I don't care that much about the truck. Ron will get a deal on something better anyway. I'm just pissed that the bastard didn't die with the truck. They still haven't found him. He must have jumped out before it went over."

Claudia shuddered at the memory of his face close to hers, lit beneath by the flashlight.

Maryanne came back into the room, cheery and unaware of the new heaviness. "I have an idea—let's watch *To Catch a Thief*, she said. "Kinda reminds me of you, Kate—befriending a criminal and all."

Kate laughed. "If you're comparing me to Cary Grant, I'll take it. But don't you remember who the real criminal was in the movie?"

"Don't tell me! I haven't seen it in forever and I can't remember," Claudia said.

They filed into the guestroom and Claudia put in the disk and pushed play. They made themselves comfortable on the bed, all propped against pillows supported by the headboard. The sweeping orchestra of the opening credits played, and the ladies swooned when Grant appeared on screen.

"There she is again," Claudia said about Grace Kelly, fifteen minutes into the film. "She is just too perfect."

"I think my mother had a bathing suit like that," Kate said during the ocean scene in Cannes. "She always looked a little out of place here in Joshua Tree."

"I wish bathing suits were still that modest," Maryanne said.

"I wish I looked like Grace Kelly did in a bathing suit," Claudia said.

Unfortunately, Claudia again missed out on the ending because she fell asleep after the buzz of the mimosas wore off, sometime around the point where Grace Kelly packs a gourmet picnic for Cary Grant, and then drives like a maniac on the winding roads through the mountains of the French Riviera.

Chapter 41

When Claudia woke from her nap, she was alone in the guestroom bed and her phone was ringing.

"Hello?" she mumbled.

"Hello, wife. That sounds so weird, doesn't it? I wonder when we'll get used to that," Alex said.

"Maybe when we get an actual marriage license," Claudia said.

"Yeah, maybe then. Anyway, I just left Charles and Louisa's house, and I'm going to check on Foster now. I thought I might wait until after rush hour to head back."

"Give Foster a squeeze from me."

"I will. See you sometime after dinner."

Claudia walked into the kitchen, still wearing her wedding dress, the makeup wearing off and pillow creases pressed into the side of her face.

Maryanne was reading a midwifery book from Kate's

bookshelf and Kate was outside washing the horses.

"I don't know why these women voluntarily do this without medication," Maryanne said, grimacing. "An epidural wasn't an option when I was in labor with you. By the time we finally got you out, I was so tired I couldn't enjoy the fact that you were okay. I think I passed out right after I heard your first cry," Maryanne said.

"You don't think an epidural will trigger your addiction?" Claudia asked.

"I think not having an epidural would trigger my addiction," Maryanne said, taking one last look at the photos in the book. "How'd you sleep?"

"Great," Claudia said. "I feel like I could go into a sleep coma for weeks though."

"You have a lot to recover from," Maryanne said.

Claudia nodded and then chuckled, realizing the truth of the statement.

Kate stepped through the sliding glass door, water splashed from head to toe. "The horses smell better, but I smell worse. I'll do you guys a favor and go take a bath," she said.

Claudia nodded, walked into the kitchen and opened the bottle of Advil.

"Your ribs hurting?" Maryanne asked.

"Not too bad. It's more the champagne headache that's killing me now. It seems like such an injustice to get a headache from something as perfect as champagne."

"It seems like an injustice that ice cream makes me fat," Maryanne said.

"Yeah, exactly." Claudia sat next to Maryanne and took the book from her. "Yikes," she said, opening the book to the middle and looking at a photograph of a baby's head crowning. "How does anything ever go back to normal?" she asked.

"It doesn't," Maryanne said.

They sat in silence.

"But that's not necessarily a bad thing. In fact, it's a really good thing," Maryanne said.

Kate reappeared with wet and shiny hair. "Did you ever think you'd be spending your wedding day with two old women instead of your husband?" Kate asked.

"Well, I'm not exactly a blushing bride, if you know what I mean. And anyway, I'm still a bit too fragile for a wild honeymoon romp. We'll spend a few nights in Malibu or Laguna next week."

Maryanne cleared her throat. "I'm just going to pretend that I didn't hear any of that," she said.

"Oh, please." Kate said. "You still can't stomach talking to your own daughter about sex?"

"We never really had that conversation, did we, Mom?" Claudia said.

"No, I guess we didn't. But it looks like you figured it out for yourself," Maryanne rolled her eyes.

"Kate, you're just always trying to stir things up. Help us

out here, change the subject already," Claudia said.

"Stirring the pot is what I do best. I'm witchy that way. Anyone hungry, speaking of caldrons?"

"Tiny bit, but not much," Claudia said. "Why don't we just eat leftovers for a change?"

"Really? There's frittata left and salad from last night. Are you sure? I feel like I should make dinner for your wedding night."

"Just hang out with us. I'd rather you do that than be in the kitchen working," Claudia said.

As the sun sunk in the sky, the women went outside. Kate poured mint-iced tea into glasses. She served the frittata at room temperature and added some chopped apples to the salad of greens, cucumbers, and spiced pecans. They looked out onto the mountains, shadows moving across the pocketed surface. There was still a smattering of clouds in the sky, creeping on an otherwise unnoticeable breeze.

The ice in Claudia's glass made a crackling sound as it melted and called her attention. She took a sip through the straw, looked at Maryanne and Kate, both lost in thought, and turned her gaze back to the landscape. She thought this must have been what Kate's family did in the evenings long ago. When they weren't hunting buffalo or performing sacred rituals.

Jackson Browne crawled out from under the table and looked at something in the distance. He crept toward the edge of the fence, with his head lowered and his tail pointed.

Kate stood up, walked over to him and led him back toward the house. He relinquished with hanging head and tail and came back to the table, but he still looked to the mountains, quietly whining. "Come on, in you go," Kate said, walking him to the door and putting him inside. He stared out the glass for a minute, then turned around and walked toward the couch.

"That's weird," Claudia said, "I haven't heard him do that before."

"He doesn't do it very often. Sometimes he just gets spooked, and I never figure out why. Maybe he sees things we can't."

"Maybe he sees angels," Maryanne said.

"Maybe he sees dead people," Claudia said, and thought of Gram.

The sky shifted into a ceiling of stained glass; the white clouds divided sections of pink quartz, mandarin citrine, and amethyst. The tone of the women's skin changed and glowed with the warm light.

"Shhhh," Kate said, and stood up from her chair slowly. She reached for a handful of greens from the salad bowl. "Follow me."

Claudia looked at Maryanne and they both stood and tiptoed behind Kate to the side of the fence. Kate opened the gate and walked steadily, crouched like an animal or the hunchback of Notre Dame. Claudia almost laughed out loud when she thought of what Alex would say if he saw the three of them tiptoeing across the desert like this. They walked toward the mountains, Claudia still clueless as to what they were looking for. She turned around to see Maryanne, whose face lit up as she pointed to the distance, and Claudia turned to follow her gaze. This must have been what Jackson was barking at and Kate somehow sensed. The white deer was back.

"Stop," Kate whispered, and they paused, crouched low. The deer continued to walk toward them, its nose to the ground. Claudia was unsure if it had seen them. She hardly breathed, watching the pale animal come closer. She wasn't sure how much longer she could stay in the same position; her side was killing her and she was suppressing a wheeze. She heard Maryanne take in a sharp breath behind her and anxiously watched for the deer to run away at the slight noise; but it kept moving closer, its nose still to the ground. Finally she was only feet away and Kate held out her hand filled with greens, a peace offering to the animal. It looked up, its ears twitching from side to side, its body frozen, eyes blinking. Claudia watched intently, the sleeves of her wedding dress fluttering in the breeze that carried the scent of the greens to the deer. It fixed its gaze on Kate's hand and walked cautiously forward. Claudia saw Kate's hand quivering. Maryanne tried to straighten her back a little. Oh, don't move; don't scare her away.

The deer stopped just a foot in front of them, leaned her long elegant neck forward and reached for Kate's hand, her white muzzle straining for contact with the leaves. Kate inched forward. Claudia and Maryanne moved in behind her. The deer took another step, and then grabbed a leaf of arugula with her tongue. Kate inched closer still, and while she held the lettuce under the deer's nose and let her nibble, with her other hand she reached for her side. The deer allowed the touch. Kate breathed with relief. "Come here," she whispered to Claudia and Maryanne. Claudia held her hand out, keeping her movements fluid. Her fingers shook, and as she made contact, a surge ran throughout her body. She saw the image as if from afar—her in a white dress, touching the white deer, both bathed in the last light of the day, an ending and a new beginning all at once. She motioned for Maryanne to come next to her. She removed her hand from the deer's flank, took Maryanne's wrist and placed it on the animal. Maryanne sighed, and Claudia felt warmth around and within. The deer ate the last piece of lettuce and looked up from Kate's hand. She turned to Claudia and Maryanne, nodded her head twice and leapt away.

Chapter 42

Maryanne went quietly to the guestroom and Kate to her bedroom. Claudia was reading when Alex walked through the door—she had finally started *Franny and Zooey*, setting the creased photo of Kate, Gram and Keith on the mantle where it belonged.

"Hey," he whispered, and sat next to her.

"It feels good to be home," Claudia said, burrowing her nose into his neck.

"What do you mean?" Alex said.

Claudia looked in his eyes, and then pointed to the small space where his neck and shoulder met, just above his collarbone. "Here. This is home."

They pulled out the couch-bed and laughed beneath the blanket, trying to be quiet and hoping that neither Maryanne nor Kate would suddenly appear for a glass of water from the kitchen. Jackson whined from his cushion on the floor as if to say, "Really? What are you guys, sixteen?" Alex was careful with Claudia's wounded body, which made her laugh, as he found inventive ways to stay off her ribs. The couch mattress was old and slanted, and she was sure they were going to tumble onto the floor in a loud crash at any moment. Afterward she lay on top of him and breathed into his chest. The scent of his skin eased the pain in her side, and breathing wasn't such a chore when she had someone to do it with, in and out, matched in time.

In the morning, butterflies of anticipation fluttered from Claudia's stomach to her chest. She was excited to leave and be in her own space again, if only for a little while, but she was sad to leave Kate.

"Are you sure you're ready to make the trip back?" Alex asked, and Claudia nodded.

"Well, I guess you and Maryanne will follow me back in Ramona," he said, handing her a cup of coffee.

She blew on the top of the warm mug and thought for a moment. "Or. . ." she said, cocking her head to the side.

"Uh-oh, I know that look," Alex said.

"Kate!" Claudia called to the kitchen, still looking at Alex as she jumped off the couch, overestimating her body's condition. "Ouch!"

"I'm right here, you don't have to yell," Kate said.

"Sorry. I don't know why I didn't think of this before— it's the perfect solution really. Why don't you take Ramona as a replacement for your truck? Ron said it himself; she should run forever now. I won't be taking her to New York with us."

Alex smiled at Claudia and Kate. "Wow. I didn't expect you to say that. Do you know how huge this is, Kate? I don't know if Claudia would even let me drive Ramona."

"I know," Kate said. "Are you sure about this?" she asked Claudia.

Maryanne watched from the kitchen table, waiting for the response.

Claudia smiled, "I'm positive," she said.

"Well—then, yeah—that's great! I'll gladly take Ramona."

Claudia clapped her hands in front of her chest. "Oh good. It'll make me feel so much better knowing that the two of you are together."

"I guess I'll pack everything in the Prius then," Alex said, and grabbed the bags waiting by the door.

Claudia, Maryanne, and Kate looked at each other. "I'll be back in just a minute," Claudia said to them.

She opened the heavy wooden door and walked into the heat toward Ramona, who was parked several feet away from Alex's Prius. He looked up at her and smiled as she opened the driver's side door. She sat down, closed the door, and placed her hands on Ramona's steering wheel. "Thanks," Claudia said. "Thanks for carrying me all those years when I needed someone to take me away, and thanks for stopping when you knew it was time for me to stop running. I'm sure you have plenty of adventure ahead of you—there's no telling what you'll see and do with Kate. Keep her safe, like you kept me. I have a feeling I'll see you again some day." Claudia ran her hands around the steering wheel and touched Ramona's dashboard. She got out and closed the door and walked back to the house, Alex following behind her.

"Okay, this is how we do it," Kate said, like a football coach. "No plans, no promises, because that's even worse when it fails. I don't have to say it, you guys already know—"

Kate and Maryanne nodded their heads at her.

"Well, as long as you ladies are ready, we're all packed," Alex said.

"Vamanos," Kate said, shooing them away.

Claudia and Maryanne hugged Kate and Alex gave her a kiss on the cheek.

"Don't forget your stick," Kate said to Claudia, motioning toward the door where it leaned against the wall.

"Oh yeah," Claudia said, and smiled at Kate. "A souvenir from wandering in the desert."

"Who knows—maybe it will come in handy in the city," Kate said.

Claudia gave her the keys to Ramona and looked her deep in the eye, nodding twice like the deer had the night before.

They got into Alex's car, the long stick propped against the seat next to Maryanne. Kate waved goodbye once more from the front door. Jackson Browne wagged his tail next to her, and then she quickly closed it and they both disappeared. Maryanne wiped the tears from her face.

Alex started the engine as they buckled their seatbelts. Claudia slid one of her mixed CDs into the player and leaned back into the seat when the guitar intro started. As they pulled onto the freeway, she sang along: *Standing stretching every nerve, I had to listen had no choice . . .*